MOORINGS

Proofread by Jay G Arscott

Special thanks to Lorraine Swoboda,
John Kincaid, Ali Dunn, Anna Burke and Kath Middleton

Published by Black Oak Publishing Ltd
2nd edition published in Great Britain, 2020

Cover photograph 56819550 © Sniperscott · Dreamstime.com

ISBN: 978-1-9163479-2-2

DEDICATION

For Akiko, Akira and Kai.

MOORINGS

A DI Tanner Mystery

- Book Three -

DAVID BLAKE

www.david-blake.com

BOOKS BY DAVID BLAKE

CRIME FICTION
Broadland
St. Benet's
Moorings
Three Rivers
Horsey Mere

CRIME COMEDY
The Slaughtered Virgin of Zenopolis
The Curious Case of Cut-Throat Cate
The Thrills & Spills of Genocide Jill
The Herbaceous Affair of Cocaine Claire

SPACE CRIME COMEDY
Space Police: Attack of the Mammary Clans
Space Police: The Final Fish Finger
Space Police: The Toaster That Time Forgot
Space Police: Rise of the Retail-Bot
Space Police: Enemy at the Cat Flap
Space Police: The Day The Earth Moved A Bit

SPACE ADVENTURE COMEDY
Galaxy Squad: Danger From Drackonia

ROMANTIC COMEDY
Headline Love & Prime Time Love

"It is mine to avenge; I will repay. In due time their foot will slip; their day of disaster is near and their doom rushes upon them."
Deuteronomy 32:35

· PROLOGUE ·

Sunday, 6th October

THE SUDDEN SOUND of the cattle shed's door being rattled from the outside made Harry Falcon's heart jump with a start.

He remained motionless for a few seconds, straining for further sounds. Hearing boots being scuffed on the ground outside, he slowly sank into the water trough until his ears lay just above the surface.

Face down on top of him was the stinking corpse of a dead German soldier, its cold bristly skin pressed firmly against his own, a pair of rubbery lips gently touching his ear.

The soldier was one of many he'd butchered a few days before, in and around the French farmyard. Since then he'd been using the farm to take shelter, plundering the soldiers' medical supplies to tend to his many wounds whilst gorging himself on their food. He knew it wouldn't be long before another troop came sniffing about, but with a bullet wound to his leg and only a few rounds of ammunition left, he had no choice but to remain where he was. If everything went according to plan, it shouldn't be long before the allied forces arrived, the ones for whom he and his long-dead fellow members of the SAS had been sent behind enemy lines to clear the way.

The cattle shed's door rattled again. Then came the noise of German voices. From what he could make out, there were at least three of them, maybe four. As to what they were saying, he'd no idea.

He remained where he was, as still as the corpse lying on top of him. Should the soldiers force their way in, he thought it was unlikely they'd lift the body to peer underneath; at least he hoped to God they wouldn't.

The talking continued, but thankfully the shed door was left alone.

After what felt like hours the voices began trailing away to be followed by the sound of a truck's doors being opened and closed, presumably the same one he'd seen being driven up to the farm a few minutes earlier, and the diesel engine turned over before rumbling into life.

Harry waited in earnest for it to drive off, but it didn't. It just stayed where it was, the engine ticking over.

Becoming increasingly desperate to shove the decomposing corpse off and to claw his way out of the trough's freezing cold water, he muttered to his late enemy, 'What are they waiting for?'

The soldier's face twitched in response.

Shock mixed with revulsion as he screwed his eyes closed and turned his head away, his mind racing to understand how the nerve endings could still be active. He'd seen dead people twitch before, many times, but only in the brief moments following death. This one had been killed three days before! And there was no question that he was dead. Apart from the stiffness of his joints, and of course the smell, Harry knew he was because he'd slit his enemy's throat himself, holding a quietening hand over the man's mouth until he'd felt his life force ebb slowly away.

As Harry's heart began pounding deep inside his chest, every sinew of his body was screaming at him to push the disgusting rotting corpse off and climb out; but his mind refused to obey. Until the truck left he had no choice; he had to remain where he was.

Then something truly terrifying happened. He felt a breath of stale air escape the body's decaying lungs to brush against his ear, whispering out a name as it did. And it wasn't just any name. It was his!

Fractured thoughts exploded inside his mind, leaving his body convulsing under the corpse, desperate to shove it off. But the more he tried, the more it seemed to force him back down.

'Harry,' it whispered again, its flaccid head flopping against the side of his face.

Kicking and punching, Harry tried to force it away, but every time he thought he'd been able to roll it off, somehow it managed to fall back down.

'Harry, my love,' came the voice again. 'I'm not finished with you yet.'

'Get the fuck off me!' he screamed, pushing up against it with all his might.

For a moment he thought he'd done it. But when he dared to open his eyes, he saw he'd done no such thing. The body was now sitting directly on top of him, smiling. But what had been a dead German soldier had somehow transformed itself into a beautiful naked young woman, with luminous blue eyes, full red lips, flowing auburn hair and a pair of mesmerising white breasts which heaved up and down as she took in a series of deep, passionate breaths.

Harry's mind began to tear itself into two, one half still desperate to claw itself away, the other left longing for the pleasures this beautiful temptress seemed to be offering.

As the woman rested her hands gently down on his chest, she stared deep into his eyes, and with a voice full of enticing promise, bent her head to say, 'This one's on me.' She leaned forward as if to kiss him, but instead she raised up her hips to push down hard on his chest, plunging his head under the water's cold, unwelcoming surface.

Waking with a start, Harry gasped at the air, his hands clawing at nothing more sinister than a bath full of lukewarm water.

Darting his eyes about, it took him a few moments to remember where he was – at home in his bath – and that he'd been having a nightmare, the same one that had been darkening his sleep every night for the past few weeks.

As the water he'd been wrestling with returned to its natural placid state, so did the peaceful serenity of the bathroom.

Grateful for being alive, he took a moment to

4

stare down at his body as it lay stretched out before him, just under the water. What he saw left him feeling old and depressed. What had once been a lean, strong and athletic physique was now nothing more than a skeleton wrapped in pale sagging skin.

A creaking noise came from out in the hall.

Blinking, he stared at the closed bathroom door, listening hard. His hearing wasn't as good as it used to be, though it was far better than most people's his age. But all he could hear was the repetitive drip of water coming from the tap just a few inches above his feet.

He was about to rest his head back against the bath's smooth curved end when the sound came again. He knew what it was. It was the creaking noise of someone coming up the stairs.

'Hello?' he called out, wondering who could be creeping around his house at such an hour. Realising that he didn't have a clue what time it was, he stole a glance over towards a large carriage clock that he kept on the shelf above the sink. But there was no way he could see what it said, not from where he was lying.

Trying to remember what time he'd run the bath, he heaved himself into a sitting position. Had it been before dinner, or after? Looking out of the bathroom window only told him that it was dark, but as it was October, all that meant was that it was sometime after six.

Remembering he'd left his watch on the chair by the bath, he lifted a hand out of the water. After letting it drip for a moment, he reached over to retrieve it. It had been a gift from his wife, decades before, and he liked to keep it close by.

Bringing it to within just a few inches of his eyes, he squinted to try and see what it said, but it had been a 'long time since he'd been able to do so with any accuracy. As far as he could make out it was either five minutes to seven, or half-past eleven.

At another noise from the hallway, he replaced the watch, calling out, 'Phillip? Is that you?'

Phillip was the name of his elder son who lived in a small cottage just down the road. He'd often come around unannounced.

He stopped again to listen.

After about a minute of hearing nothing other than the steadily dripping tap, he began to question whether he had heard someone on the stairs. It could easily have been just the noise of the water pipes expanding as the central heating turned itself on.

A thought crept into his mind which made his heart jolt hard in his chest.

Did I lock the back door?

Like so many things recently, he simply couldn't remember.

Then he definitely did hear something: the weight of a foot creaking a floorboard, directly outside.

It must be Phillip, he thought, and began the slow, painful process of heaving himself out of the bath. But he'd only managed to lift his pelvis up when someone opened the door and stepped inside.

Plonking himself back down, he glared over to be greeted by the sight of a complete stranger, smiling back at him.

'Who the hell are you?' he demanded, his heart beginning to race.

The stranger's smile fell away to be replaced by a look of disappointed irritation. 'Don't be daft. You know who I am.'

'I've never seen you before in my life!' the old man insisted. 'And if you don't get the hell out of my house, I'm calling the police!'

Ignoring the remarks, the seemingly unwelcome visitor glanced around the larger than average bathroom. 'Where's your towel?'

'I don't want a towel! I want you out of my house!'

'I see. So you want to go to bed soaking wet, do you?'

Furious at being talked to as if he were a five year-old child, the old man shouted, 'Of course I don't! But there's no way I'm having someone I don't know stand there and watch me get out.'

'As I've said, you already know who I am.'

'Well, you're not my Phillip, I know that much!'

Stepping over to the bath, the visitor leant over to dip a hand into the water. 'Good God! It's stone cold! How long have you been in here? You must be freezing!' A hand reached out for the hot water tap and began frantically twisting it around.

As steaming hot water began to pour out, thundering down into the bath below, the old man shouted, 'None of your damned business!'

'Well, don't worry. We'll soon get the temperature up. Now then, let's see if we can lie you back down. Then I'll go on the hunt for that missing towel of yours.'

The old man muttered a series of protests about being physically manhandled by a complete stranger as a guiding hand was placed onto a bony shoulder to ease him gently down, until his head was resting back against the end of the bath. Laying the other hand on the opposite shoulder, the visitor stared at him to say, 'Now, if you relax, this shouldn't take too long,' before pushing down hard, so that his head slipped off the edge to plunge into the water below.

· CHAPTER ONE ·

Monday, 7th October

'WHAT THE HELL'S all that bloody noise?' moaned Tanner, his head half-buried in his pillow.

He waited a moment for some sort of a response from Jenny, lying to his right, but there was none.

Lifting his head, he stared down at her through dawn's early light to see if she was awake, or was just doing her best to ignore both him and the noise. But the way in which the black curls of her eyelashes rested gently against the tops of her soft lightly flushed cheeks, and her full red lips hung half open as she breathed with rhythmic ease, it was obvious that she was still fast asleep.

'How can you possibly sleep through this?' he asked, but the question went unanswered.

Jenny was a far heavier sleeper than him, something he'd become discreetly envious of. Unlike her, it would normally take him ages to drift off, and the slightest noise would have him wide awake. He had been sleeping better since moving on board a boat, but it was still a struggle.

Jenny, on the other hand, would nod off within

seconds, and she didn't seem to move again until the alarm went off.

Tanner reached around for his phone. Seeing that it was only seven in the morning, he let his head fall back onto the pillow, making disgruntled mutterings to himself as he did.

From outside their relatively new home, a forty-two foot traditional Broads cabin cruiser, came the steady rumble of what sounded like a platoon of tanks, but was more likely to be some sort of heavy plant machinery. It certainly couldn't be a boat. He'd heard some noisy old diesel engines grumbling their way past before, but that wasn't one of them. Nothing that floated on the water could have made anywhere near that much noise. With the sound growing louder, whatever it was seemed to be heading in their direction.

The alarm was not set to go off until half past seven. Tanner turned over onto his back and just lay there for a moment, staring up at the sloping low ceiling, trying to decide whether to remain where he was for another half an hour or to drag himself out of bed and find out just what the hell was making such an unwelcome racket.

As the rumbling grew ever louder, he came to the conclusion that he might as well get up. After all, it wasn't as if he was going to get back to sleep again. That much he did know.

Rolling out of bed, doing his best not to wake Sleeping Beauty, and feeling an autumnal chill in the air, he dressed himself as quickly as he could, a job made far easier than it had been on his previous boat thanks to the additional headroom that this new, larger version provided.

Ducking out into the cockpit, he pulled an old navy fisherman's jumper over his head for warmth before taking a look out of the canvas awning.

There, just beyond their mooring platform where they had their electrical hook-up, manoeuvring around on the lush green open field was an enormous dirty yellow digger, spewing out thick black diesel smoke into an uninviting grey sky.

After giving the driver a dirty look, Tanner slipped on a pair of trainers before pushing out through the awning and stepping down onto the decked footway. With his head hung low and his hands buried deep inside his pockets, he marched over to where the digger had come to a standstill.

He saw the driver glance over at him and roll his eyes, shutting off the engine as he did.

As it juddered to a halt, and the normal tranquillity of the Broads returned, the wide-set man, who had a large pair of orange ear-defenders clamped over his head, shoved open the door with a booted foot and leaned forward to call out, 'Are you all right, mate?'

'I was just curious to know what you're doing here, exactly.'

Pulling his ear-defenders down to leave them draped around his short thick neck, the driver cupped a hand around his ear. 'Sorry, mate. I didn't catch that.'

'I asked what you were doing here,' Tanner repeated.

'Parkin' up. Why? What's it got to do with you?'

'Because I live on board that boat,' replied Tanner, pointing behind at his home, one of three yachts tied up to the jetty behind him.

With an unhidden smirk the driver asked, 'What, by choice?'

Seeing the look on Tanner's face, the man stopped grinning. 'Sorry, mate, but I didn't know anyone was living in 'em.'

'Anyway,' continued Tanner, 'you've still not told me what you're doing here?'

'I've got four of these to bring in before we can start work.'

'Start work on what?'

'Has nobody told you?'

'No, nobody's told us about any work.'

From his cockpit's elevated position, the driver looked over at Tanner's boat and said, 'Er, I think they have. There's a notice stuck on top of your roof.'

'A notice...' Tanner spun round to look for himself.

Following where he was being directed, he saw that indeed something had been taped up there, enclosed inside a clear plastic bag.

As the driver began hauling himself out from his cockpit, Tanner stepped back to his relatively new floating home to hop on board and retrieve the notice he'd been referred to.

After taking it out of the bag, he scanned through it. 'How long's this been here for?'

'Dunno, mate,' the man answered, jumping down from the last of the digger's steps onto the grass. 'Not my job.'

'But this says that there's going to be a luxury

block of flats built here.'

'Uh-huh.'

'But – nobody's told us.'

Pointing at the notice held in his hand, the driver said, 'What's that then?'

'A soggy piece of paper that couldn't have been here for long, else we'd have seen it.'

'Well, there's another one up at the site entrance, where the billboard is; the one with the pictures of new-build flats plastered all over it. There's no way you could have missed that.'

'Surprisingly, we don't use the entrance to the field,' replied Tanner, indicating over to his left. 'We use the car park's entrance, like everyone else.'

'There's nothin' I can do about that. You'll just 'ave to find somewhere else to keep your boat.'

'But we've only just paid a year's worth of mooring fees!'

'Then you'd better ask for your money back, 'adn't you,' he replied, before pulling his ear defenders back over his head, 'else you're gonna need a pair of these.' With that, he turned back, stomping over the field following the tracks his digger had left along the grass.

'I don't bloody believe this,' moaned Tanner, staring back down at the notice.

Remaining where he was, he read through it again, but this time with more attention. Seeing a number for a site office at the bottom, alongside where it said Jackson Developments, he climbed back on board his boat to duck into the cabin, searching for his phone.

Seeing it resting beside his pillow, he reached

over to grab it, just as Jenny finally began to stir.

As he sat on the side of the bed, he thumbed the number displayed at the base of the notice into the phone. Jenny blinked open her eyes. 'Don't tell me I slept through the alarm again?' she muttered, still half asleep.

'No, but you managed to sleep through just about everything else.'

'What's everything else?'

Waiting for the phone to be answered, Tanner glanced down at her. 'There's a bloody great digger parked in the field outside, and another three are on their way in.'

'A digger?'

'Here,' responded Tanner, handing her the notice. 'Take a look at this.'

Taking the flier in one hand and rubbing her eyes open with the other, Jenny sat up to begin reading it through.

'A luxury riverside block of flats called the Moorings?'

'That's what it says.'

'How come nobody told us?'

'Apparently, that's what the notice is for.'

'But we've only just paid the annual mooring fee.'

'And that will be my next call.'

When the phone was finally answered, Tanner stood up, saying, 'Can I speak to the site manager, please?' and ducked back out into the cockpit.

'I'm sorry, but he's not here at the moment,' came the dreary monotone sound of a woman's voice. 'Can I take a message?'

'How about the business owner?'

'Mr Jackson?'

'If that's who the owner is, then yes.'

'This is the site office. You'd need to call head office if you want to speak to him, but they don't open till nine.'

'OK, can you give me that number, please?'

'May I ask who's calling?'

'Sure. It's Detective Inspector Tanner, Norfolk Police,' he replied, thinking that should get her attention.

Having scrawled the number she recited on the back of an old copy of the Sunday Times, Tanner added, 'And if you could get the site manager to call me as soon as he can, I'd appreciate that.'

'May I ask what it's in connection with?' questioned the woman, beginning to sound more awake.

'It's to find out why nobody's bothered to tell us that you're building a bloody great block of flats right next to the moorings we've only just paid for.'

'Oh, I see,' she said, sounding considerably less impressed than when Tanner had told her he was from the police. 'You'll have to speak to the Broads Waterways about that.'

'That's as may be, but nobody's bothered to inform us about the proposed development.'

'I can assure you that we've followed all the legal necessities to ensure that the general public's been made fully aware.'

'Everyone apart from us, it would seem, and we're the ones who are moored up right next to it!'

'Well, we placed public notices around the site

six months ago. If you had a problem with the proposed plans, you should have said something then.'

'But we've only just moored up here, having paid for an entire bloody year!'

'Then the Broads Waterways should have advised you of what was planned before allowing you to pay. If you have a complaint, you'll have to speak to them.'

'I will, thank you, but I'd still like a word with the site manager.'

'He'll only tell you what I just have.'

'I appreciate that, but I'd like to speak with him anyway.'

'Very well. I'll leave a message for him to call. What's your number?'

As Tanner relayed it to her, along with his name, again, Jenny ducked out into the cockpit, pulling a long cardigan over her shoulders.

Peeking out of the canvas awning to see the digger for herself, on hearing Tanner end the call she turned to ask, 'What did they say?'

'According to them, they made all the necessary public announcements months ago, along with posting up various notices around the site.'

'But we've only just moored up here. How could we have seen them? And I don't remember hearing anything about it. Word normally gets around about this sort of thing. Even if I didn't read about it somewhere, my parents would have told me.'

'Well, I've asked the site manager to call, but it looks like I'm going to have to get in touch with the Broads Waterways. They really should have told us about this when we paid for the mooring.'

Hearing her alarm going off down inside the cabin, Jenny said, 'Then you'll have to call them later. There's no way they'll be open this early.'

· CHAPTER TWO ·

A LITTLE OVER an hour and a half later, with Jenny sitting beside him, Tanner pulled his black, slightly grubby Jaguar XJS into Wroxham Police station car park and edged it between a gleaming 7 Series BMW and a brand new Audi A3 saloon.

They'd been driving to work together since moving onto their new yacht. By that time everyone seemed to know that they were an item, at the police station and beyond, so it didn't matter that they'd always show up at the same time. Even their boss, Detective Chief Inspector Forrester, was fully aware, and although he'd never given the relationship his blessing, or condoned it, at least publicly, it was fairly obvious to everyone at the station that he didn't approve. But once it had become public knowledge that they'd bought a boat together, and were living on it as a couple, he'd probably reached the conclusion that there wasn't a lot he could do about it and had decided to leave it at that.

'You know,' began Tanner, glancing around at the two vehicles, 'looking at the cars around here, anyone would think Germany won the war.'

'If you mean the second one,' Jenny said,

unclipping her seatbelt, 'then they definitely came last. I remember that much from school. I think the same thing happened with the one before that as well.'

'Sometimes I'm not so sure,' continued Tanner, wrenching on the handbrake. 'In fact, I'm beginning to think that they only pretended to lose the last one in order to begin a third, straight afterwards, one that involved invading our green and pleasant land with an endless stream of luxury saloon cars.'

'There's nothing wrong with German cars,' she said, as she pushed open the door of Tanner's distinctly British one, which screeched loudly as it did. 'You should try one sometime.'

'If you mean like your Volkswagen Golf,' he said, climbing out, 'then I think I'll stick with this one, thank you.'

'To be honest, it's not you I'm worried about,' she said, 'it's your car,' and as if to demonstrate what she meant, she slammed the door and stood there for a moment, watching as the whole vehicle wobbled like a freshly made trifle, but one that was about to collapse into an untidy pile of welded steel, plush leather and heavily varnished wood.

Hearing what she'd done, Tanner spun around with his hands held out, ready to catch anything that might fall off.

Fortunately, nothing did.

As a look of relief swept over his face, he said, 'You see! She's still got a few years left in her,' and closed his own door with a little more care.

'You mean a few weeks,' muttered Jenny, just loud enough for Tanner to hear.

'No doubt it would last a lot longer if you didn't keep slamming the doors all the time.'

'It's a structural integrity test,' she replied, as they began making their way towards the building's entrance. 'If it is going to collapse, then I'd rather it did so in the safety of a car park than when I'm being driven in it down the A47 at 80mph. Besides, if it can't survive having its doors closed, then maybe it's time for it to be towed into the middle of a field and shot.'

'Do you want a lift home, or are you happy to walk?'

'But we've only just got here.'

'Then maybe you should drive yourself in tomorrow. I'm not sure my car can take much more of your constant abuse.'

'I'll make it up to it, I promise.'

'I see. And just how do you intend to do that?'

As Tanner held the door open for her, she thought quietly for a moment as they stepped inside. After they'd nodded a greeting over at the duty sergeant, she eventually piped up with, 'I know! I'll buy some shoulder pads and get a perm. I reckon it would appreciate that.'

'What, that the passenger was making an effort to look more Eighties?'

'Uh-huh. Then maybe we could take it for a drive down to London to take in a show. Something like Dynasty the Musical.'

'I wasn't aware they'd made a musical version of Dynasty.'

'Oh, they must have by now. And you never know, there might even be a part in it for your car.'

With that, she sent Tanner one of her most mischievous smiles, before pushing through the double doors and leading the way through to the main office.

· CHAPTER THREE ·

A S THEY STEPPED inside, they couldn't help but notice that someone had left a large pile of old box files stacked up on top of Jenny's desk.

'Who's dumped all these here?' questioned Tanner, pulling his coat off.

'It must have been Forrester,' she said, doing the same. 'He's probably trying to find us something to do.'

Removing the one off the top to look at what had been written on the spine label, Tanner said, 'I suppose it has been a little quiet recently.'

'What does it say?'

'Missing persons: 1960 to 1965.'

'Seriously?'

'I'm afraid so.'

'I know it's quiet, but that's taking the piss, surely?'

More out of idle curiosity than any form of professional interest, Tanner placed it down on the desk to open the lid. Finding it to be crammed full of beige-coloured folders, he lifted out the first to discover an old Norfolk Police Missing Person's Report hidden inside. At the top of the first page had been stapled a couple of faded colour photographs. The first was of a beautiful young girl with short blonde hair, wearing a sleeveless knitted jumper and a belted mini skirt. Parked behind her was a sumptuous E-Type Jag, a car almost as attractive as the girl leaning against it. The second picture was the close-up image of a gold jewel-encrusted bangle.

'Who is she?' enquired Jenny, peering over his shoulder.

'Stephanie Denton. Local socialite, by the looks of her. She went missing in Horning, back in 1964.'

'She certainly is pretty enough,' commented Jenny, with just a hint of envy. 'Love that Sixties look!'

'I hope Forrester doesn't expect us to start a door-to-door search for her!'

'It wouldn't surprise me. Anyway, first things first, I'm going to make us a coffee.'

'And I'd better give the Broads Waterways a call about our mooring fees,' said Tanner, replacing the file back into the box. 'We can take a look at this lot later.'

As Jenny headed off to the kitchen, Tanner sat down at his desk, turned on his computer and checked the time. Seeing that it was just gone nine, after waiting for the computer to whir into life he searched up the relevant website, found their number and picked up his desk phone.

After following a seemingly endless series of automated instructions, the phone was eventually answered by a human being.

'Hello,' Tanner began, 'I'd like to talk to someone about my mooring fees.'

'Yes, sir,' said the girl on the other end of the line. 'How may I be of service?'

'Well, we've only recently paid for an entire year's moorings, but when we woke up this morning we discovered that the land opposite is about to be converted into a block of flats.'

'I see. And how is it that you think we can help?'

'Well, for a start I'd like to know why nobody told us that the mooring was about to become a building site, and secondly, if we can have our fees transferred over to cover us for somewhere else?'

'You mean, for another mooring?'

'That's right, yes.'

'I'm very sorry, but unfortunately we're unable to do that. Was there anything else I can help you with?'

Feeling his temper rise, Tanner was forced to take a calming breath. 'I wasn't aware that you'd helped me with my second enquiry, let alone the first.'

'I'm, er, not sure I know what you mean.'

'Why did you give us a mooring directly opposite what is about to become a building site?'

After a brief pause, the girl said, 'Would you be able to give me your mooring number?'

Prepared for that, Tanner picked up the print-out of the email that they'd sent to him and read out the information.

'And your name?'

'Tanner.'

'Mr John Tanner?'

'That's correct.'

'And is the mooring on the River Ant, just upriver from Falcon's Yard?'

'Correct again.'

'OK, well, it looks like you're right in that there is a housing development being built on the land opposite, but it isn't expected to be finished for another two years. It would also appear that we have an agreement in place with the developers that current berth holders won't have to move for another eighteen months.'

'And how does that help us?'

'As I said, you won't have to move until the work's nearly completed.'

'But why, may I ask, would we want to live directly opposite a building site for the next two years?'

'It's actually only eighteen months. After that I'm afraid you will have to find another mooring.'

'Sorry, let me rephrase the question. Why would we want to live directly opposite a building site for eighteen months?'

'Well, Mr Tanner, you've only paid for twelve, so you'd have to apply for another six if you'd like to.'

'You don't seem to understand the question. Why would we want to live opposite a building site for another day, let alone a whole year?'

'I've no idea, but we do have plenty more moorings for you to choose from.'

'Good, then we'd like to have our fee transferred over to one of those, please.'

'As I said at the beginning, we're unable to transfer mooring fees between sites.'

'Then may I ask why nobody told us that there

was going to be a block of flats being built directly opposite before we paid over two and a half thousand pounds for the annual mooring fee?'

'I'm not sure, but as I said before, you won't have to move your boat away for another eighteen months.'

'Or fork out another two and a half grand for the opportunity to move somewhere else?'

'That's correct.'

'Well, gee, thanks for nothing.'

'You're very welcome, Mr Tanner. Now, was there anything else I can help you with?'

Slamming the phone down, Tanner glanced up to see Jenny return with two mugs of what he hoped was good strong filtered coffee.

'What did they say?' she asked, although judging by the colour of Tanner's face, and the way she'd seen him end the call, she already had a pretty good idea.

'Almost nothing, at least nothing that was of any use.'

'Can they transfer our mooring fees?'

'You'd have thought so.'

'You mean they can't?'

'Not can't as much as won't. If we want another mooring, we're going to have to fork out another two and a half grand.'

'But that's...'

'Criminal? Probably, yes, but I doubt there's much that even we can do about it.'

From the corner of his eye, Tanner saw DCI Forrester approaching, and stood to take one of the coffees from Jenny, directing her attention towards their boss as he did. 'Anyway,' he muttered, 'we'd better talk about it later.'

'I trust you two had a good weekend?' Forrester asked, giving them each the look of parental disapproval he always managed to offer when asking them about something unrelated to work.

Turning to face him, Tanner replied, 'Apart from a slight problem with a mechanical digger this morning, we did, thank you, sir, yes. How about you?'

'Oh, just the normal,' he replied, squirming a little. Like Tanner, Forrester rarely felt comfortable talking about his personal life.

'We saw the box files,' said Tanner, glancing over at them. 'I assume you'd like us to go through them?'

'Only when you get a moment. For now a call's come through on a matter which I'd like the two of you to take a look at. The owner of Falcon's Yard was found in the bath this morning.'

'Dead, I assume?' asked Tanner, raising an eyebrow.

'Of course he's dead, Tanner! Why else would someone have called the police?'

Unable to stop himself, Tanner replied, 'I don't know, sir. Maybe he got his toe stuck in the plug hole.'

From the corner of his eye, Tanner could see Jenny was busy suppressing a smirk.

Realising his senior detective inspector was being his normal jocular self, Forrester choose to ignore the remark. 'According to the person who found him, he was ninety-four years old, so he probably just had a stroke and drowned. However, it could be something more dubious. Either way,

I'd like you two to head down there and take a look.'

· CHAPTER FOUR ·

TANNER AND JENNY knew Falcon's Yard, as did most people who lived on the Broads. Not only was it located down a narrow channel only a couple of hundred metres from where they were moored, they'd been there only a few months before when viewing a yacht that was up for sale.

Falcon's Yard had been an operational boatyard since before most people could remember. Founded shortly after the Second World War, it started out building a range of traditional Norfolk cruising yachts for a cash-strapped post-war Britain, an enterprise that proved very successful. It had quickly expanded to provide what were considered at the time to be exclusive moorings before going on to offer charter yacht holidays during the summer months, something they continued to do to this day.

Neither Tanner nor Jenny knew much more about the yard than that, and they'd certainly no idea who its founder and former owner was, until then.

Having followed what was effectively their route home, Tanner turned his XJS into a spacious walled courtyard outside a substantial

Edwardian farmhouse with a grey tiled roof, red-brick walls and small cottage-style windows.

At the front door, a young constable led them inside, up a dark wooden staircase and into a Victorian-style bathroom. There they stood for a moment as they quietly stared down at a wiry, prune-like body lying half-submerged under the water of a free-standing porcelain bath. At one end dripped an ornate chrome tap, sending ripples fleeing over the surface which distorted the macabre image of what lay underneath, whilst at the other was the head of an old man with unusually long grey hair, paper-thin skin and a pair of hollowed out eyes that were staring forever up at the ceiling.

'Cause of death?' enquired Tanner, breaking the rhythmic noise of the dripping tap that echoed out around them.

Dr Johnstone, their forensic medical examiner, to whom Tanner had directed the question, looked up from where he was crouched down beside the edge of the bath. 'I'm going to have to go with drowned, for now at least.'

'Foul play?' asked Tanner again, keen to know if there was any real need for him to be standing there, staring down at the body of a naked old man.

'Well, he didn't do it on his own, if that answers your question.'

'So he couldn't have had a heart attack, and then gone under?'

'It's certainly possible that he had a heart attack,' agreed Johnstone, 'but if he had, it still wouldn't have been possible for him to have drowned because of it.'

'Are you sure?' asked Tanner, puzzled.

'About as sure as I can be, at this stage.'

Glancing up to see the questioning look on Tanner's face, Johnstone took it upon himself to explain further.

'It's the way his nose and mouth are lying above the surface. Heads naturally float, as this one is doing. To have died from drowning it would have had to have been held under the water by someone else. If he'd had a heart attack, or maybe even a stroke, then someone would still have had to hold his head under the water long enough for him to drown.'

'So how do you know that he drowned, and didn't die from a heart attack?'

'It's the petechiae in his eyes and here, around his nose and mouth.'

Leaning forward to examine the areas Johnstone was pointing out, Tanner said, 'Sorry, but what am I looking for?'

'The small red dots. Petechiae is haemorrhaging of the blood vessels caused when they're forced apart by intravascular pressure. But there are other signs to make me think that someone else had a hand; two, in fact.'

Heaving himself to his feet, he indicated the body's bony white shoulders, where a series of pale purple marks could just about be seen.

'I'd say that's where someone held him under. But there's also the amount of water that's been spilled out onto the floor, a clear sign that he didn't go down without a fight.'

As Tanner and Jenny glanced down at their

feet to see that they'd been standing in a puddle without even realising, Johnstone pulled off a pair of latex gloves to add, 'But as I said before, I'll have a better idea when I get him back to the lab.'

- CHAPTER FIVE -

EAVING THE MEDICAL examiner to continue with his work, Tanner and Jenny made their way out of the bathroom, down the creaking staircase, their hands taking advantage of newish handrails strategically placed on either side, presumably for the benefit of the elderly owner.

Once downstairs, they were soon able to locate the person they'd been told had found the body. He was pacing up and down a threadbare patterned rug within the confines of a small but cosy living room with a low beamed ceiling and a modern Edwardian-style gas fire that flickered with gentle reassurance.

'Mr Phillip Falcon?' enquired Tanner, as he and Jenny stepped into the room.

As the tall balding man turned a gaunt grey face towards them, Tanner pulled out his ID to formally introduce himself.

'Detective Inspector Tanner, and this is my colleague, Detective Constable Evans, Norfolk Police.'

'Yes?'

'We understand that you found the man who you've said is your father?'

'I did,' he replied, his deep-set eyes reflecting the many emotions associated with someone who'd just lost one of their parents: shock, confusion, and sadness, all mixed together with a child-like sense of deep-rooted insecurity.

'May I first of all express my condolences.'

'That's kind of you, thank you.'

'I know this is hardly the best of times, but we have a couple of questions we'd like to ask before we head off.'

'Of course. By all means.'

After a momentary pause, Tanner said, 'We've been told you found him early this morning.'

'That's right.'

'What time was that?'

'It must have been just before eight o'clock. I come in every morning around then, to make sure he's OK and to see if he needs any help with anything.'

'And did he usually?'

'What? Need help? Well, he'd never admit to it, but there weren't all that many things he could do on his own; not any more. He was all right physically, just about, but he'd been struggling with his memory for a good number of years, short-term especially. Even his long-term was beginning to slip, so much so that sometimes he didn't know who I was.'

'That must have been difficult.'

The man shrugged. 'It had been a gradual decline, and the doctors had told me to expect it. But even so, it still came as a shock.'

'Has there been anyone else around to help?'

'Not really, but I do use a local care service,

and a cleaner comes around once a week.'

'I assume you'll be able to provide us with their details.'

'I have them back at my house.'

With a nod, Tanner went on, 'About him having a bath – was that a regular occurrence?'

'It was, yes. As far as I know, he had one every day, either straight after supper or just before bed. He said it helped with his arthritis.'

'When was the last time you saw him?'

'Yesterday evening. We always had supper together; I'd come round and make it for us. I only live down the road, you see.'

'So, you were close?'

'I suppose you could say that. More so as he grew older. Before then we had what would probably best be described as a working relationship.'

'And Falcon's Yard: was he the sole owner?'

'Sole owner and sole founder. He started building boats here when he was twenty-one, back in 1946, but I've been managing the place for him over the last ten years or so.'

'And I suppose you're due to inherit his estate?'

'That obviously depends on what it says in his will. I'd have thought it likely to have been left equally between myself and my brother.'

Tanner glanced over to make sure Jenny was taking notes. 'Older or younger?'

'Younger.'

'May I ask where he lives?'

'Dartmouth, in Devon; at least, he does now. He used to live in London, but moved down there with his yacht when he retired.'

'Not up here?'

'Er, no. Despite having been brought up here, he never liked the place. He always said that it was too quiet, and moved away as soon as he could to take up a career in banking. We never saw much of him after that.'

'Do either of you have a family – wife, children?'

'I don't, no. I left that sort of thing to my brother. He's got both, or at least he had. His wife left him a long time ago.'

'And where do they all live?'

'I've no idea about his wife, but his children are down in London. Canary Warf, to be more precise.'

'Their names?'

'Edward and Tessa. They're twins.'

'And what do they do?'

'Edward's a senior hedge fund manager for the Instathon Bank. Tessa's some sort of a lawyer. I'm not sure who she works for.'

'Do you know when they were here last?'

'It must have been for my father's ninety-fourth birthday party, a couple of weeks ago.'

'And the name of your brother's ex-wife?'

'Oh...er...' After gazing up at the ceiling for a moment, he eventually replied, 'Margery? Or was it Margo? To be honest, I can't remember.'

'I assume you'd be able to provide us with your brother's contact details, should we need to speak to him?'

'Of course, yes, but I've already told him what's happened.'

'Let's just say that it may be useful to have,

just in case.'

Looking confused, the man asked, 'In case of what?'

'In case we need to speak to him.'

With it finally dawning on him why the police had been asking him so many questions, a sudden look of horror passed over his face. 'You don't think that someone...?'

'We're not thinking anything at the moment, Mr Falcon, but there is a chance that his passing came sooner than perhaps it should have.'

· CHAPTER SIX ·

MAKING THEIR WAY out of the cosy
living room, back into the dark wood-
panelled hallway, they heard raised
voices coming from the courtyard directly outside.

Heaving open the solid oak front door, Tanner
and Jenny found that the uniformed police officer
who'd shown them in earlier now had his hands
full trying to prevent a robust middle-aged
woman from entering the premises.

'You can't stop me from going in!' the woman
declared, as she tried shoving her way past.

Forced to push her back, the young officer
grunted, 'I'm afraid I can, madam!'

'But I have to see Mr Falcon. He needs me!'

Squeezing his way between the police constable
and the door frame, Tanner caught the eye of the
freckle-faced woman. 'I'm afraid Mr Falcon is
dead, madam.'

The woman glared back at him as if he'd just
slapped her around the face. 'Nonsense!' she
exclaimed. 'Mr Falcon can't be dead! The man's as
strong as an ox!'

'And now he's as dead as a dodo.'

Seeing how the woman's face reddened and
that her bottom lip began to tremble, regretting

having made the remark, Tanner asked, 'May I enquire how you knew Mr Falcon?'

'I'm his carer!' she declared, as if it was the most important job in the world.

Fighting the temptation to say, 'Not any more,' he asked, 'May I ask your name?' glancing around at Jenny as he did as a cue for her to make a note of it.

'Pauline. Pauline Denney. I assume you're his doctor?'

'Norfolk Police.' Pulling out his ID, he added, 'Detective Inspector Tanner.'

Staring at it with a confused look, the woman spluttered out, 'But – what? Did someone break in and – and…?'

'I'm afraid we don't know yet.'

'But – something must have happened, else you wouldn't be here.'

'Mr Falcon died, Ms Denney. For now, that's all we know.'

After pausing for a moment, the woman shifted her gaze to the door to which she was being denied access. 'Do you think I'd be able to see him?'

'I'm afraid that won't be possible.'

'May I at least go in to pick up what I left when I was here last?'

'When was that?'

'On Friday.'

'OK, well, if you tell Constable Walker here what the items are, we'll make sure that they're returned to you.'

'But I only need to pop in for a moment,' she said, taking a sudden step forward in a bid to slip past.

'Again, sorry, but that won't be possible,' said Tanner, blocking her way.

'Fine, but you'd better make sure I get my stuff back!'

'And what was it exactly that you left behind?'

With a more guarded look, the woman shifted from one foot to the other. 'Nothing important. Just some personal items.'

'And whereabouts did you leave them?'

'I'm not sure, which is why it would probably be easier if I just went inside to have a look.'

Addressing the young police officer, Tanner said, 'Make sure to take down Ms Denney's address and contact details, as well as a full list of the items she thinks she's left behind.'

'Yes, sir.'

'As I said,' the woman repeated, 'it's nothing of any value.'

'Don't worry, Ms Denney, I can assure you that anything you've accidently left inside will be returned to you.'

With that, he turned to lead Jenny away.

Crunching over the gravel-lined courtyard towards Tanner's car, as soon as they were out of earshot, Jenny said, 'She certainly seemed keen to get inside.'

'Almost as if she'd left something incriminating behind,' observed Tanner, glancing over his shoulder at the supposed carer.

'Do you think she could be the killer?'

Reaching his car, Tanner shrugged. 'It's possible, I suppose, but if she is, she'd have needed a pretty good reason.'

'Maybe she lost her temper when giving him a bath?'

Seeing that Jenny wasn't being serious, Tanner turned to look around at some of the more prestigious cars parked in amongst the emergency vehicles. 'I suppose we'll have to wait and see what forensics have to say, but at this stage I think it's more likely to have been money-motivated.'

Seeing what he was looking at, Jenny said, 'The Rolls Royce must be worth a fair penny, as must the Bentley Continental.'

'In their day, but they're both older models.'

'And how about the number plates; Falcon 1 and Falcon 2?'

'They're probably worth more than the cars.' He looked back at the house. 'I suspect most of their wealth is tied up in the property, and the land it sits on.'

'So we need to find out whoever had the most to gain?'

'Possibly; although if that is the case, it does strike me as odd that whoever decided to drown him chose to wait until now to do so, and didn't simply hang about for another few months. At ninety-four, he couldn't have had much longer to go, no matter what the carer may have thought.'

'Maybe they just got tired of waiting? I mean, it's not uncommon these days for people to live to be over a hundred. It could be that they simply weren't prepared to wait that long, especially if they had financial problems.'

'If that was the case, and whoever did it has an

urgent need for money, then they're going to find themselves with a fairly long wait before they can get their hands on it. For a start, it will take a while for the estate to go through probate, and then they'd need to sell everything, which would take time in itself. But before then there's the question of the will.'

'The older son seemed to think everything would be divided equally between himself and his brother.'

'Maybe he was just saying that. If his brother hasn't been around, as was suggested, and if the old man's mind was going, it probably wouldn't have been too difficult to persuade him to change the will in his own favour. If he had been looking after him all these years whilst his younger brother has been mucking about in boats in Dartmouth, he could have easily been spoon-feeding his father some sort of story about how his youngest son wasn't worthy of his inheritance, and that he should leave it all to him. For all we know, he could have told him that his youngest son was dead.'

'Or maybe he'd simply had enough of having to look after him all the time.'

'Now that is a possibility,' said Tanner. 'It's hardly an easy job. Far from it!'

'Your father?' enquired Jenny. Tanner had mentioned to her before that he'd had Alzheimer's for a number of years before passing.

'It's not easy having to watch one of your parents fade away before your eyes,' he remarked, cupping his hand under the Jag's chrome door handle. 'It's harder still when they don't even know who you are. At that stage you start asking yourself what the point is of keeping them alive. It's almost as if their soul has already gone. And when they start pleading with you to end it...'

Tanner turned his head away to prevent Jenny from seeing that he was becoming emotional. 'It may simply have been that the older son couldn't bear to watch his father suffer anymore, and decided to take the matter into his own hands.'

Jenny studied the side of Tanner's face over the car's sloping low roof. She could tell he was crying. She knew him well enough by then to know.

'Anyway,' he eventually continued, using the back of one of his hands to wipe away an escaping tear, 'I'd better give Forrester a call, but assuming we're going to have to wait until Johnstone can give us a definitive cause of death, we may as well take lunch.'

Glancing down at her watch to see that it was already gone twelve, Jenny suggested, 'How about we have it on board our boat? After all, it's not every day we have a case that's virtually next door to where we live.'

· CHAPTER SEVEN ·

Wednesday 9th October

I T WASN'T UNTIL Wednesday when the final reports came through from both forensics and Dr Johnstone, their conclusions giving reason for Tanner to ask for an impromptu office-wide briefing.

'OK, listen up everyone,' called Forrester, standing with his senior DI in front of the whiteboard. 'I'm sure you've all heard by now that the founder and owner of Falcon's Yard, Mr Harry Falcon, was found dead in his bath on Monday morning.'

Using a marker pen, he wrote the name under a photograph that had already been posted up. The image depicted an elderly man leaning on a cane, with a wooden boat propped up on stilts behind him.

'What some of you probably don't know is that he founded the yard at the tender age of just twenty-one, way back in 1946, and that it's the longest running boatyard in the whole of the Broads. He also founded the Broads Wildlife Trust, something to which he gave generously of both his time and money throughout his life. On top of that, and this is something that even I didn't know about, not only did he see active service during World War Two, but he was one of the earliest, and youngest members of the Special Air Service, more commonly known as the SAS. It was for his war record that he was awarded an OBE along with the King's Gallantry Medal for bravery. So I think it goes without saying that Harry Falcon was a pillar of our local community, one who will be sorely missed.

'Consequently, it's with a heavy heart that I have to report that the conclusion of our medical examiner is that he didn't die from natural causes. Dr Johnstone's findings are that he was killed by having his head forced under water, sometime between ten o'clock on Sunday evening and one o'clock the following morning.

'It would appear that we therefore have a murder on our hands, and as the victim was a ninety-four-year-old war hero, I for one am particularly keen to find the person responsible.

'I'm now going to hand you over to DI Tanner, who'll be the SOI for this investigation, overseen by myself of course. I've no doubt you'll all give him your one hundred percent commitment and support.'

Thanking his DCI, Tanner opened a folder to take out two photographs which he proceeded to stick up directly underneath the picture of Harry Falcon.

'At the moment,' he began, 'due to the size of the estate owned by the victim, we're considering this to be financially motivated. However, we're not ruling out more personal reasons which we'll touch on later.

'We've yet to see a copy of the will, but for now we're assuming that the main beneficiaries are his two sons; Phillip, the elder on the left, and James. Phillip has never married and doesn't have any offspring, whilst James is divorced with two children, Edward and Tessa Falcon. We don't have pictures for them yet, but we know that they're both in their late twenties and live in London. As they could also be beneficiaries of the will, we need to treat them as suspects, for now at least.' Glancing over at DS Vicky Gilbert, Tanner asked, 'I don't suppose there's been any news from the victim's solicitors yet?'

'They've still not sent the will over, no.'

'OK, it's a priority, so keep chasing.'

Seeing her nod, Tanner returned his attention to the board.

After scrawling out the names of the sons and the two grandchildren, Tanner pointed at the eldest son.

'Phillip lives in a cottage just down the road from Falcon's Yard. From what he's told us, he's lived in Norfolk all his life, during which time he's learnt the ropes of the business. He's now the yard's managing director. He's also played a significant role in looking after his father. According to him, Harry Falcon had been suffering from the latter stages of dementia for a number of years. This had reached the point where Falcon senior would often be unable to remember those closest to him, including Phillip. This is where the second possible motive may come into play. For those of you with relatives who suffer from severe cognitive decline, I'm sure you can appreciate just how challenging it can be, for both the relatives and the person affected. We therefore need to keep in mind that someone may have decided to take matters into their own hands, possibly even at the request of the victim. That may have been Phillip, but it could equally have been someone else, including one of his carers.'

Turning his attention back to the whiteboard, Tanner pointed at the next photograph. 'James Falcon is a retired banker. He lives down in Dartmouth, Devon, where he apparently has a yacht, probably together with some other toys. We all know how much bankers like their money, even retired ones, so he's also at the top of our list of suspects.

'We don't know much about his children at the moment, other than that Edward is a banker, like his father, and Tessa is a lawyer. If the will includes them, then they'll also need to be on our suspect list.

'Looking at the forensics report, a total of eleven distinct sets of fingerprints have been found within the property and around the bathroom, where the body was found. Now we know from the eldest son that Harry Falcon had a cleaner coming in once a week as well as numerous carers, one of whom we've already met. At the moment I'm not prepared to rule any of them out, so we need to find out exactly who they all are, when they were last there, and where they all were on Sunday evening. We'll also need to do background checks on them all. Did any have a personal connection to Harry Falcon? For all we know, one of them could be an illegitimate child who thinks they have some sort of a claim over the estate. Or it could be that Harry Falcon asked them to end his life for him, and they elected to oblige. DI Cooper and DS Gilbert, I'll leave them with you. DC Evans and I are going to focus on the immediate family.

'OK, that's it for now. Any news, let me know.'

· CHAPTER EIGHT ·

SINCE THE SCHOOL summer holidays had come to an end in September, traffic in the Broads had been noticeably lighter. That meant it took less than fifteen minutes for Tanner and Jenny to make the journey from Wroxham to Stalham, where Falcon's Yard was located, along with their own boat.

Leaving the XJS in the courtyard, next to a brand new Aston Martin Vanquish, they crunched over the gravel towards the yard's warehouse-sized boatshed, at the end of a dyke in which numerous yachts were moored.

They were eventually pointed in the direction of the office, where they found Phillip Falcon sitting behind an untidy desk, busily rummaging through a pile of paper with a pained expression etched over his weathered face.

'I hope we're not disturbing you?' asked Tanner, having knocked on the already half-open door.

Jumping with a start, Phillip glanced up to say, 'Not at all!' before staring back down at the documents he was going through. 'Our accountant's asking for all the receipts for our annual tax return. It doesn't have to be done till the end of January, but he always insists on doing it early, God knows why. He doesn't seem to understand that my father's just passed away. Anyway, sorry, how can I help?'

'May we sit down?'

'Where are my manners? Of course. Can I get you anything to drink?'

'No, no, we're fine, but thank you.' He and Jenny pulled out a couple of chairs.

Once seated, crossing one leg over the other, Tanner pushed on by saying, 'We're here with news of your father's post-mortem.'

Noticing the way the man grabbed hold of the arms of his chair, as if bracing himself, Tanner returned to studying his face. 'Unfortunately, it looks like your father didn't die of natural causes.'

'You mean, he was...?'

'I'm afraid so.'

'But... Who could have done such a thing?'

'That's what we're here to find out, Mr Falcon, and to initiate that process, we'll need to ask you a couple of questions.'

'Absolutely.'

'And to take copies of your fingerprints, and a DNA sample.' Seeing a look of deep concern descend over his face, he added, 'They will help us eliminate you from our enquiries.'

'Right.'

'We also need to ask where you were on Sunday night, from ten o'clock through to one o'clock the following morning?'

'I was at home. I'd had dinner with him earlier that evening. I left him sitting in his favourite armchair, beside the fire in the living room.'

'What time was that?'

'It must have been around half eight – maybe nine. Then I went home, watched the news, read a little, and went to bed.'

'I assume nobody would be able to vouch for you?'

'I'm afraid not.'

'And you didn't see him again until the following morning?'

'That's right. He'd normally be pottering about in the kitchen, but when I couldn't find him, I went upstairs and... Well, there he was.'

'Has there been any news on the will?'

'There has, yes. My brother came up yesterday for the reading.'

'May I ask what it said?'

'It was as I'd expected. The estate's been left equally between myself and my brother. There have been some items bequeathed to his children, but only a few pieces of my mother's old jewellery and some furniture.'

'So, what are you planning on doing now?'

'Sorry, but how do you mean?'

'Do you intend to sell the yard?'

'God, no! It's a family business, and so it will continue. That's what my father would have wanted. He even said as much in the will.'

'And what does your brother think about that?'

'Frankly, it's got nothing to do with him.'

'But he now owns half the estate.'

'Which means he can't do anything without my approval.'

'Do you think he'd like to sell it?'

'Well, probably, but only because he has no

particular interest in the business. He never has. And as he doesn't exactly need the money, I can't see it being an issue.'

'You said that he came up yesterday.'

'That's correct. You probably saw his Aston Martin parked in the courtyard.'

Tanner thought for a moment. 'Do you know where he's staying?'

'Yes – on board my father's yacht.'

'Which is where?'

'Oh, sorry. It's moored up at the end of the dyke – called Vanessa.'

'OK, well, I think that's it, for the time being.'

'Before you go, I don't suppose you know when my father's body will be released? It's just that I have a funeral to arrange, and, well, it's difficult to do so without being able to set a date.'

'Yes, of course,' replied Tanner, as he and Jenny rose from their chairs. 'I'll ask our medical examiner and come back to you.'

As Phillip Falcon got up to show them out, Tanner remembered about the flats being built opposite, and for more personal reasons than professional, turned to ask, 'Whilst we're here, you wouldn't happen to know anything about the housing development going up next door?'

'Oh, that! Unfortunately I do, yes.'

'I assume you objected?'

'Naturally, but it didn't seem to make any difference. And with the builder's reputation, it was fairly obvious that it was going to go ahead, no matter what anyone said.'

'You mean Jackson Developments?'

'That's the one. The owner's called Jim

Jackson. Not a particularly pleasant individual. I've even found him round here, trying to persuade my father to sell him the yard.'

'Really?' said Tanner, his interest piqued. 'When was that?'

'Twice in the last six months. If it wasn't for the fact that I was around, he'd have probably succeeded as well. He's well known for preying on the elderly.'

'Is he now?' Tanner raised an intrigued eyebrow at Jenny.

'According to what people say, he's built half his business by taking advantage of them.'

· CHAPTER NINE ·

THE MOMENT THEY stepped outside, where the dyke stretched out before them, Jenny turned to Tanner. 'It sounds like we need to make an appointment with Jackson Developments.'

'And in particular its owner,' agreed Tanner. 'But whilst we're here, before he disappears back to deepest darkest Devon, I suggest we have a chat with the younger son – James, isn't it?'

'James, yes,' she nodded, 'and the boat he's staying on is called Vanessa.'

Stepping carefully over a narrow channel of water that led into the boatshed's entrance, they followed a dull grey wooden walkway down the dyke, towards the river at the end. On their right was a neat row of near-identical traditional mahogany Broads yachts with matching white awnings, all very similar to their own. On their left was a grass verge on which stood some old sagging wooden picnic tables, looking as if they'd collapse if anyone were to actually sit on them.

Admiring the yachts, they studied the names painted on the backs of each, all with the same elaborate gold lettering, until they found the one they were looking for, moored up at the far end.

With its canvas awning closed, and no front door to knock on, Tanner was forced to call out, 'Hello? Is anyone home?'

Movement inside was followed by a muffled voice saying, 'Hold on.'

They were happy to spend a few moments looking over the boat they were waiting beside, and it wasn't long before the entrance flap was pulled back to reveal a heavily tanned older man with jet black hair that had obviously been dyed.

Staring out at Tanner, then Jenny, in a tone thick with disdain the man demanded, 'And you are?'

Taking an instant dislike to him, Tanner pulled out his ID. 'Detective Inspector Tanner and Detective Constable Evans, Norfolk Police. Are we speaking to Harry Falcon's younger son, James Falcon?'

'Yes, why? What of it?'

'It's about your father, Mr Falcon.'

'Ah, I see. Well, if you've come all the way over here to tell me that he's dead, you're too late. I already know.'

'It's not so much that he's dead, Mr Falcon, but more the manner in which he died that we've come to talk to you about.'

'I thought he had a heart attack in the bath?'

'With regret, it's been concluded that someone deliberately held him under the water.'

'You mean, he was drowned?'

'I'm afraid so.'

'Well I never. And I suppose you're here because you think that I may have had something to do with it; possibly as a means to get my grubby little hands on his inheritance?'

'Something like that,' confirmed Tanner, offering him a thin smile.

'Well, good luck with that!'

'But at this stage we simply need your fingerprints and a DNA sample.'

'Now?'

'Not this minute, no. You can come down to the station, or we can send someone over to collect them from you here.'

'I'm afraid neither's particularly convenient.'

'But necessary,' said Tanner, his eyes remaining fixed on the man's.

Eventually Falcon capitulated, shrugging his shoulders. 'I suppose you'd better send someone around. But not today, mind. Sometime tomorrow. And not too early, either. I rarely get up before eleven.'

'We'll see what we can do, Mr Falcon. Oh, and whilst we're here, may I ask where you were on Sunday, between the hours of ten in the evening and one the following morning?'

'I'm delighted to say that I was nowhere near the place.'

'So where were you then?'

'Probably on board my yacht; and I don't mean this woodworm-infested floating pile of crap.'

'I assume that you're referring to the one you keep down in Devon?'

'On the River Dart,' he confirmed.

'Would anyone be able to vouch for you?'

'Probably.'

'So, you'd be able to give us a name?'

'Well, yes, but I'd have to look up to see which

girl I was with at the time,' he replied, winking at Jenny.

Tanner felt his skin crawl. 'Do you think you'd be able to find out for us?'

'To be honest, I'm not sure I can be bothered. Would it be OK if I emailed it over to you later?'

'I'd be happier if you could find it for us now.'

'Oh, very well. Wait here!'

With that, he disappeared inside, to re-appear a moment later carrying a phone.

'Sunday night, you say?'

'That's right.'

'I was with Sexy Sandra.'

'Surname?'

'Buckingham, or Fuckingham, as she likes to be called, at least she does when I'm banging her against the bulkhead,' he added, giving Jenny a lurid, salacious grin.

Sensing her squirm beside him, Tanner wondered if he could get away with punching the man in the face. Doubting he would, he gritted his teeth and forced himself to remain calm. 'And a contact phone number, if you'd be so kind?'

'I suspect she's a little out of your league, Detective Spanner, wasn't it?'

With a wry smile, Tanner said, 'Close enough.'

Once he'd read out the woman's contact details and Jenny had noted them down, Tanner pushed on. 'When was the last time you saw your father?'

'It was for his ninety-fourth birthday, a couple of weeks ago. I can't say I normally make the effort, but he was so far gone, I honestly thought it would be his last.'

'Well, it seems you were right about that.'

'Perhaps,' he replied, with a shrug, 'but you must be wondering why someone would go to the trouble of drowning him in his bath when he was about to keel over anyway?'

'Maybe they needed the money,' proposed Tanner, studying the man's face, 'and they weren't in a position to wait?'

'Don't look at me! I've got cash coming out of my ears, unlike my dear departed father.'

'Are you suggesting he was having financial difficulties?'

'I'm not suggesting. Just look at the place! It's hardly a hive of industry. Don't get me wrong, the land is probably worth a fair whack, but the business itself barely makes enough to break even; in fact, most years it doesn't.'

'Which leads me to ask about the will,' interjected Tanner. 'From what your brother has told us, you've been left half the estate.'

'So I hear.'

'And your brother intends to keep running the business.'

'We'll have to see about that.'

'I assume that you'd be keen to sell?'

'If it was my choice I would, yes. It obviously isn't sustainable. It would make far more sense to sell the land and invest the profits into something more rewarding. No doubt my idiot brother will eventually reach the same conclusion. He's already had to re-mortgage his house to keep it going. I doubt it will be long before he's left with no choice but to sell.'

'And then you'll be there, to take your half.'

'I know what you're thinking, Inspector, but

believe you me, the value of the yard is a drop in the ocean compared to my personal net worth. You don't spend forty odd years working in mergers and acquisitions to retire without having made a shed-load of cash. Half the value of this mosquito-infested swamp wouldn't even be enough to buy myself a new yacht, at least nothing decent. I'd be lucky if I could pick up a second-hand dinghy. So I can assure you, I have absolutely no reason to want the old man dead, apart from the obvious, of course.'

'And the obvious is…?'

'That he was walking around in a virtual coma. Half the time he didn't know where he was, and the other half he didn't know who he was. Having a conversation with him was like talking to a goldfish, and not an intelligent one. I've no idea how my brother coped; in fact, maybe he didn't. Maybe he cracked under the pressure of having to talk to him all the time and drowned him himself. For all I know, my father asked him to do it. It's certainly the sort of thing I can imagine him doing. All his stupid he who dares, wins crap. Thinking about it, I wouldn't be surprised if he didn't go and drown himself.'

'Am I correct in thinking that you didn't get along with your father?'

'Who, me? Er, not exactly, no. He'd probably have been OK had he not been a complete psycho. The man was like a dad from hell. He raised us as if we were on army basic training. If we didn't do exactly what he said, when he said it, he'd beat us to a pulp. He was bad enough when Mum was around, but when she upped and left the guy just went nuts. One time he hit Phillip so hard he had to be taken to hospital. That's why I left, just as soon as I could.'

'But Phillip stayed?'

'He did, yes, and to this day, I've got no idea why. Probably out of some sort of misplaced sense of loyalty.'

'OK, well, thank you for your time, Mr Falcon. I assume you're going to be around for a while.'

'I've told Phillip I will, yes, but only to help out with the funeral.'

'Maybe you could let us know if you decide to leave,' said Tanner, giving him one of his cards.

'I'll think about it,' he replied, not even bothering to look at it.

Tanner was about to lead Jenny away, when he remembered what the elder brother had said about the building developer.

'Before we go, I don't suppose you know anything about the flats being built next door?'

'What flats are those?'

'The riverside apartments.'

'I've not heard about them, why?'

'Did you know that the construction company involved has been trying to buy the yard from your father?'

'I didn't, no, but as far as I'm concerned, they're welcome to it.'

'So they've not been in contact with you?'

'Not yet, no; but I don't suppose there's any chance you can ask them to give me a call? A half-decent offer might help persuade my brother to do the right thing and sell the damned place.'

With an unamused smile, Tanner turned to

say, 'Thank you for your time, Mr Falcon,' and led
Jenny away.

· CHAPTER TEN ·

'I KIND OF liked him,' said Jenny, as they made their way back to the car. Tanner stared round at her. 'I don't suppose you've got his phone number?'

'Oh, I get it now. You're joking.'

'Joking? Why would I be joking? He's stinking rich, a real looker, clearly a natural with women, and he's got a massive yacht! What's not to like?'

Tanner thought for a moment. 'His hair?'

'Nobody's perfect.'

'Anyway, marriage material aside, what did you think?'

'You mean apart from his wealth, good-looks, his way with women, massive yacht and dyed hair?'

'Uh-huh.'

'That he's the slimiest person I've ever met in my entire life.'

'I meant in regard to the investigation?'

'Oh, that! Well, I've no idea if he did it or not, but of everyone living on the planet who may have done, I sincerely hope it was him.'

'Seriously,' said Tanner, keen to hear her professional opinion.

'Well, seriously, I suppose he lacks motive.'

'Being that he doesn't seem to need the money.'

'He would also appear to have a pretty good alibi, since he was in Devon, entertaining some tart on board his yacht.'

'Perhaps,' replied Tanner, deep in thought.

'What do you think?' asked Jenny.

'I think he was trying a little too hard to be obnoxious. There are two things I know about the rich; firstly, that they all seem to live in a bubble in which they think the normal rules of society don't apply to them, and secondly, that even though they've got more money than they could ever need, they always seem to want more – that's if he's actually got any.'

'How do you mean?'

'From personal experience I've found that it's often the case that the more people go on about how much money they've got, the less they actually have, so we'll need to look at his finances. It could well be that despite appearances, he's completely broke, and is desperate to get hold of Daddy's estate.'

'Enough to murder his own father?'

'Bearing in mind what he said about how his father brought him up, I wouldn't put it past him.'

'And he'd still need to persuade his brother to sell.'

'Yes, but if what he was saying about Falcon's Yard's financial position is true – that his brother had to re-mortgage his house just to keep it in the black, then that may not be a problem. But it's certainly something else we need to look into.'

'The company's finances?'

'Those and the older brother's.'

'There's another possibility as well,' mused Jenny.

'What's that?'

'That if the brothers are both skint, they hatched the plan together.'

'Very true; but in the meantime, I think we need to pay a visit to the property developer. What was his name again?'

Checking her notebook, Jenny replied, 'Jim Jackson.'

'That's right, him. From what Phillip was saying, he sounds even slimier than that brother of his.'

- CHAPTER ELEVEN -

W ITH JACKSON DEVELOPMENTS'
main office being based in Great
Yarmouth, Tanner and Jenny followed
the A47 heading towards the east coast.

Turning into what they discovered to be a
large, non-descript industrial estate crammed full
of iron-roofed warehouses and square concrete
office blocks, they were soon able to locate the
premises they were looking for.

After showing their police identification they
were ushered into a spacious but grubby office, at
the end of which sat a stocky red-faced man
wearing a blue-checked office shirt, open at the
neck.

'Mr Jackson,' the secretary said, leading the
way inside, 'I have Detective Inspector Tanner
and Detective Constable Evans from Norfolk
Police to see you.'

With a broad welcoming smile aimed squarely
at the approaching officers, half-standing he
offered them a seat.

As they pulled out a couple of chairs, the man
sat back, saying, 'Can we get you anything to
drink? A coffee, perhaps?'

Imagining it would be some horrendous instant

variety, Tanner smiled and declined.

'So, how can I help?'

'We understand you know Mr Harry Falcon.'

'I know of him, as do most people around here. I read about his death in the papers, but that wasn't unexpected, surely?'

'It may not have been unexpected, Mr Jackson, but it was certainly earlier than it should have been.'

'Sorry, but in what way?'

'The post-mortem concluded that someone had a hand in his death.'

Exchanging concerned glances between the two detectives, Jackson eventually said, 'You can't possibly think that I had anything to do with it?'

Tanner ignored the question. 'We've been reliably informed that you've been speaking to him about the sale of Falcon's Yard.'

'Yes, and...? So what?'

'And that he declined your offer; twice, in fact.'

'Oh, I see where you're going with this. You thought that because he'd refused to sell it to me, I decided to have him killed?'

'Either that, or you did it yourself.'

'Listen, I'm just your average law abiding businessman, not some sort of East End gangster. Everything I do is above board. I even pay my taxes, which is more than can be said of most in my profession. I certainly wouldn't go around killing some old man just to get hold of his land, especially not when he was about to keel over anyway. I may be ambitious, but I'm not stupid!'

'But you'd threatened him before, though, right?'

'You've been speaking to that older son of his, haven't you?'

'If you mean Phillip Falcon, then yes, we have.'

'Well, whatever he's told you is utter bollocks. Yes, I'd been round to see his dad, but there was no way I threatened him. If anything, it was the other way round. I mean, the guy's completely off his head, or at least he was. He even started waving some old World War Two submachine gun in my face, saying that he'd shoot me if I didn't get off his land. And his son was just as bad. After that, it probably wasn't surprising that I decided to leave them to it and let nature take its course. I knew the old man would be dead soon anyway, and if the rumours are true about the state of its finances, I doubt if it will be long before the son is round here begging me to buy the place.'

'I assume it would be worth your while if he did?'

'If you mean, would I make money from it, then yes, of course. I've got the investors in place, and have already started to build on the land opposite.'

'We know,' said Tanner, grudgingly. He was sorely tempted to tell him that their boat was moored there, but thought better of it.

'I've got planning permission to build over the yard as well.'

'And how, may I ask, did you manage that, seeing that it doesn't even belong to you?'

'Don't worry, it's quite legal. Besides, I know someone at the council,' he added, with a dry smile. 'Actually, I know quite a few people at the council, but it's only planning permission. I can't build on it until the title deeds are transferred, for which I basically just need a signature.'

'And what then?' asked Tanner.

'Good question! Tell you what, why don't I show you?'

Jumping up from his chair, he invited them to follow him to the other end of the office, where on display was a scale model of a sleek modern riverside development complete with miniature boats, cars and people.

'Here's what my architect came up with when I was pitching the idea to the council. As you can see, when it's finished, it will be the ultimate in luxury living; spacious two- and three-bedroom flats, each with either an outside space or a private balcony, complete with exclusive moorings. It even has secure underground car parking. What do you think?'

After studying it briefly, Tanner asked, 'Where's Falcon's Yard?'

'Ah, yes. I must admit that this is the model for the final stage of the development. The first stage is this section here. Where this footbridge leads to is where Falcon's Yard is at present.'

'But where's the dyke?'

'The plan is to drain it, and then build straight over the top.'

Tanner crouched down to look at it at eye level. 'I must admit, it does look good. You've clearly gone to some considerable expense already, almost as if purchasing the yard is just a formality.'

'I have to admit that I do have it on very good authority that it is.'

'And who, I wonder, could have given you that impression?'

'Unfortunately, I'm not at liberty to say.'

'Well, it's not Harry Falcon, as the man's dead, and I doubt it was his eldest son, Phillip. That leaves only one other person who could know.'

'As I said, I can't say.'

'You do realise that this is a murder investigation?'

Jackson paused for a moment. 'Well, if you must know, it was the other son, James.'

Raising an intrigued eyebrow, Tanner asked, 'And when did you speak to him?'

'I can't remember. It was a while back now.'

'Exactly?'

'If you must know, it was after Harry Falcon escorted me off his property with a submachine gun stuck in my face. I got a call from James a few days later. That was when he told me about the yard's financial position and to sit tight, as he didn't think it would be long before the old man kicked the proverbial bucket. Once he had, the estate would be as good as mine, after I'd paid for it, of course.'

'And that was when you approached the council for planning permission?'

'I had to commission the architect first, but yes, it was then that I started to get the ball rolling. So if you're looking for anyone to blame for Harry Falcon's slightly earlier than scheduled demise, if I were you, I'd have a chat with James.'

· CHAPTER TWELVE ·

As SOON AS they were back outside, Tanner pulled his phone out of his pocket, saying, 'I'd better give Forrester a call.'

'What are you going to tell him?'

'Not much. Only that we have another suspect that needs a background check.'

'Jackson?'

'Uh-huh.'

'So you still think he may have done it, even after what he was saying about the younger brother?'

'I think he may have done it because of what he was saying about the younger brother!'

'Er, I'm not with you.'

'I just thought it was a bit of an unlikely coincidence that James Falcon would have called him after he'd been chased off the premises by Harry.'

'So you think it could have been the other way round. Jackson called James?'

'It would seem more plausible, yes.'

'So, if Jackson killed the old man, or arranged for him to be killed, why would James have lied about having spoken to him?'

'Frankly, at this stage I've no idea, but I

wouldn't put it past either of them if they came up with the idea together, which would leave James denying all knowledge, and Jackson deciding that it would probably be in his best interest to shift the focus of the investigation in James's direction. Anyway, first things first, let me give Forrester a call. I also need to ask him if it's OK for us to go down to London tomorrow, to interview the grandchildren.'

'Oh, yes, please!' exclaimed Jenny, grinning at him. She'd never been, but had always wanted to.

'Well, let's see what he says first, shall we.'

When the DCI answered, Tanner said, 'Just letting you know that we're in Great Yarmouth, sir.'

'Great Yarmouth? What on earth are you doing there?'

'We had a lead, sir. Apparently, a building developer by the name of Jim Jackson had been threatening Harry Falcon in an effort to persuade him to sell him the yard. His offices are in Great Yarmouth. We've just come out of a meeting with him.'

'And what did he say?'

'In a nutshell, that he hadn't. He said that it was the other way round. Harry Falcon had threatened him. But he did at least admit to having tried to buy the land off him. He's even gone to the trouble of having arranged for planning permission to build on it, despite the fact that he doesn't own it yet.'

'So, you think it could be him?'

'Well, I wouldn't put it past him. It's fairly obvious that he's already sunk a hell of a lot of time and money into the project. He's started building on the site next door, so it could be that he'd simply run out of time waiting for Harry Falcon to die.'

'How about the younger son – James, isn't it?'

'We've spoken to him as well, sir.'

'And...?'

'I'd have to say that if he didn't do it himself, I wouldn't be surprised if he'd had a hand in it. Hardly the most charming of individuals. We asked him if he knew anything about the offer made by Jackson, but he said he didn't. However, about an hour later, Jackson told us that James had called him to discuss the deal.'

'OK, so, what's next?'

'We need to run a background check on this Jackson guy. We also need to look into the finances of Falcon's Yard. According to James, the business is on its last legs, and the only reason it's still afloat is because Phillip re-mortgaged his house to cover its debts.'

'That shouldn't be a problem.'

'We also need to pop down to London, sir.'

'London?'

'Yes, sir. According to Phillip, James's children have been named in the will, and they both live in London.'

'How much have they been left?'

'Well, not much, but as Phillip doesn't have any children, they're next in line to inherit the lot.'

'But only after both Phillip and James are dead.'

'Exactly, sir!'

'Er...I actually meant that as a reason for them

not to be involved.'

'Well, sir, one's a banker and the other's a lawyer. If they're anything like their father, they're probably thinking ahead.'

'Are you honestly suggesting that they'd murder their grandfather, uncle and even their own father, just to claim their inheritance?'

'I don't know, sir. I've not spoken to them yet.'

'I think I can answer that one for you, Tanner. Besides, I can't spare you; not with all these background checks that need to be done.'

'But can't Cooper and Gilbert cover them?'

'No, Tanner! They're still ploughing their way through all the bloody cleaners and carers.'

'But we still need to collect the grandchildren's prints and DNA.'

'We do?'

'We've been told they were at Harry Falcon's ninety-fourth birthday party, so we'll need to eliminate them, at the very least.'

'OK, then we can arrange for them to be collected via the Met.'

'We may as well speak to them as well, sir.'

'Then you can phone them up.'

'But it's better face-to-face. It will only be a day out of the office.'

There was a pause, before a heavy sigh came down the line. 'Very well, but only you, Tanner. DC Evans can stay behind and push on with the background checks.'

'But I'll need Jenny's – I-I mean – DC Evans's support when I'm down there, sir.'

'And why's that, may I ask?'

'Well, to take notes, for a start.'

'I see. Why do I get the feeling that you're attempting to use this as an excuse to have some sort of sordid weekend away together?'

'Er...but tomorrow's Thursday, sir.'

'If you want to go down to London, you'll just have to cope on your own; and that's my final word on the subject!'

With the call ending rather abruptly, Tanner was left staring at Jenny. 'Sorry, Jen, but it looks like you're going to have to stay here.'

'Oh well. Not to worry,' she replied, forcing a smile.

Seeing the disappointment in her eyes, Tanner put his phone away to say, 'Tell you what. The next free weekend we have, I'll take you down and give you a personal guided tour. How does that sound?'

'Would you take me to see a West End show?' she asked, her face brightening.

'I don't know about that. Those things cost a small fortune.'

Turning her head away, she folded her arms securely over her chest. 'Well, I suppose I could always develop a sudden and unexpected headache every night for the next, what, shall we say six months?'

Shoving his hands deep into his pockets, Tanner let out a heavy sigh. 'You'd better let me know which one you want to see, then, hadn't you?'

As she looked at him with her most dazzling smile, he added, 'But only on the condition that you start making a few less derogatory remarks about my car.'

'Really? Oh well. I suppose I'll just have to make do with a play instead.'

- CHAPTER THIRTEEN -

FTER FIGHTING THEIR way through
Great Yarmouth's traffic, Tanner and
Jenny eventually arrived back at Wroxham
Police Station. There, Jenny began the tedious
task of making background checks on the three
men who'd become the main suspects in the
investigation: Phillip and James Falcon, and the
owner of Jackson Developments. With those
underway, she put in a request to access their
personal finances, as well as the business
accounts relating to Falcon's Yard, held at
Companies House.

Meanwhile, Tanner contacted the two
grandchildren, arranging to meet with them the
following day at a café in Canary Wharf, near to
where they worked.

After organising a train down, he spent the
next couple of hours helping Jenny with the
background checks, before deciding to call it a day
at just after six.

Arriving home, they were somewhat surprised
to find a police patrol boat had moored up
between their yacht and one of their neighbours',
and that it looked as if they were each being
issued with some sort of penalty notice by a

couple of uniformed police constables.

Marching up to the one with a foot resting on top of their varnished mahogany coach roof, vaguely recognising him, Tanner called out, 'Excuse me, but may I ask what you're doing, exactly?'

Glancing up to see not one but two members of Wroxham's CID hurrying over towards him, after opening and closing his mouth, the constable eventually came out with, 'I'm, er, sorry sir, but these boats have been reported as having been moored here illegally.'

'By who?'

'Jackson Developments, sir,' he replied, pointing at a large sign overlooking the river, which definitely hadn't been there when they'd left for work.

Exchanging a dirty look with Jenny, under his breath Tanner muttered, 'Unbelievable,' before turning his attention back to the officer. 'OK, well, for a start, that particular boat belongs to us, so I'd appreciate it if you could remove your boots from the woodwork.'

Seeing him step hurriedly off the coach roof, Tanner added, 'And secondly, we've paid our mooring fees right up until this time next year, so I suggest you take that penalty notice of yours and shove it...' Hearing Jenny cough loudly beside him, he stopped mid-sentence to replace what he was about to say with, 'back into your file.'

'Er, yes sir, of c-course,' the officer spluttered, tucking the ticket discreetly into his pocket. 'But unfortunately, you'll still need to move your boat.'

'And just why do you think we'll need to do

that?'

'Well, because it's being moored here illegally, sir.'

'But I've just told you that we've paid our mooring fees for the entire year.'

'Unfortunately, that's not what Jackson Developments says, and they're the ones who own the land.'

'That's as may be, but the Broads Waterways told us they'd reached an agreement with Jackson Developments that we'd be able to stay here for another year, at least!'

'I'm sorry, sir, but you'll have to take that up with them. As the land and the moorings are now owned by Jackson Developments, they have every right to ask us to move you along.'

'Well, I'd like to see you try!'

'Er...' began the young constable, glancing over at his colleague standing on the other boat. When nothing came back from him other than a dismissive shrug, he turned back to Tanner to say, 'How about we give you till the end of next week?'

'How about you give us another eleven bloody months, which is just about how long we've paid for.'

'I'm not sure we'll be able to do that, sir.'

'I see, then I suppose I'd better bring the matter up with DCI Forrester.'

Seeing the colour drain from the young constable's face, Tanner thought he'd press home his advantage by adding, 'Now, may I suggest you get the fuck off my boat, before I have you thrown off.'

'Yes, sir! Of course, sir! Right away, sir!'

As he scrambled back to the police patrol boat, Tanner turned to Jenny. 'Can you believe that!'

In a bid to calm the situation down a little, Jenny rested her arm on Tanner's. 'It's frustrating, I know, but in fairness, I think they're just trying to do their job.'

'By issuing us with a penalty notice, despite the fact that we've paid for the whole year?'

'Then there must have been some sort of a mix-up. Tell you what, why don't I give the Broads Waterways a call in the morning, when you're on your way down to London. If I tell them what's happened, I'm sure they'll agree to refund our fee, or at least to offer us an alternative site.'

'From the conversation I had with them on Monday, somehow I doubt it. Even if they do, it's hardly the point.' Gazing out over the tranquil stretch of the River Ant, with the picturesque Hunsett Mill just beyond, he added, 'We spent ages finding this mooring.'

'And no doubt we'll be able to find something equally as good, if not better! Now, come on. Let's get a bottle of wine open and start thinking about what we're going to have for dinner.'

· CHAPTER FOURTEEN ·

Thursday, 10th October

THE FOLLOWING MORNING, after Jenny had dropped him off at Wroxham train station on her way into the office, Tanner made the three-hour journey down to Liverpool Street in London, changing only once at Norwich.

From there he jumped on the tube to Bank, and then took the driverless DLR service through London's Docklands, alighting at Canary Wharf, home to some of the largest financial organisations in the world.

As he jostled his way through the thousands of sharply dressed people, all purposefully making their way along the bustling open passageways between the many dizzyingly high skyscrapers, he couldn't help but feel like a fish out of water; either that or a scruffy-looking tourist. Despite having spent most of his life living and working in London, he'd never been to Canary Wharf before. There had been no need. Before moving to the Broads he'd lived in Mill Hill in North London, working out of Colindale Police Station. There'd never been any investigations involving him in Docklands, and he'd never thought to take his family there for a day out. However, now that he was actually there, he was thinking that he probably should have. The views were quite spectacular, and his late daughter, Abigail, would have enjoyed the boutique-style shops and restaurants, especially with their views over the open docks and the River Thames beyond.

Taking the modern but elegant steps down into Reuters Plaza, a focal point for the many restaurants and bars lying in the shadow of Canary Wharf Tower, Tanner began scanning the faces of the people eating outside the Frappuccino restaurant, where he'd arranged to meet Harry Falcon's grandchildren. Having viewed their LinkedIn and Facebook profiles the previous day, he had a vague idea of what they looked like, which was basically the modern day equivalent of two Greek Gods: thin, stylish, and annoyingly good-looking. But from what he could see, just about all the people sitting around the tables outside seemed to meet that description. The only two he thought could be them were holding hands across the table, which he hardly thought was something a twin brother and sister would be doing. However, he was soon proved wrong when the man glanced up and raised an uncertain hand at him.

Feeling suddenly self-conscious, and regretting not having had his suit cleaned and pressed before coming down, he stepped over towards their table. 'Edward and Tessa Falcon?'

'That's us!' said the man, standing to greet him with an immaculate white smile.

Fishing out his formal ID, Tanner introduced

himself. 'Thanks for agreeing to meet.'

'No problem. We saved you a chair.'

Pulling it out, Tanner glanced over at the girl, who was curvaceous, blonde and devastatingly beautiful.

Catching his eye, she asked, 'Can we get you a drink?'

'Oh, I'm, er, OK, thanks.'

'How was the journey?' enquired Edward, with relaxed ease.

'Fine, all things considered.'

'Car or train?'

'Train. It gave me a chance to do some work.' He'd just lied, and wasn't even sure why. All he'd done on the journey down was to read the latest Stephen King novel, whilst taking occasional breaks to study the Norfolk Broads tourist map he'd brought with him, looking for a possible new mooring.

'So, anyway, Inspector Tanner,' began Edward, 'you didn't say much on the phone, but we're assuming this is about our grandfather.'

'I take it that you've heard that we're treating his death as suspicious.'

'We have, yes.'

'Who could have done such a thing?' asked Tessa.

'That's what we're trying to find out. Now, from what I understand, the last time you saw him was at his ninety-fourth birthday party. Is that correct?' Tanner pulled out his little-used notebook.

'It is, yes,' replied Edward. 'We always travelled up for his birthday, at least we have been since he turned ninety. At that point I think we all felt that it could be the last time for us to see him.'

'We've been told that he'd been suffering from severe cognitive decline?'

'If by that you mean his memory was going, then unfortunately it was. It had been for a while, but it had never been as bad as when we last saw him. Sometimes he was his normal self, mind as bright as a button, but at other times it was as if he wasn't there, and didn't even know who we were, which I know we both found upsetting.'

Seeing Tessa nod in sombre agreement, Tanner asked, 'Do you have any idea who may have wished your grandfather harm?'

'Nobody, no,' Edward said, 'which was why it came as such a shock to learn that he'd been, well, murdered. After all, the man was a decorated veteran who spent his life after the war doing nothing more innocuous than running a traditional Broads boatyard. Do you know he founded the Broads Wildlife Trust as well?'

'We do, yes.'

'So anyway, it's difficult to see why anyone would want to do him harm, especially when he must have been close to passing.'

Tanner let a quiet moment slip past, before saying, 'About the will. We understand that you've both been named as beneficiaries.'

'Apparently we have, yes,' confirmed Edward, glancing over at his twin sister. 'We thought that was sweet of him, didn't we?'

Seeing her smiling at her brother, Tanner asked, 'May I ask what he left you?'

'Oh, nothing much,' Edward said. 'He's given me his old cuckoo clock, which I'm not even sure works anymore. What about you, Tess?'

'Just some of my grandmother's jewellery.'

'Nothing else?' enquired Tanner.

'Not that we've been told,' replied Edward.

'Have you seen a copy of the will?'

'We haven't, no, although I can't say that we've asked. We were invited up for its reading, but with work and everything, it was too short notice to make the trip.'

'Are you aware that the bulk of his estate has been left equally between your father and your uncle?'

'So we've been told.'

'How do they get on?'

'Who, Dad and Uncle Phil?'

'Uh-huh.'

'Well, considering how different they are – OK, I guess.'

'I don't suppose you have any idea how they got on with your grandfather?'

'I assume you're proposing that one of them might have murdered him to claim their inheritance?'

'At this stage, I'm simply trying to establish motive.'

'Then you probably already know that our father didn't exactly see eye to eye with our grandfather. But if you think he'd have murdered him for his money, then you're most definitely barking up the wrong tree. He's already got plenty of his own.'

'How about your uncle?'

'Well, he'd being looking after him for the last ten years or so, so again, I'd have thought it unlikely. Besides, our uncle has never had much interest in money.'

'Unlike your father.'

'Unlike most people.'

'Going back to your grandfather's estate: I don't suppose you have any idea what your father and uncle plan to do with it?'

'If Dad has his way, he'll sell it. He's never been much of a fan of the Broads, so I can hardly imagine him wanting to keep hold of it.'

'And your uncle?'

Edward shrugged. 'I've no idea. The land must be worth a fair bit, so if he did sell, I'd have thought he'd be able to retire. But it may be that he wants to keep running the yard. I suppose it gives him something to do.'

'Last question. I don't suppose either of you knows anything about the development being built on the land opposite?'

'What development's that?'

'They're putting up a block of flats. Apparently, the developer behind it had been trying to persuade your grandfather to sell him the yard.'

The two grandchildren gave each other a blank expression.

Looking back at Tanner, Edward shook his head. 'We've not heard anything about that.'

Catching Tanner's eye, Tessa asked, 'Do you think that it might have been the property developer who killed our grandfather?'

'As I said before, at the moment we're simply looking for possible motives, whilst doing our best to eliminate people from our enquiry. Speaking of which, may I ask where you both were on Sunday night?'

'Who, us?' enquired Edward, sitting up in his chair.

'We normally stay at home, recovering from the weekend,' said Tessa, fixing Tanner's eye.

'And on Sunday?'

'We were in,' she replied, looking at her brother. 'The King's Speech was on. Remember?'

'Oh yes, that's right,' confirmed Edward. 'Good film that. Have you seen it?'

'I can't say that I have.' He didn't offer the fact that he wouldn't be able to, since he didn't have a TV on board his boat. If their story was true, they'd clearly watched the film together, and on a Sunday night, suggesting that they shared the same residence. That again seemed odd, seeing they were brother and sister. Even with London's high property prices, with one being a banker and the other a lawyer, they must have been able to afford their own accommodation.

Filing the thought for now, Tanner began to wind up the informal interview. 'OK, well, I think that's about it. We will need you to provide us with your prints and DNA at some stage.'

'Why would you need those?' Edward asked, in an apprehensive tone.

'Don't worry, Eddie,' said Tessa, resting her hand on his. 'They only need them to help eliminate us from their enquiries. Isn't that right, Inspector?'

'That's correct, Miss Falcon. Forensics found a large number of prints at your grandfather's house, and as you were both there about two weeks ago, we simply need to be able to identify which ones belong to you. Do you think you'd be able to drop by your local police station to provide them, or would you rather I arranged for someone to come by your work?'

'We'll stop in at the police station. There's one just off the DLR at Limehouse.'

'Sounds like you've been there before?' Tanner said, with a searching look.

'I work in criminal law, Inspector, so yes. I've been there once or twice.'

'I'm sorry. I didn't mean anything by that.'

'Yes, you did, but don't worry. I forgive you,' she added, with a beguiling smile.

Hearing his phone ring, Tanner pulled it out to see that it was Jenny calling.

'Will you excuse me?' he said, standing. 'I need to take this.'

'Are we done...I mean, may we go?' enquired Edward.

'If you could wait there for just one minute.'

Hurrying out to the middle of the plaza, he answered the phone.

'Hi Jen, how's it going?'

'Good, thanks. Are you there yet?'

'I'm just finishing interviewing the two grandchildren.'

'Oh, OK. I thought you'd be interested to know that I've been checking back through the phone records of the main suspects, and something came up that I thought might be of interest.'

'What's that?'

'Phillip called Edward yesterday.'

'His uncle?'

'That's right.'

'Well, OK. It was probably about the will.'

'That's what I thought. But why would their uncle call and not their father? And the duration of the call was of interest as well. It went on for over an hour, which seems like a long time to be discussing the contents of a will in which they barely had a mention.'

Tanner thought about that for a moment. 'What about their father? Has he called his children?'

'Not recently, no.'

'Do the grandchildren speak to their uncle often?'

'I've only gone back six months so far, but that was the only call I've found between them.'

'Right. Then I suppose I'd better ask them what they talked about. Thanks for that, Jen.'

'No problem. When do you think you'll be back?'

'I'm not sure. I'm going to find myself something to eat after I'm done here, then I may as well have a look around. Canary Wharf is quite a place. We'll have to come down together sometime. It's got a stack of restaurants and shops, and some quite spectacular views.'

'Sounds good. Give me a call when you're on your way back, and I'll pick you up from the station.'

'Will do. Thanks, Jen. Bye for now.'

Putting his phone away, Tanner returned to the restaurant's enclosed outdoor seating area.

'Sorry about that,' he said, resuming his seat.

Looking at Edward, he said, 'My colleague's just informed me that you received a call from your uncle yesterday.'

'That's right.'

'May I ask what you talked about?'

'From what I remember, it was mainly about our grandfather's will. Why?'

'It's just that you were on the phone with him for over an hour, which seems like a long time to be discussing a will in which you'd only been left a broken clock and some old jewellery.'

Taking a defensive tone, Edward replied, 'We discussed the funeral arrangements as well.'

'I see, but with your uncle; not your father?'

'Yes, well, we don't really get along with our dad.'

'Have you not spoken to him since your grandfather died?'

'He hasn't bothered to phone us, no.'

'OK, just curious. Anyway, I'm pretty much done. If I could just take down your addresses, I'll be on my way.'

'We actually live in the same apartment.'

'Oh, really?' questioned Tanner, feigning surprise.

Seeing the expression on his face, Tessa said, 'No doubt that seems odd to you. It does to most people. But we've always been close, Eddie and I, and it just makes good financial sense for us to live together. It also means that we can afford something a little special.'

Pen poised, Tanner repeated, 'So, your address is...?'

'It's the penthouse suite at the top of Aerial

View.'

Making a note of the name, Tanner asked, 'And where's that?'

'Overlooking Crossharbour.'

'Does it have a flat number?'

'Er, no. It's just called the Penthouse Suite. It takes up the whole of the top floor, so there's only one of them.'

With a raised eyebrow, Tanner put away his notebook. 'Well, thank you both very much for your time.'

As the three of them stood, Tanner asked, 'Will you be in London for the next few weeks?'

'I've got a business trip to Tokyo at the end of November,' replied Edward, 'and then we have a skiing holiday booked for Christmas.'

Handing each of them one of his cards, Tanner said, 'We'll have to see how it goes, but for now, if you could let me know if either of you needs to leave the country before then, I'd be very grateful.'

'Will do.'

'OK, thanks again for your time. Oh, and don't forget that we'll need your fingerprints and DNA samples as soon as possible.'

· CHAPTER FIFTEEN ·

LEAVING REUTERS PLAZA, his visit to London bringing back memories of his former life, Tanner ambled back to Canary Wharf station. There he toyed with the idea of giving his ex-wife a call, to ask if she'd like to meet up for lunch. She was an orthodontist at the UCL Eastman Dental Institute, near King's Cross, only a few stops on the tube away from Liverpool Street station. As he had to go back that way anyway, he eventually decided that he may as well and gave her a call.

After her initial surprise that he was in London, she agreed to meet, albeit with some reluctance.

Their divorce had come about through what had happened to their daughter. Prior to that they'd had what would probably have been described as a normal marriage, one that survived more on compromise than everlasting love. But Abigail's death had brought an end to that. Each side had blamed the other; Tanner his wife, for having been a career mum instead of a stay-at-home one, and she him, for not being able to prevent what happened despite the fact that he worked for the Metropolitan Police.

During the divorce proceedings, as the natural grieving process drifted from anger through to eventual acceptance, the hostility shared between them softened into general friendship, and although they were hardly on the phone to each other every day, they did exchange the occasional text and email.

'So, how have you been?' asked Tanner, taking a sip from the glass of wine the waiter had just poured.

'OK,' she replied, lifting her own as she began studying the menu. 'How's life in Norfolk?'

'Surprisingly busy. And London?'

'Same old,' she replied, before glancing up. 'Matthew told me that you've been living on board his boat?'

Commander Matthew Bardsley of the Metropolitan Police, one of the most senior ranking members of the British police, was a close family friend. It was he who'd provided Tanner with the personal recommendation that helped him to secure the job at Wroxham Police Station.

'I was living on board his boat, yes.'

'I was going to say. It didn't sound like you. A little too bohemian, I thought.'

'It actually caught fire a few months back, so I had to move out.'

'You're joking?'

'About it catching fire, or me moving out?'

She offered him a generous smile. It was a very typical John Tanner sort of a joke, humour she'd always described to her friends as being almost funny, but never actually so. Returning to study the menu, she asked, 'Not with you on board, I hope?'

'Well, I was, but a friend helped me off.'

Glancing up to look at his hands, she asked, 'Is that how you got those scars?'

As soon as they were mentioned, he attempted to cover them up. 'It was around that time, yes,' he replied, but didn't say anymore. He rarely felt comfortable talking about events that took place at work with Sara, which was probably another reason why their marriage had ultimately failed. The only person he seemed able to share with was Jenny, but that was because they worked together.

'What did Matthew say when you told him that you set fire to his boat?'

'Er, to be honest, I haven't told him yet.'

'You're not serious?'

'Well, yes, but I'd bought it off him the month before, so I'm not sure he'd be all that bothered.'

'You bought Matthew's boat?'

'Uh-huh.'

'And then you set fire to it?'

'Er, no, someone else did.'

'Did you at least have it insured?'

'Fortunately, yes. And they paid up as well, which was handy.'

'That's something, I suppose. So, where are you living now?'

'I bought another one.'

'You bought another boat?'

'Uh-huh,' Tanner repeated, glancing nonchalantly down his menu, leaving his ex-wife to stare at him with her mouth hanging open.

'And that's where you live now?'

Looking back up at her, Tanner decided that it was probably a good time to tell her about Jenny.

'I met someone, from work, and we decided to buy it together.'

'Oh!' she exclaimed, her face and neck flushing unexpectedly.

Seeing her surprise, with an odd sense of guilt for having entered into another relationship without telling her, Tanner attempted to take the edge off his announcement by adding, 'It all happened rather quickly. She's a local who just happens to be into boats. She's even teaching me how to sail, or at least she's trying to.'

'You mean, it's a sailing boat?' she asked, sounding even more surprised.

'A forty-two foot gaff-rigged Norfolk cabin cruiser,' Tanner confirmed, with some pride.

'Right!' The description clearly meant nothing to her.

Placing her menu down on the table, holding her hands together on top of it, she looked into Tanner's eyes. 'Then I suppose I should tell you that I've started to see someone else as well.'

Now it was Tanner's turn to be surprised. For some reason he thought she'd remain single. He didn't know why. It wasn't that she wasn't attractive enough to catch the eye of another man. For a woman in her late forties, she was. She'd even managed to keep her figure. It was probably because she'd always been so fiercely independent throughout the course of their marriage, so much so that he honestly didn't think she had any particular need to be with anyone else.

With a twinge of jealousy, Tanner asked,

'Someone from work?'

'We actually met through an online dating site,' she replied, as a flicker of a smile passed over her lips which was about as fragile as it was brief.

As it dawned on him what her admission meant – that she must have been actively looking for someone – for some reason his mind was taken back to the time when he'd told her what had happened to their daughter; that he'd found her body lying in a gutter down some disgusting rat-infested side street. He'd been so distraught himself, he'd hardly given a second thought to how the news must have affected her.

With a deep sense of guilt for the way he'd allowed his anger to dominate his emotions at the time, he found himself feeling genuinely pleased.

'I hope he's better looking than me,' he said, tagging a roguish grin onto the end.

'Infinitely,' replied Sara, looking relieved to have told him.

After they'd ordered, and the waiter had wafted away, she dug out her phone to check for any messages, saying, 'You know, it's funny that you called.'

'How so?'

'I had your old boss on the phone the other day.'

'DCI Baxter?'

'That's the one.'

'What the hell did he want?'

'He was calling to say that they'd had a witness come forward.'

'About Abigail?' asked Tanner, his heart picking up a beat. When she nodded, he demanded, 'Why didn't you tell me?'

'I don't know. I suppose I assumed that he'd already spoken to you.'

Knowing that it was highly unlikely that his old boss would have called him, mainly because he knew Tanner didn't want him to be involved in the investigation in any way, feeling himself already beginning to lose control of his emotions, he stated, 'Well, he hadn't!'

Pausing for a moment to calm down a little, he eventually asked, 'Did he say anything else?'

'Only that the witness has provided them with a photofit of someone they thought they saw leave the scene.'

'But...it's been over a year.'

'I'm only telling you what he said.'

'Anything else?'

'They're hoping to hold a press conference, and was asking if I – well, if we wanted to take part.'

A cold silence descended over the table. This had been one of the key areas of contention between them at the time; that Sara had wanted to take part in the press conference the police were organising, calling for witnesses, but Tanner had refused. He wanted to be leading the investigation, not playing the part of some pathetic parent, sobbing his heart out in front of the British media for all and sundry to gawp at. And as Sara hadn't had the confidence to do it without him, the Met decided not to go ahead, since without the parents' participation they didn't think there would be much point.

'You know how I feel about that,' said Tanner, with brooding malice.

'I'm fully aware, yes!' spat Sara.

'And you know why. They had no right excluding me from the investigation.'

'They had every right, John! You were totally out of control!'

'I was angry.'

'No, John, you were psychotic. There was no way you'd have been able to find who'd murdered her, not without killing a few innocent people along the way.'

Tanner didn't answer. Deep down he knew she was right. He could already feel that same uncontrollable fury boiling up inside him just thinking about it.

After they'd both taken a steadying sip from their glasses, Sara went on more calmly, 'So anyway, that's why he called.'

'When are they hoping to do the press conference?'

'I think that depends on us.'

'And what did you say?'

'Same as before. I can't do it without you, John.'

Cradling her glass in both hands, Sara sent him an imploring look. 'Would you do it? For me?'

Seeing the waiter approach with their meals, Tanner straightened his cutlery in preparation. He knew it would help the investigation if they agreed, although it would have been far more beneficial had he swallowed his pride the first time they'd been asked. The press would have liked nothing more than to cover the story of a couple of distraught parents whose beautiful teenage daughter had been cut down in the prime of her life, especially given his position in the police.

Before the waiter reached their table, he took another quick sip from his glass before glancing at Sara. 'I'll think about it.'

· CHAPTER SIXTEEN ·

STANDING ON THE bustling street outside the restaurant in the heart of King's Cross, Tanner said goodbye to his ex-wife with a kiss on the cheek before jumping back on the tube, heading for first Liverpool Street, then Norwich and Wroxham beyond, all the while thinking about whether or not he should take part in the press conference.

It was only when he was about an hour into his journey that he decided to give his old boss, DCI Baxter, a call. Perhaps unsurprisingly, he didn't answer, so Tanner left him a brief message, asking him to get back to him when he got the chance. He then phoned Jenny, telling her that he was about halfway home, and that he'd call again when he was about twenty minutes out.

A little over an hour and a half later, Tanner stepped off the train at Wroxham Station to see Jenny's silver Golf parked directly outside. With her opening the door for him from the inside, he climbed in to say, 'Hey Jen, good to see you,' whilst leaning over for a kiss.

Noting the smell of alcohol on his breath and perfume on his collar, intrigued by both she asked, 'How'd it go?'

'Good, yes.'

'Worth the trip?'

'I think so.'

On the train he'd been unsure whether or not he should tell her that he'd had lunch with his ex-wife. Obviously there wasn't any reason for him not to; he just didn't know how she'd react, especially given the fact that he'd not told her before he decided to, which, now that he thought about it, he probably should have.

'What were the two grandchildren like?'

'Thin, tall, attractive and rich.'

'Edward as well?'

'Uh-huh.'

'I do hope you're not turning gay on me.'

'Not yet, no; however, if I lived down there, I could be persuaded. Canary Wharf seems to be heaving with exceptionally good-looking banker types, most of who look as if they're barely old enough to drive.'

'Sounds like my sort of place.'

'It's got loads of boutique shops as well, and some quite spectacular views.'

'Did anything useful come from the trip?'

'I'm not sure. It's a shame you weren't there. Two people can always pick up more than one. I was hardly able to take any notes, just their address, which was interesting in itself.'

'How so?'

'They live in the penthouse suite of a tower block called Aerial View.'

'What, together?'

'That's what I thought; and they were unusually close. When I was first looking for them, outside where we'd arranged to meet, they were holding hands.'

Jenny turned to raise an eyebrow at him.

'Did you ask them why they were?'

'Holding hands or living together?'

'Living together, obviously,' replied Jenny, turning to frown at him.

After a brief smile, Tanner replied, 'They just said that it made good financial sense, and allowed them to afford the penthouse.'

'Do you think they could be...?'

'Having an incestuous relationship? I've no idea, but even if they are, I can't see how it can have a bearing on the investigation.'

'What about the call between Edward and his uncle?'

'He said it was about the will.'

'For over an hour?'

'He said they also discussed the funeral, but even so, I'd have to agree it seems overly-long, especially as they'd only been left an old clock and some jewellery.'

'And why didn't their dad call them instead of their uncle?'

'Because they don't get on with him, which, having met the man, I'm sure is something we can both relate to.'

'Fair enough.'

As Jenny drove out of the station, heading for home, Tanner asked, 'Any news from this end?'

'Not really. I spent the day ploughing through the Falcon family's phone records, emails, texts and social media. Apart from the call to Edward from his uncle, I didn't find anything out of the ordinary.'

'I don't suppose you had a chance to do a background check on Jim Jackson?'

'I'm sorry, I didn't.'

'What about Cooper and Gilbert? How are they getting on?'

'They spent the day interviewing various carers and cleaners.'

'Do you know if anything came from that?'

'They only said that they needed to check through all their alibis.'

'James Falcon's finances?'

'We haven't been given access to them yet.'

'And the will?'

'Lucy said that it still hasn't been sent over.'

'What's taking everything so long?' wondered Tanner, with mounting frustration.

Sensing that it was a rhetorical question, Jenny elected to remain silent.

'I'm sure this one comes down to money,' he mused, staring out of the car window. 'It's either Jim Jackson who's promised his investors that he'd be able to build over Falcon's Yard, or it's James Falcon, who's not quite as rich as he's making out to be.'

'You don't think the grandchildren had anything to do with it?'

'Not unless they're planning on killing both their father and uncle, but even if they are, they don't exactly seem to be strapped for cash.'

'Unless they're also struggling. Maybe one of them has lost their job, and they can't afford the mortgage on their penthouse suite?'

'But they'd still have to kill their father and

their uncle to get the estate. If that was the case, surely they'd have given their grandfather a miss and gone straight for their father's inheritance.'

'Unless he is broke, and they know it.'

'True.'

'Maybe their grandfather by-passed his two children and has left his entire estate to them, which was what the uncle was talking to Edward on the phone about? And there's still the possibility that it was the older son, Phillip, who'd simply had enough of having to look after his dad all the time. Or maybe it was one of his carers, with mental problems of their own? Maybe one who Harry Falcon didn't like very much, and didn't mind saying so?'

Tanner thought about all that for a moment. 'I'm afraid you're right, Jen. Everyone's still a suspect, and until we can see the will, and get access to the key suspects' financial accounts, we're going to be none the wiser.'

As he continued to watch hedgerows flicker past, he eventually said, 'Anyway, at least we have the view of a building site to look forward to when we get home.'

'I'd forgotten about that. I wonder how much more they've done?'

'Judging by how fast they're working, they've probably finished the build and have nothing left to do except screw in the lightbulbs.'

· CHAPTER SEVENTEEN ·

'NOPE! IT STILL looks like a building site,' observed Tanner, as they ambled their way along the towpath, heading for their boat.

'I see our neighbours have gone,' observed Jenny, seeing that theirs was the last one still tied to the moorings.

'I can't say I'm surprised,' said Tanner. 'They probably couldn't afford to keep paying all the penalty notices; which reminds me. At some point we're going to have to start looking for another mooring.'

'I don't see how we're going to have time, not with a murder investigation in full swing.'

'I suppose it depends on how long it takes to get hold of the will and financial statements. Hopefully we'll be able to get some time off over the weekend.'

A distant siren caught their attention. Glancing towards where it was coming from, Tanner said, 'Someone's late for their dinner.'

'Either that or England's playing,' added Jenny.

As the sound grew louder, Tanner hopped up on to the side of the boat for a more elevated view.

'Looks like they're heading this way,' he said, watching a flashing blue light dance over a group of trees, just beyond the churned-up field still littered with unsightly yellow diggers.

'I hope they're not coming to arrest us for mooring illegally.'

It was then that they heard the sound of raised voices drifting towards them from Falcon's Yard.

'Can you see anything?' asked Jenny.

'No, but something's going on,' he replied, jumping back down to the tow path. 'Come on. Let's take a look.'

- CHAPTER EIGHTEEN -

TAKING THE XJS, with Tanner spinning the wheels out of the carpark, less than two minutes later they were driving into Falcon's Yard.

On entering the courtyard, ahead of them they saw a large silver Mercedes parked in the middle, directly opposite a white van with the name of Jackson Developments written down the side. Beyond that, outside the farmhouse's front door, were three men, all crowding around Phillip Falcon.

As they pulled up, the men surrounding Phillip glanced over to see who it was. Immediately Tanner recognised one of them as being Jim Jackson. The other two must be a couple of his larger than average builders, each one wielding an ominous-looking sledgehammer.

With the wail of the siren coming ever nearer, Tanner leapt out, yelling at Jackson, 'Just what the hell is going on here?'

'Shit,' Jackson mouthed, then turned to whisper something to the two men standing either side of him. Backing away, they lowered their sledgehammers so that they were held innocuously down by their sides.

As Tanner approached, he saw Jackson lifting a threatening finger up to Phillip, before turning to face him.

'Nothin' to concern yourself with, Inspector,' he declared. 'Isn't that right, Phil?'

Despite it being abundantly obvious that the man was scared out of his wits, Phillip replied, 'It's n-nothing, really.'

Hearing the squad car pull in behind them, Tanner stormed up to Jackson. 'It doesn't look like nothing to me.'

With his two heavies fetching up their sledgehammers again, Jackson took a step forward. 'I suggest you stay out of this, Mr Tanner.'

'Must I remind you that the use of threatening behaviour in order to persuade someone to do something against their will is a public order offence, Mr Jackson?'

'But you'd 'ave to 'ave someone who felt they was being threatened first though, wouldn't you?'

Tanner glanced over at Phillip, hoping he'd be able to support his accusation, but he'd taken to staring at his feet, his face a mask of stone.

Hearing car doors being slammed behind him, with his anger rising Tanner fixed his eyes on Jackson. 'But in this instance, there's a witness, i.e. me!'

'But what did you see? A group of men 'aving a friendly chat? Hardly grounds for charging me with a public order offence now, is it?'

'You'd be right, if it wasn't for your apes here with the over-sized tools.'

'We just came off a job, one that just happened

to involve the use of sledgehammers. Now, if you don't leave us alone, I'm the one who's gonna be filing charges,' he said, digging a stumpy finger into Tanner's chest.

Being touched in such an aggressive manner by such a repulsive man sent Tanner over the edge. 'Don't you dare lay your disgusting fingers on me,' he growled, and shoved him back with such force, he fell over backwards to land hard on the gravel-lined courtyard.

As his two heavies rushed forward, looking as if they were about to pummel their sledgehammers into Tanner's face, two uniformed police constables appeared beside Tanner, the nearest one saying, 'All right, all right. That's enough of all that!'

'It was him!' stated Jackson, pointing an accusatory finger up at Tanner as he picked himself up off the ground. 'He started it!'

Pulling out his ID, Tanner turned to the police officer to say, 'Detective Inspector Tanner and Detective Constable Evans, Norfolk Police.'

'Yes, sir. We recognised your car.'

Facing the building contractor, Tanner continued his conversation with the constable. 'We heard raised voices and came over to find Mr Jackson and his two friends here threatening Mr Falcon, no doubt trying to persuade him to sell his father's estate.'

Looking over towards the supposed victim, the policeman asked, 'Is that correct, Mr Falcon?'

Another cautionary glance from Jackson left Phillip stuttering, 'We were just t-talking.'

'What utter bollocks!' stated Tanner.

As a wide grin spread out over Jackson's face, he leered at Tanner to say, 'As the man says, we was just talking. Now, if you move aside, we'll be on our way, all peaceful-like.'

'You're not buying that, I hope?' asked Tanner, staring round at the uniformed officer.

'I'm afraid if Mr Falcon says that they were just talking, then I'm not sure that there's a whole lot we can do about it, sir.'

With a wink aimed squarely at the young police constable, Jackson said, 'Thanks, son,' and shoved his way past Tanner, then Jenny, deliberately forcing his elbow into each as he did.

Fuming with indignation, Tanner was left standing there, with nothing more he could do other than to glower at the back of Jackson's anvil-shaped shaved head as it bobbed its way back to his car.

· CHAPTER NINETEEN ·

Friday, 11th October

A S SOON AS they arrived at work the following day, Tanner and Jenny jumped into a briefing with DCI Forrester inside his office, along with DI Cooper and DS Gilbert, to update them on the events that had taken place the previous evening at Falcon's Yard.

'OK, so what do we know about this Jim Jackson?' asked Forrester, catching the eye of the person who'd been at the station the longest, DI Cooper.

'Well, sir, he does have a certain reputation.'

'Does he have any form?'

'I'd need to check, but I wouldn't be surprised. I've heard his name mentioned often enough, normally in connection with some dodgy housing development. He's known for targeting old people, coercing them into selling him their homes for less than the market value. Rumour has it that he started his company by befriending a wealthy old lady, persuading her to change her will in his favour to leave her family with nothing.'

'I assume it was never proved?'

'Well, as I said, it's just a story I'd heard. If he

did, it was before my time, but there'd probably be a record of it somewhere.'

'What do you think, Tanner?'

'From what we found out when we interviewed him, he's clearly got a lot riding on this new development of his, including a number of investors he's going to have to keep happy. One of them may even be the younger son, James Falcon.'

'What makes you think that?'

'When we asked him if he knew anything about the development, he said he'd never heard of it, but Jackson later told us that he'd already been in touch with him.'

'So you think the younger son could be involved in his father's murder?'

'Well, it's possible. There was clearly no love lost between them. However, I think it's equally possible that it was Jackson acting on his own. OK, maybe not him directly, but certainly one of the ape-like builders he seems to have at his beck and call. If he does have investors breathing down his neck, possibly threatening to pull out their money if they don't get what they were promised, with the way he's treated the elderly in the past, I wouldn't put it past him.'

'Cooper, how're you getting on with all those carers and cleaners?'

'We've managed to get statements from them all, sir, as well as their DNA and prints, but we've yet to confirm any of their alibis.'

'Did any come over as being suspicious in any way?'

'Not that we could tell, at least not in relation

to having murdered Harry Falcon.'

Remembering the carer they'd met on the very first day, Tanner asked, 'What about the woman who was trying so desperately to get into his house, the morning we found him?'

'Which one was that?'

'She said she'd left something inside. I mentioned her to DS Gilbert.'

As everyone turned to look at her, Gilbert nodded. 'We found her bag with all her personal items hanging up behind the door in the downstairs cloakroom.'

Recalling the way she'd been trying to force her way inside the house, Tanner asked, 'Was that it?'

'That's all we know so far, although what we found inside the bag would probably explain her behaviour.'

'Why? What was in it?'

'A steamy romance novel and a...er...'

'And a what, Gilbert?' Tanner demanded.

'Well, it was a vibrator, sir.'

Jenny snorted through her nose, leaving Tanner to shift awkwardly from one foot to another.

Thinking it was probably best to move the conversation along, Forrester stepped in. 'Anyway,' he said, 'today I think you'd all better focus on Jackson for the time being. Dig up anything we have on him and his company. If we've got his prints and DNA on file, get them over to forensics to see if any match what was found at Harry Falcon's house. Then see if we can find out who his investors are.'

'I think it would also be useful if we could get

statements from the two men he had with him yesterday, sir,' proposed Tanner, 'along with their prints and DNA.'

'Do we know who they are?'

'I didn't recognise them, no. Jenny?'

'Not a clue, sir. Sorry.'

'We can ask the two officers who were at the scene,' said Tanner. 'They might know them.'

Forrester leant back in his chair and thought for a moment. 'OK, but at the moment, all we seem to be doing is growing a seemingly endless list of suspects, but without ever ruling any of them out.'

To Gilbert, Tanner asked, 'I don't suppose there's been any news on that will?'

'Nothing so far, no. I was going to chase the solicitors again this morning.'

'OK, let me know when you see it. If the main beneficiaries are just the two sons, as we've been told, then I think we can at least rule out the grandchildren. They seemed to have even more money than their father!'

The phone burbled on Forrester's desk, which he picked up to say, 'Yes?'

The room fell into an awkward silence as everyone stood around, not sure if they should stay or leave.

As Forrester listened, he began staring around at them all, raising a finger in the air to hold their attention.

After no more than thirty seconds, he ended the call, saying, 'Understood. We'll be straight down.'

Dropping the receiver back into its cradle, he

stood up. 'A body's been found inside the boatshed at Falcon's Yard. By the sound of it, it's Phillip Falcon.'

· CHAPTER TWENTY ·

WITH IT DECIDED that Cooper and Gilbert had better stay behind to continue chasing leads, Forrester opted to accompany Tanner and Jenny to Falcon's Yard.

As they raced out to the car park, Tanner's phone rang.

It was his old boss.

Realising Baxter must be returning his call from the other day, and given the sensitive nature of the subject, he unlocked his XJS with the key fob, saying to Jenny, 'Give me a sec, will you?'

She sent him a curious look, but Tanner peeled away past a couple of parked cars to answer in privacy.

'Tanner, it's DCI Baxter.'

'Good morning, sir. Thanks for returning my call.'

'Sorry it's taken me a while. You know how it is.'

'Yes, of course.'

'I assume you heard from your wife that we had a new witness come forward.'

'I did, yes.'

'He was arrested as part of an enquiry into a drugs-related crime, one that we believe was

115

linked to what happened to Abigail. I know it's a bit late in the day, but he's been able to provide us with some useful information, including a photofit of someone he says he saw at the scene.'

'I see.'

'Which was why I called Sara, to see if she'd be up for taking part in a press conference.'

'But you didn't call me,' said Tanner, holding up an apologetic hand to Forrester who was driving out of the station car park, glaring at him as he passed, no doubt wondering why he was standing around talking on the phone when he had the scene of a possible murder to attend.

'Well, no,' continued Baxter, 'but only because I didn't think you'd be interested, especially after what you said when I asked you before.'

'Yes, sir, but I was a little upset at the time, as I'm sure you can imagine.'

'Of course, which was also why it was impossible for us to allow you to lead the investigation.'

'Or to even help out!' stated Tanner, feeling the resentment he'd been harbouring all these months begin bubbling up to the surface.

'Listen, Tanner, I've no interest in going through all that again. Sara's already told me that you met up the other day, and that, as before, she's only prepared to take part if you do it with her. So I was hoping that's why you were calling – to say that you would.'

Tanner took a moment to turn and stare over to where he'd left Jenny, who was now leaning up against his Jag's passenger door, checking her phone.

Seeing her glance up at him, he turned away. 'To be honest, a lot's happened since then. No doubt you know that Sara and I aren't together anymore.'

'Which was another reason why I didn't call. So, I take it that's a no?'

'I think it's going to have to be; but do you think you'd be able to send over the case files, just for me to have a look?'

'You know I can't do that.'

'Then how about the photofit?'

'I can only do that after we've made it public.'

'You're seriously telling me that you won't even send me the bloody photofit?'

'If you're not prepared to help us find who killed your daughter, then no.'

'But all I've ever wanted was to find out who murdered her.'

'I meant, as a member of the public, Tanner, as you well know.'

'Then I suppose I'll just have to wait until you make it public, won't I?'

'I suppose you will, yes.'

Feeling his blood boil, Tanner ended the call.

'Twat!' he muttered, shaking his head in a bid to clear the many emotions that were crowding his mind.

As he hurried back to his car, Jenny looked up to ask, 'Everything all right?'

'It was nothing,' he replied, forcing a smile at her. 'Nothing important, at least. Anyway, we'd better get going, or else Forrester's going to wonder where we've got to.'

· CHAPTER TWENTY ONE ·

'WHAT DO YOU think?' asked Forrester, talking to the back of Dr Johnstone's head, as he crouched down on the dusty concrete floor.

The body of a man lay on its back in the middle of the yard's boatshed. There was no question about whether or not he was dead. His head had been crushed under the hull of a large cabin cruiser, bloody fragments of bone and brain splattered out around it.

'I think he's long past his sell-by date,' replied the doctor, with his normal sanguine sarcasm. 'More than that I can't say at the moment, but only because he would appear to have a boat moored on top of his head.'

'Is it Phillip Falcon?'

'So I've been told.'

'Time of death?'

'At a guess, I'd say around nine to twelve hours ago.'

'So, sometime last night,' estimated Tanner, looking around. 'I don't suppose anyone knows who found him?'

From out of a group of yard workers huddled behind a line of blue and white Police Do Not

Cross tape, over by the shed's wide entrance, one of the more senior of them stepped forward.

'That be me, sir,' he said, with a thick Norfolk accent.

'When was that?' asked Tanner, turning to look at him.

'When I opened up the yard this morn'.'

'Did you touch anything?'

'No, sir! I took one look and called the police.'

'And this was exactly how you found him?'

'Just like this, yes.'

Taking in the scene, Tanner asked, 'Has it ever happened before – a boat falling over like this?'

'It has, sir, yes; but only once, and that was when someone drove into one of the blocks by accident, when we had one out in the courtyard.'

'So it couldn't have toppled over on its own?'

'I don't see how, sir, no.'

'What if Mr Falcon kicked it by accident, when he was underneath?'

'It's not very likely, sir,' replied the old man, screwing up his face.

'But would it have been possible?'

'He'd 'ave had to have given it a fair old kick, and I doubt he would've been able to, not if he was lyin' under it like that.'

'Was there any reason for him to be underneath it?'

'Well, he'd oft'n check the work we've done, but I'm not sure he'd 'ave been able to with this one, not from down there.'

'How do you mean?'

'Well, sir, the boat was in for repairs to the hull, but not to the bottom of it. A hire boat had put a hole in its side, up near the stanchions.'

'Would Mr Jackson have known that?'

'Of course!'

Turning back to his colleagues, in a discreet tone, Tanner said, 'It has to be foul play. It's beyond coincidental that a Broads cabin cruiser just happened to fall on top of his head in such a way, only a few days after his father was killed.'

'And only a few hours after Jackson's men had been threatening him with sledgehammers,' added Jenny.

'Well, as always,' said Johnstone, picking himself up off the floor, 'I should be able to have a better idea when I get him back to the lab, but I'm not going to promise you anything. Not with this one. If he was killed by a blow to the head, for example, and whoever did it used this as a means of covering it up, then I think they may have been successful.' Peeling off his latex gloves, he looked around to ask, 'But first things first. I don't suppose anyone knows how we'll be able to get this boat off him?'

- CHAPTER TWENTY TWO -

LEAVING DR. JOHNSTONE with Forrester, the forensics unit, and the yard's employees to discuss the best method of lifting the boat high enough to enable them to slide what was left of Phillip Falcon from underneath, Tanner and Jenny headed outside to their first port of call: Phillip's brother James, who was hopefully still staying on board his father's yacht at the end of the dyke.

Placing his foot on the boat's wooden side, Tanner called out, 'Hello, is anyone home?'

There was no response.

Checking his watch to see that it was gone half-past ten, he called out again, 'Mr Falcon, are you on board? It's Detective Inspector Tanner and Detective Constable Evans, Norfolk Police.'

'What sort of time do you call this?' came the eventual muffled response.

'Er, I make it twenty-five to eleven.'

Falcon cursed audibly. Jenny whispered to Tanner, 'I think we may have woken him up.'

'Oh dear. What a shame.'

'Do you think he had a busy night?'

'We'll have to wait and see.'

After keeping them waiting patiently on the

grass verge beside the boat for about a minute, the cheerless unshaven face of a bedraggled James Falcon eventually appeared from behind the canvas awning to stare out at them through a pair of bloodshot eyes.

'What the hell do you two want?'

'Sorry to disturb you, Mr Falcon, but I'm afraid we have some rather bad news.'

'Let me guess; the clocks have gone forward and I've lost an hour's sleep.'

'It's about your brother.'

'He hasn't gone and robbed a bank, has he?'

'I'm afraid he's dead, Mr Falcon.'

The man stared first at Tanner, then Jenny. 'Is this some sort of a joke?'

'No joke. His body was found this morning, inside the boatshed. A boat that was in for repairs was found lying on top of him. We think that he was either checking the work when he accidently kicked out one of the blocks, or someone knocked it over on purpose.'

'You're not serious?'

'So anyway, Mr Falcon, we were wondering what you were doing last night, between the hours of say, eleven o'clock and one o'clock this morning?'

'You can't possibly think that I would have killed my own brother?'

'If you could just answer the question.'

'If you must know, I was out, seeing some old friends.'

'Whereabouts was that?'

'Down at the Bittern.'

'I see. They had a lock-in, did they?'

'Not that I know of, why?'

'So what did you do after they closed?'

'I came back here.'

'And then?'

'And then I went to bed.'

'Would anyone be able to vouch for you?'

'Unfortunately not, but only because the quality of the totty in Norfolk has always been abysmal.' Leering at Jenny, he added, 'Present company excepted, of course. Had I been down in Devon, I'd have probably pulled at least two girls who'd no doubt be just as fuckable as your Detective Constable Evans.'

'Of course, yes,' snarled Tanner, taking short shallow breaths in through his nose as he did all that he could to prevent himself from climbing on board and bashing the man's brains in with a mud weight. 'And I'd love to believe you. However, given the fact that we've just told you that your brother's dead, you don't seem very upset about it. In fact, you seem more interested in acquiring my colleague's phone number.'

'Well of course I'm upset about it. But as you've pretty much gone and accused me of being the one who killed him, what am I supposed to do? Own up and let you lead me away to spend the rest of my life doing time for a murder I had nothing to do with?'

'No, Mr Falcon, but I would expect you to show a little more sympathy for your brother's passing.'

'OK, look, I'm sorry about what's happened to him, but as I think I mentioned before, we didn't exactly get on.'

'So, you're pleased he's dead, then?'

'Not pleased, no.'

'Even though it means you're going to be the sole beneficiary of your father's inheritance?'

'Well, I would be delighted, naturally, were it not for the fact that I've now got two funerals to arrange instead of one.'

'Wow! You're all heart, aren't you?'

'And besides, as I've told you before, I don't exactly have a desperate need for any more money, not unless the Footsie 100 crashed overnight, along with the global housing market.'

'Speaking of which,' began Tanner, 'how's your friend over at Jackson Developments?'

'Who?'

'You know, Jim Jackson. A charming individual, very much like yourself, who'd been trying to persuade your father to sell Falcon's Yard and who, incidentally, was round here yesterday evening with a couple of his builder chums, threatening your now deceased brother with sledgehammers?'

'I've got no idea what you're talking about.'

'You don't?'

'No! I don't!'

'You know, that's funny.'

'And why's that?'

'Because we were having a good old chat with Mr Jackson yesterday, down at his offices in Great Yarmouth. He even showed us the model of the brand new riverside development they've started working on next door.'

'Yes, and...? So what?'

'Well, it's just that it was interesting for us to find out that he said he had spoken to you about the development when you said that he hadn't.'

'Then I must have forgotten about it. After all, I do invest in rather a lot of property. I must speak to dozens of building contractors every week.'

'And yet you can't remember talking to one who'd been speaking to you about buying your father's estate?'

'Oh, I get it now. You think that me and this Jackson guy are somehow in this together, and that I've helped him bump off both my father and my brother just to be able to sell him a poxy piece of marshland that's probably worth no more than £3 million.'

'So, are you saying that you haven't spoken to him?'

'Funnily enough, I am, yes.'

'So why do you think he's told us that you have?'

'Er, I'm no Sherlock Holmes or anything, but I'd have thought it was pretty bloody obvious to anyone with even half a brain that he's the one going around murdering my family, and is now attempting to pin the blame on me.'

'And yet you've already told us that you have every intention of selling your father's estate, something you'll now be able to do as your brother's not around to stop you. I even seem to remember you asked for Jackson's phone number.'

'I was joking!'

'I see. So you're saying that you're not intending to sell your father's estate?'

James paused for a moment. 'I've no need of it, so yes, I'd have to admit that it would still be my intention to sell it, but that doesn't mean I've had anything to do with what's happened to my father and brother.'

'Maybe not, Mr Falcon, but you may have a job convincing a judge and jury of that.'

· CHAPTER TWENTY THREE ·

'**H**OW'D YOU GET on with the boat, sir?' asked Tanner, seeing Forrester about to climb back into his car out in the courtyard.

'It was easier than we first thought,' he replied, leaning one of his thick-set arms on the edge of his open car door. 'They levered it off with about six planks of wood, enough at least for Johnstone and his team to ease the body out.'

'Was he able to get any more of an idea as to a cause of death?'

'Apart from the boat, nothing obvious, but he seemed confident that he'd be able to reach a conclusion by examining the skull fragments. Anyway, how's the younger son?'

'As belligerent as always. If he did have something to do with it, he's certainly doing a good job of hiding the fact.'

'So, you don't think it was him?'

'Not on his own, no. At this stage I think it's more likely to be Jim Jackson, especially after yesterday's incident with his sledgehammer-wielding henchmen. I wouldn't be surprised if they didn't come back after we'd left to continue their conversation, ending up with them smashing his head in and having the bright idea to use the boat to help cover it up.'

'Yes, well, hopefully Johnstone and forensics will be able to give us a better idea. Do we have James Falcon's prints and DNA on file yet?'

Tanner glanced around at Jenny.

'We do, sir, yes,' she replied. 'They were collected from him yesterday.'

'Good. Well done!' Taking her in for a moment, Forrester asked, 'You've got your sergeant's exam coming up soon, haven't you?'

'At the end of the month, sir.'

'I assume DI Tanner has been helping you to prepare?'

'On occasion,' she replied, giving Tanner a sideways glance.

'OK, well, good luck with it, when the time comes. No doubt you'll pass with flying colours.'

'Thank you, sir.'

'I assume you're both going to be heading off to have another chat with Jackson?'

'I think that's the next sensible step,' replied Tanner.

'OK. I'd better head back. Let me know how you get on.'

'Will do, sir.'

After watching him climb into his car, Tanner pulled out his phone, saying to Jenny, 'Before we go, I'm going to give Cooper a quick call, to see if he's come up with anything we can use against Jackson.'

A minute later, Tanner was deep in conversation with DI Cooper, asking him for an update.

'We're making progress,' replied Cooper. 'I've just started going through Jackson's phone records. It looks like there have been a number of calls made between him and James Falcon, from both sides.'

'I bloody knew it! I bet they've been planning this for months. OK, we're going to head back down to Great Yarmouth to have another chat with Jackson. I don't suppose you've had a chance to see if we have his DNA and prints on file?'

'Not yet, no, but it's next on the list. Speaking of prints, forensics have said that they've managed to identify all but three sets from Harry Falcon's house, so I was thinking that one of them could belong to Jackson.'

'Possibly,' replied Tanner, 'although I think it's unlikely he'd have had a direct hand in any of this, not when he's got those apes of his to do his dirty work for him. I don't suppose you can find out the names of the officers who attended the scene at Falcon's Yard last night, and ask if they recognised the gorillas who were with him? If we can find out who they are, and those unidentified prints are theirs, then we've got him! Maybe even James Falcon as well.'

'I'll add it to the list, although Vicky was wondering if the others might belong to the grandchildren.'

'Haven't they provided theirs yet?'

'Not the last time I checked. Hold on. Let me ask her.'

As he was doing that, Tanner quietly filled Jenny in.

'Cooper's found out that Jackson and James

Falcon have been having regular chats on the phone, and forensics says that there are only three sets of prints left to identify at Harry Falcon's house.'

'Two of them are most likely to belong to the grandchildren, aren't they?'

'That's what's being suggested. Cooper's just checking to see if we have them.'

Cooper came back on the line. 'Nothing from either grandchild,' he said.

'OK, I suppose I'm going to have to chase them.'

'Whilst we're on the subject,' continued Cooper, 'I'm not sure it's relevant, but Vicky's just mentioned that the grandson, Edward Falcon, called his uncle yesterday evening.'

Raising an intrigued eyebrow over at Jenny, Tanner asked, 'How long was the conversation?'

'Only about five minutes.'

'I wonder what that was about.'

'I've no idea, but it probably means that Edward was the last person to speak to him.'

'Interesting. OK, let me know if you find out anything else. Hopefully we'll be back in the office in a couple of hours.'

· CHAPTER TWENTY FOUR ·

ALMOST HAVING TO show themselves into Jim Jackson's office, with a perturbed secretary left protesting in their wake, Tanner and Jenny were greeted by a wide but altogether spurious smile.

'What a most pleasant surprise,' said Jackson, standing to greet them. 'But perhaps you could 'ave the decency to make an appointment next time, instead of just barging your way in 'ere like this.'

'Don't worry,' retorted Tanner, 'we won't be long. We just have a few more questions.'

Glancing over at the flustered-looking secretary, Jackson said, 'Don't worry, Tracy. You can go now.' The moment the door was closed, he continued, 'Look, if this was about last night, I apologise if I was a little off with you, but as I said at the time, we were only 'aving a friendly chat.'

'So you said, and if it wasn't for those sledgehammer-wielding gorillas of yours, I'd be inclined to agree with you.'

'I can see how 'aving them there may have seemed a little 'eavy-handed, but I wasn't taking any chances, not with what 'appened last time. I think I told you how his dad had threatened me with a submachine gun.'

'You did mention something about that, but you weren't there to speak to Harry Falcon, seeing that he's dead.'

'No, but his older son has his father's temperament. He may not seem like it, but believe you me, he can easily fly off the 'andle. For all we knew, he could have 'ad the machinegun locked and loaded, propped up behind the front door. So I brought Bazzer and Gazzer with me, just in case.'

'I assume those are nicknames for Barry and Gary?'

'I guess so,' replied Jackson, with an ambivalent shrug.

'I take it that you know their surnames?'

'Not a clue, no. Sorry.'

'I see. And you expect me to believe that, do you?'

'No offence, Inspector, but I couldn't give a rat's arse what you believe. Everyone just calls 'em Bazzer and Gazzer. I don't even know which one is which.'

'But they are employees of yours?'

'I wouldn't go so far as to call them that. They're what are known in the trade as casual labour. I suppose you want to charge them with the illegal possession of an unlicensed sledgehammer.'

As Jackson laughed at his own joke, Tanner said, 'No, but an address and phone number would be useful.'

'Look, what's all this about anyway? Phillip

hasn't gone and done something silly has he, like making an official complaint?'

'Surprisingly no, he hasn't, but I suspect you already know that.'

'Well, I did advise him against it, if that's what you mean.'

Tanner was silent for a while, before eventually asking, 'How are you getting on with that brother of his?'

'Who? James?'

'That's the one.'

'I've not spoken to him since the last time you were here.'

'I see, but you two have been having regular phone conversations?'

'Well, yes, but I'd already told you as much.'

Glancing over at Jenny, Tanner asked, 'Is that what he said?'

After finding the relevant page in her notes, Jenny replied, 'Not exactly. He told us that James Falcon had called him, after he'd been escorted out of Falcon's Yard by James's father.'

'Which implies that you'd only spoken once,' continued Tanner, redirecting his attention back to Jackson. 'And yet we've since learnt that there have been numerous conversations held between the two of you.'

'OK, I admit that we 'ave been talking for a while.'

'Am I correct in thinking that he's one of your investors?'

Jackson didn't answer, but just continued to stare at Tanner.

'I can caution you and ask the exact same

question down at the station, if you prefer?'

'All right, yes! He is an investor, but he's 'ardly a significant one.'

'I therefore take it that you have been discussing the sale of his father's land for some time?'

'It was before I went to all the expense of 'aving the architect's plans drawn up and getting the planning permission. If it wasn't for him telling me that his father was about to keel over, after which he and his brother would be more than happy to sell me the estate, and for a bargain price I may add, I wouldn't be in the position I'm in now.'

'And what position is that?'

'Well, if you must know, I've got a number of people breathing down my neck, all who are expecting me to 'ave had both phase one and two started by now, whereas I 'aven't even secured ownership of Falcon's Yard yet, as his older brother isn't willing to sell it to me, despite what James promised.'

'Then it's probably a good job Phillip Falcon is dead then, isn't it?'

'Sorry, you mean Harry Falcon?'

'The body of Phillip Falcon was found this morning, inside Falcon's Yard's boatshed. But you already knew that, right?'

As his eyes darted between Tanner and Jenny, the colour fast draining from his face, Jackson spluttered out, 'B-but...you can't possibly think it was me?'

'Given the fact that only a couple of hours before you were seen by not only me, but my colleague here, along with two uniformed police officers, encouraging a couple of your so-called casual labourers to bash his head in with some sledgehammers; and with what you've just told me about your postponed building development, then I think that puts you at the top of an increasingly short list of suspects.'

'You can think what you like, but it wasn't me, and I can prove it!'

'To be honest, Mr Jackson, I'd have been surprised if you couldn't.'

'What do you mean by that?'

'I mean that in my humble experience, a man like yourself would rarely go around killing people.'

'Well, I'm pleased you're finally seeing sense.'

'Not when you can pay a couple of your chimpanzees to do the job for you.'

'But – I didn't!'

'How much did you give them? Fifty quid each? No, that's sounds far too much. It was probably more like fifty pence.'

As Jackson regained control of his emotions, he eased himself back down in his chair to fix his eyes firmly on Tanner's. 'Before I say anything else, I want to speak to my lawyer.'

'Don't worry, Mr Jackson, we're not arresting you. Not yet, at any rate.'

Leaving him to whatever it was that he'd been doing before they'd arrived, Jenny reminded Tanner to ask the secretary for his so-called casual workers' contact details, before heading outside.

Stepping over the industrial estate's concrete-lined car park, heading for Tanner's car, Jenny said, 'I must admit, I thought he came over as being quite genuine, inasmuch as he didn't seem to know anything about what had happened to Phillip Falcon.'

Pulling open the car door, Tanner turned to glance up at the window he guessed belonged to the office they'd just been in. Seeing Jackson's head disappear behind a blind, he said, 'We'll have to see about that, but it's worth remembering that it's not all that difficult to play the part of someone who's innocent, especially when that person has probably had a fair amount of practice doing so. If he did have a hand, he'd have been expecting our visit, giving him plenty of time to rehearse what he was going to say, and how he was going to say it. And don't forget that he probably didn't do it, but paid someone else to. It's a lot easier to spin a lie when it's based on truth.'

'Well, we'll soon know if he was involved,' said Jenny, 'shortly after we get the prints and DNA off his two thugs.'

'That's if they did it. He may have had the good sense to use someone else.'

'But is Jackson that intelligent?'

'Good point. However, even if he was stupid enough to send the same two men who he'd used to threaten Phillip only a few hours earlier, if we do find their DNA inside the boatshed and they admit to having done it, they may not be quite so willing to say who directed them. And even if they did, it would only end up being his word against theirs.'

Inside the XJS once more, with their seatbelts on and the engine started, Jenny turned to Tanner. 'So, what do we do now?'

'What we always do. Keep chasing the leads until we find a guilty dog attached to the end of one.'

· CHAPTER TWENTY FIVE ·

'I DON'T SUPPOSE there's been any news from Dr Johnstone or forensics yet, sir?' enquired Tanner, as he entered DCI Forrester's office with Jenny following behind.

'I assume you mean from the boatshed?' he replied, a little absently. Dragging his eyes off the screen, he eventually looked over at them. 'Not yet, no. How'd you get on in Great Yarmouth?'

'It's difficult to tell,' Tanner replied, resting his hands on the back of a chair. 'As you'd expect, he denied knowing anything about what happened to Phillip Falcon.'

'No surprises there.'

'He did admit to having investors breathing down his neck over his latest development, though. He was supposed to have started building at Falcon's Yard by now. He also admitted to having had discussions with the younger brother, James, about selling the yard, and that they'd been talking about it for some time. According to him, it was James who'd given him the idea to buy the land, promising that his father didn't have long to live, and that his brother would be agreeable to sell once he'd gone.'

'Which he wasn't.'

'As it turned out, no. He also told us that James is one of his investors, so they have a mutual incentive for the development to be completed. That means James needs Jackson to purchase Falcon's Yard, and Jackson needs to be able to finish what he's started.'

'And now that Harry and Phillip are both dead, there shouldn't be anything to stop them. Unless, of course, we can find them guilty of murder first,' mused Forrester.

'Absolutely. However, if they did do it, acting alone or together, I doubt if either would have done the killing. I think it's more likely that they'd have paid someone else. If that is the case, then I think it could be difficult to prove, especially if they concluded their business over the phone, made sure not to keep a note of anything on paper or electronically, and paid whoever actually did it in cash.'

With his elbows resting on his desk, Forrester steepled his fingers together. 'OK, so I suppose we need to wait and see what forensics comes up with from inside the boatshed.'

'Yes, sir. In the meantime, we have the names and addresses of the two thugs Jackson used to threaten Phillip Falcon, so I think it would definitely be worth having a chat with them, and make sure we get their prints and DNA. I also think it would be useful to find out who all Jackson's investors are. Someone like him is bound to know some dubious characters. At the end of the day, I think anyone with a financial interest in seeing the development completed has a motive.'

'That sounds like you're intending to start growing our list of suspects again, Tanner, but still without being able to eliminate anyone.'

'We've managed to rule out one of the carers, sir.'

'Wow.'

'As well as Phillip Falcon.'

'I suppose that's you're idea of a joke?'

'More of a statement of fact, sir.'

After narrowing his eyes at him, Forrester continued. 'What about the two grandchildren? Can't we cross them off?'

'We're still waiting on them to provide us with their prints and DNA.'

'What, still?'

'I'm afraid so, sir.'

There was a knock, closely followed by DI Cooper putting his head round the door.

'Sorry to disturb you, sir, but we've just been given access to James Falcon's and his two children's bank accounts, and Harry Falcon's will has come through as well.'

'It's like buses,' muttered Tanner to Jenny.

'Have you had a chance to look through any of it?' asked Forrester.

'Only briefly, sir. The will doesn't say anything we didn't already know, apart from the two grandchildren being named, but not just for an old clock and some jewellery. Harry Falcon specifically said that he wanted them to inherit his estate, in its entirety, after his two sons.'

'Why would he have done that?'

'Probably to try to prevent his sons from selling.'

'What about the finances?'

'Well, sir, it's going to take us a while to go through,' Cooper said, 'but on the face of it, it looks like the younger son, James Falcon, isn't quite as well off as he's been making out.'

Leaning in towards Jenny, Tanner murmured, 'Told you.'

'He's only got just over £21,000 in the bank, but has monthly outgoings that easily exceed that, and without all that much coming in to make up the difference.'

'Where's the money going out to?'

'The largest payment seems to be to cover a sizeable mortgage. The next is to a marine finance company.'

'That must be for his yacht,' mused Jenny.

'The others are to Aston Martin and at least three credit card companies.'

'So, in other words, he's broke.'

'It looks that way, yes, sir.'

'How about his children?'

'Well, the first thing I thought was interesting was that they have a joint bank account.'

Hearing that, Forrester exchanged glances with Tanner and Jenny.

'Again,' continued Cooper, 'we've only had a quick scan through, but they've also got a hefty mortgage, and regular payments are going out to several car finance companies, including Porsche and Ferrari. And there's more going out to cover credit card debt. However, they do at least have substantial incomes, which is more than their father has.'

'Are their incomes meeting their expenditures?'

'Just about.'

'But I assume they wouldn't if one of them were to lose their job?'

'Judging by how much each of them seems to earn, I'd say that's a definite no, sir, they wouldn't.'

'So, the younger son is broke, and his two children are a redundancy away from being so.'

'That's about how it looks, sir, yes.'

Forrester leaned back in his chair, swivelled it to look out of the window, then round to face Tanner and Jenny. 'What else do we know about the grandchildren?'

'DI Cooper told me earlier that Edward had phoned his uncle yesterday evening,' began Tanner, 'only a few hours before he was killed. But it was only a five minute conversation.'

'So, Edward was the last person known to speak to him?'

'It looks like it. And that wasn't the only conversation they'd had either. The one before that, Edward denied even having, or at least he said he'd forgotten about it, which seemed odd, given that it had gone on for over an hour.'

'Did he say what they'd been talking about for such a long time?'

'He said it was about the will, and that they'd been left a couple of items, but he certainly didn't mention anything about them being directly named as beneficiaries of the estate.'

'Cooper, what time was the call? The one yesterday, from Edward to his uncle?'

'Just after eight in the evening, sir.'

'Does anyone know how long it would take to

drive up from Canary Wharf to Falcon's Yard?'

'I've already checked, sir,' replied Cooper. 'With no traffic, just over two hours, so he could have easily driven up in time.'

'Didn't someone mention something about the two grandchildren having some sort of an incestuous relationship together?'

'Only that they seemed unusually close, sir,' replied Tanner.

'In what way?'

'Just their mannerisms; and the way they were holding hands over the table, when I first saw them.'

'And now we find out that they have a joint bank account, as if they're married, and are a redundancy away from being broke, and that Edward was the last person to speak to Phillip, just two hours before his estimated time of death, which is exactly how long it would have taken for them to drive up.'

Nobody responded to that, leaving Forrester to ask, 'Has anyone told them that their uncle is dead yet?'

'Their father may have done,' replied Tanner, 'although, as he's not spoken to them in months, at least not on the phone, he may not have bothered.'

With his attention focussed on Tanner and Jenny, Forrester asked, 'I don't suppose either of you have been trained in taking fingerprints and DNA samples?'

'I have, sir,' piped up Jenny.

'OK, tomorrow is Saturday. I want you two to give the grandchildren a call and ask if you can meet them inside their flat tomorrow. Jenny, make sure you take a forensics kit down with you. Once there, you can tell them that their uncle is dead. Find out where they were, and why Edward phoned his uncle yesterday. Then tell them that you'll need to take their prints and DNA, there and then. That way they won't be able to wriggle out of it. And finally, try to have a look around their flat. See if you can find any signs that they're having an incestuous relationship.'

'For what purpose?' questioned Tanner.

'Because, if they're sleeping with each other, then as far as I'm concerned, they've got some serious mental issues. I also think that would mean it would be more likely that they planned the murders of their grandfather and uncle together, simply to get their hands on the estate.'

'But in that scenario, they'd have to kill their father as well.'

'That's what I'm worried about.'

'Unless...' began Jenny, hesitantly.

'Unless what?' encouraged Forrester.

'Unless the reason why they were talking to their uncle for so long was to try and persuade him to sell the estate, which would suggest that they're also investors in Jackson's development.'

'All the more reason for you two to head down there tomorrow. We need their alibis, prints and DNA; find out what they've been talking to the uncle about, and why they didn't tell us that they were next in line for their grandfather's inheritance.'

- CHAPTER TWENTY SIX -

Saturday, 12th October

THE FOLLOWING DAY, with Cooper and Gilbert focussing their attention on tracking down Jackson Development's investors, along with the two thugs known simply as Bazzer and Gazzer, Tanner and Jenny caught the train at Wroxham Station, their destination Liverpool Street. They'd arranged to meet Edward and Tessa Falcon at their penthouse apartment at the top of Aerial View, which turned out to be a spectacular high-rise residential development near St Katharine Docks Marina, in the heart of London.

After being granted access to the lifts by the concierge in reception, they were ushered into the apartment by the grandchildren, each of whom had replaced their smart city clothes with a humble pair of jeans and a t-shirt.

Once Tanner had formally introduced them to Jenny, he went on, 'Thank you for agreeing to see us at such short notice.'

'We're happy to help, of course,' replied Edward, 'although we're not sure how.'

Stepping inside the vast opulent open-planned

space, for a moment they were both unable to do anything other than to gaze around with their mouths hanging open, especially when they saw the view of St. Katherine Docks, with the iconic Tower of London and London Bridge beyond, all of which sparkled with magnificent splendour on this perfect Autumn day.

'You mentioned on the phone yesterday that you'd already heard about what happened to your uncle,' said Tanner, turning his attention back towards the people they'd come down to see.

'That's right. Our father called with the news yesterday afternoon.'

'So, you do speak to him sometimes then?'

'On occasion.'

Leaving Jenny gazing out at the view, Tanner began to wander around the apartment, his two hosts following closely behind.

'It's a fine place you've got here,' he said, circling a suite of white leather chairs nestled around a large opaque glass coffee table. 'No TV?'

'It comes down from the ceiling.'

'Nice!'

As he strolled over to the luxurious kitchen area, Tessa asked, 'May we get you both a coffee?'

Seeing her brother shoot her a dirty look, Tanner replied, 'I'd like that very much,' before calling over to Jenny, 'Detective Constable Evans, we're being offered coffee. Would you like one?'

'I would,' she replied. Peeling her eyes away from the view, she fished out her notebook to join them, ditching her handbag and the forensics kit she'd brought down onto the immaculate white carpet next to the coffee table.

As Tessa glided into the kitchen, with its shiny bold red units that looked as if they'd only just been polished, with neither Tanner nor Jenny speaking, Edward eventually said, 'Our father told us that you think our uncle's death was intentional; that you think someone killed him?'

'Well, we found a Broads cabin cruiser lying on top of his head, and we've been reliably informed that it would have been challenging for him to have placed it there himself, at least not without help, so at the moment we are, yes; which reminds me. May I ask where the two of you were yesterday, between the hours of ten and one o'clock in the morning?'

After flickering their eyes at each other, Edward replied, 'We were out.'

'Whereabouts did you go?'

'It was a friend's birthday party, at Fabric.'

'Sorry, but what's Fabric?'

'It's a nightclub, in Farringdon.'

'I see. I suppose I am a little out of touch with London's nightlife scene. And how did you get there?'

'By tube, of course.'

'So you didn't drive?'

'Why would we have driven?'

'No reason. Will there be someone who'll be able to vouch for you?'

'May I assume by that question, and the reason for your journey, is that you've come to the rather bizarre conclusion that we murdered our own uncle?'

'Not at all.'

'I'm relieved to hear it.'

'Well, not only your uncle.'

'You mean to say that you think we killed our grandfather as well? Now that really is the most ridiculous thing I've ever heard in my entire life. What possible reason could we have for murdering half our family?'

Sidestepping the question, Tanner said, 'You still haven't told us if there'd be anyone there who'd be able to vouch for you.'

'Apart from the other fifty or so people who were invited?'

'Big party then?'

'About average.'

'Easy enough to get lost in a crowd, though.'

'You can ask Lynn Bryson, if you like,' chipped in Tessa. 'I have her number.'

'And she is...?'

'A friend from work. It was her birthday party.'

Seeing Jenny make a note of that, Tanner pushed on. 'Going back to the time you spoke to your uncle?'

'You mean, the five minute chat I had with him yesterday?'

'I was thinking more of the hour long conversation you had with him on Wednesday?'

'OK, yes, what about it?'

'The last time we met, after initially not having been able to even remember it, you said that it was about your grandfather's will.'

'The will and the funeral, yes.'

'And that you'd inherited a broken old clock and some jewellery.'

'What of it?'

'Did he mention anything to you about the

estate?'

'Only that our grandfather had left it equally between him and our father.'

'He didn't say anything about you both being named as the ones next in line to inherit it, should anything happen to your father and uncle?'

'Er, nothing about that, no,' he replied, raising an eyebrow at Tessa.

'I see. So your grandfather had already told you?'

'Why on Earth would he have discussed the contents of his will with us?'

'I don't know. Maybe it came up in conversation during his ninety-fourth birthday party?'

'Well, it didn't. Before just now, we didn't know anything about it, did we Tess?'

'We didn't, no.'

'And besides,' continued Edward, 'as you can see, we don't exactly need our grandfather's inheritance.'

Taking in their surroundings again, Tanner said, 'I must admit that you certainly seem to be doing very well for yourselves. I assume you've got a couple of cars to match?'

'Er, more than that, I'm afraid.'

'How many?'

'I've got a Range Rover Vogue, an Aston Martin Vantage and I recently bought a Ferrari 488 Spider, although I can't say that I've had much of a chance to use it yet.'

'Gosh!' exclaimed Tanner, with sarcastic indifference. 'They all sound very expensive! How about you, Miss Falcon?'

'Oh, I don't really go in for cars. I'm more of a shoes and handbags sort of a girl.'

'She's got a rather sad five-year old 911,' ribbed her brother, 'although it's not much to look at.'

'Still, it's a nice car though,' remarked Tanner.

'My brother doesn't care for it,' Tessa replied. 'He doesn't even let me keep it in the car park. I have to leave it out on the street.'

'I take it that you own them all?'

'We don't rent them, if that's what you mean,' sneered Edward.

'I actually meant if you paid for them in cash, or if you bought them on hire purchase?'

'Well, hire purchase, but...'

'And I assume you have a mortgage on this place?'

'Yes, but who doesn't?'

'So, when you go around telling everyone how rich you are, what you really mean is that you're in debt up to your ears?'

'Hardly!'

'What happens if one of you loses your job?'

'Er...we'd get another one. We're both Oxford graduates, working for two of the largest firms in the City. And as we both get inundated with calls from head-hunters on a daily basis, if we needed to, I should think it would take either one of us about ten and a half seconds to find another job; probably one that pays more as well. Oh, and if you're still seriously thinking that we woke up one morning with the cunning plan of murdering our entire family just to inherit our grandfather's estate, Tessa and I have been investing in property in and around London since before we graduated, which must be worth ten times our grandfather's mosquito-infested swamp.'

'You're property investors as well!' exclaimed Tanner, glancing over at Jenny.

'We are, yes. Why? I suppose the government has just passed some new anti-property investment law, making it illegal for us to own any?'

'I don't think they have,' mused Tanner, 'but I assume that means you've been approached about the Moorings development, the one being built next to Falcon's Yard?'

'We haven't, no.'

'I see. But you did know that your father's been speaking to the developers about selling the yard to them, and that they've already got planning permission to drain the dyke and concrete over the whole place.

Hearing that, Edward stared at Tessa, his face visibly draining of colour.

His surprising reaction wasn't lost on Tanner, who caught Tessa take a rather sudden sip from her coffee, spin around and totter over to the sink.

Pressing home whatever advantage he seemed to have gained, Tanner asked, 'Are you two bunking up together, or what?'

Looking as if he'd just been brought out of a trance, Edward's eyes drifted back into focus to say, 'Er...no. As I said before, it just makes financial sense for us to live together.'

'But even so, you do seem very close.'

Tessa finished her drink, leaving her cup in the sink before heading back to join her brother. 'We always have been, ever since we were children.'

Draping one of her elegant long arms over Edward's broad square shoulders, she added, 'And yes, we know that we have a tendency to give the impression that we're involved in some sort of incestuous relationship, but the truth is, I don't fancy men, certainly not my brother!' Turning to face him she gave him a pitying look. 'Sorry about that, Eddie darling.'

As he wound his arm around her tiny waist, Edward said, 'And I fancy girls, but not my sister, which she well knows, don't you, Tess?'

As she began pawing at his chest, she gave him a desperate, pleading look. 'What, not even a teeny bit?'

Ignoring her, Edward returned his gaze to Tanner. 'We respect each other's space. When Tess brings back one of her girlfriends, I keep out of their way, and she does the same whenever I do.'

'So, you two have the perfect relationship?'

'Well, I wouldn't go that far, but I would say that we have the perfect apartment, which we feel more than makes up for any minor inconveniences. And until one of us meets someone we want to settle down with on a more permanent basis, we're happy enough.'

With both of them now offering him sickeningly content, near-perfect smiles, Tanner was beginning to feel an annoying mixture of envy and frustration. On the surface, they really did seem to have what most people would consider to be the perfect life together. However, he knew they were hiding something. Their reaction to being told about the Moorings development was proof of that, but for the life of him, he couldn't guess what it could be.

Unable to think of anything else to ask them, Tanner began to wind up the informal interview. 'OK, well, thank you both for your time. Before we go, would it be OK if Detective Constable Evans here takes your fingerprints and a DNA sample?'

Their perfect smiles fading, Edward said, 'We were actually going to go down to the police station today.'

'Yes, well, we thought we'd save you the journey. Unfortunately, with what's happened to both your grandfather and your uncle, we're going to need them as a matter of urgency.'

'Of course.' Looking over at Jenny, Edward asked, 'Which one of us do you want first?'

'Either or,' she replied, finishing her coffee and collecting the forensics kit from her bag.

'How about Mr Falcon goes first,' proposed Tanner, 'and then maybe Ms Falcon can give me a quick guided tour of your apartment?'

- CHAPTER TWENTY SEVEN -

WITH JENNY HAVING successfully taken samples of both their fingerprints and DNA, and Tanner having had a look around their flat, once they were back in the lift and the doors were closed, he said, 'Did you see their expressions, when I mentioned about the Moorings Development, and that their father was trying to sell Falcon's Yard to Mr Jackson?'

'I did,' Jenny said, as she watched the lift's numbers count down. 'They're clearly hiding something.'

'Yes, but what?'

'Well, whatever it is, they seemed genuine about not being investors.'

'And they didn't appear to be worried about their finances, or their job situation, which rules out any financial incentive.'

'Neither did they seem to be having an incestuous relationship.'

The conversation lulled, before Jenny eventually asked, 'What are you going to tell Forrester? Do you think we can rule them out?'

'If it wasn't for how they reacted when we told them about the development, I'd have said so. I'm also not convinced that the only thing Edward was talking to their uncle about was the will and the funeral. Not for over an hour.'

'But they don't seem to have a motive, and you're always telling me that that's the key to any murder.'

'Pre-meditated, yes.'

'Well, I can't see them killing Phillip after having some sort of an argument, unless it was about whatever it was they'd been discussing with him over the phone. Something that would have so enraged them that they'd sneak out of a party and drive all the way up to Norfolk to drop a boat on his head.'

'It doesn't seem very likely, does it.'

'Not really, no,' said Jenny. 'It also doesn't explain why they would murder their grandfather; unless their uncle killed him.'

'And he'd confessed as much to his nephew, which is what the phone call was about.'

'So they decided to kill their uncle to avenge their grandfather?'

Tanner thought about that for a moment before saying, 'OK, no. I think that seems even less likely than the first idea. We're just going to have to wait and see what forensics comes up with, and if they're able to match either their prints or DNA to the scene at the boatshed.'

With the conversation about work having reached a natural conclusion, Jenny said, 'So anyway, whilst we're down in London, are you going to take me shopping?'

'I suppose,' replied Tanner, not sounding too keen. 'But may I suggest we find something to eat first. I don't know about you, but I'm starving!'

· CHAPTER TWENTY EIGHT ·

IN THE WARMTH of the autumn sun, having enjoyed a pleasant lunch in one of the many outdoor restaurant enclosures, they spent a while doing nothing but wander around Canary Warf, occasionally stopping to gaze up at the many vast concrete and glass buildings, most of which were so high they seemed to disappear into the sky.

After a while, Tanner led her into Cabot Place shopping mall, where they found a vast underground labyrinth of high street banks, supermarkets, and, of particular interest to Jenny, a vast range of up-market boutique shops.

Seeing something in the window of one, Jenny grabbed Tanner's hand and led him inside.

'This is nice,' she soon said, holding up a Dolce & Gabbana puff-sleeved top with a bold poppy print.

'For £675, no doubt it is!' exclaimed Tanner, unable to take his eyes off the price tag.

Picking it off the rack, she held it up to the artificial light. 'If I wore it with my white skinny fit jeans and some heels, I think it would work.'

'Er, I think it would make you look like an up-market gypsy.'

'Exactly!'

Shaking his head, Tanner said, 'Anyway, I thought you were going to buy yourself something with shoulder-pads, to go with my car?'

'Yes, I know, but I'm still looking for a working time machine. Surprisingly, shops these days don't tend to sell clothes from the 1980s.'

'Charity shops do!' announced Tanner, as if he'd managed to solve the problem of climate change, world hunger, and his lack of disposable income, all at the same time.

Unimpressed, Jenny glared at him. 'I'm not buying my clothes from a charity shop!'

'Why not? I do.'

'Please God, tell me you're joking.'

'OK, well, I used to. I bought my first suit from one. It was Yves Saint Laurent, no less, and it only cost me a tenner.'

'What a bargain,' Jenny muttered, but in a way that suggested they must have seen him coming.

'I know!' agreed Tanner. 'And it fitted me like a glove.'

'Did you buy them there as well?'

'What's that?'

'Gloves.'

'Not that I remember, but just about everything else.'

'Not your underpants; although, if you did, it would explain a lot.'

'No, but I'd buy my socks there on a fairly regular basis. 10p a pair, I seem to remember.'

'I'm surprised you decided to stop shopping from them.'

Tanner thought for a moment. 'You know, I

can't even remember why I did. It was probably a combination of the smell, and the fact that I was walking around in clothes whose previous owners had probably died wearing them.'

'Not the lack of choice, then?'

'That wasn't the reason, no. I'd always be able to find something that fitted.'

'So anyway, back to reality; how do you fancy buying me this top for the bargain price of only £675.'

'I think I'd have to get a mortgage on our boat first, especially if we're going to have to pay for another year's worth of mooring fees.'

'So that's a no then?'

'Um...' he began, wondering how he'd be able to wriggle out of having to buy it without upsetting her too much. 'Maybe we could haggle?'

'What, here? In front of everyone?'

'You know what I mean.'

'I suppose we could have a quick one in the changing rooms.'

'Haggle, as in when two people argue over the cost of something.'

'Oh, I see.' Jenny glanced over at the pretty stick-like girl standing behind the counter who looked as if she had a broom-handle stuck up her bum. 'I'm not sure they do that. Look, there's even a sign. No haggling!'

Tanner glanced over to see where she was pointing, before realising she was winding him up.

'How about some jewellery instead?' proposed Tanner, spying some cheap-looking earrings and bracelets hanging from a display rack where the girl was standing.

'Oh, go on then.'

As soon as they reached the stand, Jenny cupped her hand around a bracelet. 'This one's nice.'

The moment Tanner saw it, he turned abruptly away to examine the others.

'Don't you like it?'

'Well, I do, it's just…'

'It's just…what?'

Looking down at it again, he said, 'Well, I'm not sure it's really you. How about this?'

'Er, no. That is truly hideous. I like this one, and it's only £25.'

Tanner turned to look into her eyes. There was a reason why he didn't like the bracelet she seemed to have set her heart on. It was almost identical to the one he'd bought his daughter for her 19th birthday, the same one she'd been wearing when he'd found her twisted crumpled body lying discarded in the gutter of a London side street. But he couldn't tell her that; at least, he'd no idea how.

Beginning to look genuinely pissed-off, Jenny eventually said, 'Well, if you're not going to buy it for me, I suppose I'll have to pay for it myself.'

'No, it's not that, it's just that I wanted to buy you something a little more special, that's all.'

'But not the gypsy top.'

'Sorry, look, I'm being silly. Of course I'll buy it for you. Now, are you absolutely sure that this is the one you want?'

With her pout beginning to fade, she replied, 'Yes, please,' before handing it over for him to pay.

· CHAPTER TWENTY NINE ·

Monday 14th October

ON THE WAY home, with Jenny delighted with her gift, and Tanner doing his best not to think about it, he called Forrester to let him know how they'd fared with the Falcon twins, and to ask if there'd been any news from the scene inside the boatshed.

Neither forensics nor Dr Johnstone had come back, and were now not expected until Monday, so Tanner requested for Jenny and himself to be given the following day off, as it was a Sunday, briefly explaining to Forrester the situation concerning their moorings. Perhaps unsurprisingly, Forrester said a flat no. With alibis that still needed to be corroborated, finances to be gone through, and potential suspects that had to be tracked down, there was just too much going on. But he promised that they'd be able to leave early, as long as nothing of any great significance arose during the day.

So they spent their Sunday stuck inside the office, taking their turn to plough through financial and witness statements, whilst Cooper and Gilbert were out and about trying to track down Bazzer and Gazzer, and any other of Jackson's more dubious known associates. When their colleagues eventually returned, having had no luck, Tanner and Jenny decided to slink off quietly to spend what was left of the day using the excuse of having to find new moorings to go for a sail.

A little before half past nine on Monday morning Forrester called Tanner into his office, which was normal enough; it was the way he was summoned which left him wondering what it was about, as Forrester phoned him on his direct line, instead of shouting his name across the office as he normally did.

'You wanted to see me, sir?' he enquired, stepping inside, leaving the door ajar behind him.

'Take a seat, will you?' Forrester replied, still staring at his monitor.

Again, that was unusual. Tanner would normally be left to stand.

With a prickle of apprehension, he did as he was told.

Eventually Forrester looked over at him and frowned. 'I've just had Superintendent Whitaker on the phone.'

'Oh yes?'

'It was concerning a conversation you apparently had with a certain DCI Baxter, who I believe is your old boss.'

Tanner shifted uncomfortably in his seat. He knew where this was going.

'He was saying that you called Baxter last week, demanding information about the ongoing investigation into the death of your daughter. Is that true?'

'Not in so many words, no, sir, it isn't.'

'But you did phone him up?'

'Well, yes, but only because he'd already been in contact with my wife – I mean my ex-wife – saying that they had new information regarding the investigation, and to see if she'd be interested in taking part in a press conference to make a public appeal for more information.'

'OK, but that doesn't explain why you felt it necessary to call him?'

'Because I met up with her for lunch when I was down there, and she asked me if I'd be willing to do the press conference with her. So I called him to discuss the idea.'

At that moment there was a knock at the still open door. Glancing around, Tanner's heart stopped as he saw Jenny's head appear through the gap.

Blanking Tanner, with a stern flushed face, she stared over at Forrester. 'Excuse me, sir, but the final report has come in via email from Dr Johnstone. He's concluded that Phillip Falcon was hit from behind. The boat must have been pushed on top of him to cover it up.'

'So, we were right with our assumption. OK, thanks for the update, Evans. We'll be out shortly.'

'No problem, sir.'

As Tanner sat there, wondering if she'd overheard what he'd been saying about how he'd met his ex-wife for lunch without telling her, he was just beginning to think that she hadn't, when she caught his gaze to send him an icy look of stern indignation, before ducking out.

Leaning back in his chair to watch Evans through the partition's window, stomping back to her desk, Forrester eventually looked over at Tanner to say, 'I sincerely hope that you two aren't arguing about something?'

'Not at all, sir,' Tanner replied, with a calming smile, before muttering to himself, 'at least, not yet.'

'Well, she doesn't seem to be very pleased with you – that much is obvious. I have told you about how I feel about inter-personnel relationships, haven't I?'

'You have, sir, yes,' confirmed Tanner.

'OK. Anyway, going back to your conversation with DCI Baxter; if you were only discussing the press conference, why was he left with the impression that you were attempting to involve yourself with the investigation, in particular that you demanded to see the case files, as well as a photofit of a potential suspect?'

'I didn't demand, sir, I simply asked if it would be possible for me to take a quick look at them.'

Forrester took a moment to study Tanner's face. Although he knew very little about the investigation into his senior DI's daughter's death, he knew Tanner had been the one who was called to the scene to find her body, and that he'd gone on to insist that he led the investigation, only to be ordered to stay clear. Such a scenario would have been difficult for any officer to cope with, let alone a DI who was used to taking the lead on such cases.

'Listen, Tanner, I can't imagine how hard what

happened must have been for you, though I can
certainly understand your frustrations that
they've still not been able to identify who was
responsible; but there are long-establish reasons
for not allowing a victim's relatives to work on a
criminal investigation.'

'Yes, sir, I know.'

'Even if it has been over a year since it
happened.'

Tanner didn't respond to that, but just stared
vacantly at the top of his desk.

After a moment's pause, Forrester added,
'Now, I need to know that I have your undivided
attention on what we've got going on here, not
with how London CID is progressing with the
investigation into the death of your daughter.'

'You do, sir, yes.'

'OK, good. That's all I want to know. Right, so,
what's your plan for the day?'

'Well, sir, Cooper's still trying to track down
Jackson's two heavies whilst also looking into his
business finances. That should allow us to put
together a list of his investors.'

'What about Gilbert?'

'I've told her to carry on checking through the
alibis from the cleaners and carers. Hopefully
she'll be able to finish that today, allowing us to
finally cross them off our list.'

'And you and Evans?'

'Well, ideally I'd like to bring both James
Falcon and Jim Jackson in for questioning, but we
don't have the physical evidence needed to charge
either of them, so for now I think we should keep
the pressure on by going round to see them again,

and just hope forensics can come up with something tangible for us to work with.'

'What about the two grandchildren?'

'To be honest, sir, I've yet to make up my mind about them. I really don't think they have any financial interest in their grandfather's estate, but they're definitely hiding something.'

'You don't think they've invested in the Mooring development?'

'No. They genuinely didn't seem to know anything about that. It was their reaction to the news that Jackson intends to build over Falcon's Yard that was of interest.'

'Maybe they were simply surprised by the news?'

'Maybe,' agreed Tanner, 'but neither seemed the type to be easily shocked. I couldn't help but feel that there was another reason.'

With Tanner staring thoughtfully off into space, Forrester said, 'Anyway, it sounds to me like you're on the right track with James Falcon and Jim Jackson. I'd maintain your focus on them for now, and see how you get on.'

· CHAPTER THIRTY ·

T HE MOMENT TANNER stood to leave, his thoughts turned to Jenny, and how bad the fallout was going to be that she'd found out he'd met his ex-wife for lunch in London without telling her.

Approaching their desks, he knew from the way she was glaring at her monitor whilst occasionally stabbing an accusatory finger at the keyboard that she was fuming.

'You OK?' he asked, attempting to catch her eye as he pulled his chair out.

'Fine!' she replied. 'You?'

'Good, yes,' he responded.

A frosty silence followed, with Tanner left wondering what to say next, and Jenny continuing to try and murder her computer using nothing more than her bare fingers.

The most obvious thing for him to do was to simply apologise for not telling her. However, doing so would almost make it seem as if there was something going on that he had to apologise for, when there most definitely wasn't. There was also the chance that she'd not overheard him, but was upset about something completely different, and telling her would only exacerbate her current forbidding mood.

Eventually Tanner decided that it was probably best to just leave it. It wasn't as if Jenny didn't know that he'd been married before, and that he would therefore have to occasionally communicate with his ex-wife. In fact, thinking about it, he wasn't even sure why he had to tell her whenever he did.

He glanced over at her face. Her narrowed eyes, pouting lips and flushed cheeks made him think that even if he should bring up the subject and apologise, it may be more sensible to wait until she'd calmed down a little, or at least until they were away from the office, just in case it escalated into a full blown argument.

Having made up his mind, he said, 'Forrester thinks we should be focussing our attention on James Falcon and Jim Jackson.'

'At what point were you going to tell me that you'd met your wife for lunch when you went down to London?' demanded Jenny, glaring at him.

OK, time to apologise, he thought.

'Sorry, yes. I should have told you about that, but it wasn't planned. It was when I was on my way back. Liverpool Street Station isn't far from where she works, so I thought I'd give her a call, to touch base. It's not often that we talk, and it just seemed to make sense to use the time whilst I was down there to catch up.'

'Over lunch?'

'Over lunch, yes.'

'And then for you to not tell me about it.'

'It wasn't that I made a conscious decision not

to,' he lied. 'It was more that by the time I got back, I had more important things on my mind.'

'I see. And did you do anything else when you were down there that you thought best not to mention?'

'Nothing, no.'

'Apart from phoning up your old boss, of course.'

Wondering just how much of the conversation she'd overheard, Tanner replied, 'That was to do with what I'd been discussing with my wife.'

'I sincerely hope you mean your ex-wife?' sneered Jenny.

'Of course, yes. My ex-wife.'

'I suppose it's not my place to ask what you two were talking about?'

'Oh, you know. Just stuff.'

'Stuff, as in…?'

Tanner could feel his temper beginning to rise. As far as he was concerned, what he'd been discussing with his wife of some twenty-odd years was none of her business, especially as the bulk of the conversation had centred around their daughter. However, he also knew that he should have mentioned the fact that they had met up for lunch when he got back. The way Jenny had found out, by overhearing him tell their boss, was the result of him not having done so when he should have.

It was with that thought held firmly at the front of his mind that he was able to calm himself down enough to say, 'My old boss told her that they had new information surrounding Abigail's death, in particular a photofit of the possible murderer, and he wanted her to take part in a press conference, to release the photo and make a call for witnesses.'

'Oh, I see,' said Jenny, the tide of her emotions turning from scornful indignation to guilty self-reproach.

'She wanted to know if I'd be able to do the press conference with her.'

Jenny paused for a moment. 'And what did you say?'

'I told her that I'd think about it.'

'And have you?'

'That was what I spoke to my old boss about. I told him that I thought it would be inappropriate if I did, as the world would see me with Sara, my ex-wife, when I'm with you now.'

Jenny stared over at him, emotion sparkling in her deep blue eyes. Any words she had were swallowed back down.

Taking her hand across the desk, Tanner gazed into her eyes. 'But you must know that, Jen. My life is here, with you. It's most definitely not with Sara.'

'I suppose,' she replied, blinking away rising tears before they sent rivers of mascara running down the sides of her face. 'But what about Abigail? You must still want to know who was responsible for her death?'

'I do, of course I do, but it's been abundantly clear to me on numerous occasions that I'm not to get involved. Forrester just gave me a lecture about it as well.'

'But surely there's no harm, not after it's been such a long time; especially as they seem to have made so little progress in finding out who was responsible.'

'That's what I thought. When I spoke to my old boss to say that I didn't want to do the press conference, I asked if I could see the case files, and the photofit of the suspect they've recently acquired. He turned me down flat! He must have then called Head Office to complain about me interfering in their investigation.'

A moment's pause followed. 'Did he say when they're going to do the press conference?'

'I'm not sure they're going to anymore.'

'But why?'

'He said there wasn't much point, as neither of the parents would be involved. What I'd like to know is where they're going to publish the photofit of the suspect, or even if they're going to bother.'

'How about asking that family friend of yours? The one you bought the boat off.'

'You mean Commander Bardsley.'

'That's the one. I'm sure he'd be able to get hold of that photofit for you. He may even be able to send you the case files.'

'It's worth asking, I suppose.'

'So anyway,' continued Jenny, 'back to our own investigation, what's next?'

'I think we need to pay James Falcon another visit, to make sure we keep up the pressure whilst waiting for forensics. I'm also keen to tell him that we met with his children in London yesterday, and to ask him why they seemed a little shaken by the news that he was selling the land for it to be built over by his contracting chum.' Glancing towards Forrester's office, he added, 'And I think we should probably go now, or at least we should maybe stop holding hands, just in case Forrester comes out and thinks that we're about to start banging each other on the desk.'

· CHAPTER THIRTY ONE ·

AVING SPOKEN TO Commander
Bardsley, who promised to see what he
could do, Tanner and Jenny made their
way back to Falcon's Yard.

Parked in the courtyard was a car neither
Tanner nor Jenny had seen before, there or
anywhere else. It was a sleek, dangerously
attractive canary yellow Ferrari.

Assuming it to be the one Edward Falcon had
been boasting about – his brand new and hardly
used 488 Spider – Tanner leaned in to Jenny to
say, 'Looks like we're not the only ones looking to
pay our Mr James Falcon a visit.'

'Maybe we should have made an appointment.'

'We should be OK, but we might need to form
an orderly queue.'

Crunching their way to the end of the
courtyard, they crossed the dyke in front of the
boatshed's entrance to head down the narrow
channel towards Harry Falcon's Broads Cruiser,
moored up at the end.

As they grew nearer, raised voices could clearly
be heard coming from inside the cabin.

'Sounds interesting,' said Tanner. 'Maybe we
should get a little closer.'

'Are you suggesting that we deliberately attempt to eavesdrop?'

'I wasn't, but now that you've suggested it...'

'But wouldn't that be illegal?'

'If you mean, wouldn't anything we overheard be inadmissible in a court of law? Perhaps. However, if we just happened to find ourselves standing in line outside the boat which James Falcon is living on board, whilst waiting to speak to him, I can't see it being a problem.'

Tanner and Jenny edged nearer to the boat in question until they were able to overhear what was being discussed within the depths of the cabin.

'But not once have you ever said that you wanted to sell the yard,' came Edward Falcon's strained voice. 'You've always told us that your plan was to keep it for us.

'I've never said any such thing!' they heard his father say in return. 'Besides, what do you care? Neither of you are ever here, and neither of you need the money.'

'Tessa must be on board as well,' whispered Jenny.

'And neither do you!' came Edward's voice again.

'Unlike the two of you, I'm retired, which means I don't have the income I used to.'

'So you're saying that you do?'

'My portfolio has had a rough couple of years, that's all.'

'Look, if you needed money, you should have asked us.'

'I don't need money, at least I won't when I've

sold this place.'

'But you can't do that.'

'Why not? It's not as if Uncle Phillip's around to stop me.'

'Yes, but we are!'

'Er, the property belongs to me now, not you. You only get it if something happens to me.'

'Well, I'm sure something can be arranged.'

'Are you threatening me?'

'Of course not. We just don't want you to sell, that's all.'

'So you keep telling me, but what you haven't said is why.'

'Because it's not what Grandfather would have wanted. He started this place by digging out the dyke with his bare hands. If he'd not done so, none of us would be where we are today. We were going to hand it down to our children, and theirs after that. You can't just sell it because you're having a slight cash flow problem.'

'I'm afraid it's a little more than that.'

'Then we can lend you the money, can't we Tess?'

'Of course we can, Daddy,' came the voice of the sister. 'We're always here for you.'

'I'm sorry, but I'm not begging my children to lend me a few quid, and besides, I'd need more than what I suspect you have.'

'How much?' asked Edward.

There was a pause, before their father said, 'I lost over two million last year, and I'm set to lose even more this year. So unless you've got a spare five million knocking about, I'm afraid I've got no choice. I'm going to have to sell.'

'You're telling us that you're five million pounds in debt?'

'And that doesn't include the mortgage on my house, the loans on my yacht and cars, and my credit card debt as well.'

'But...why can't you just sell your house instead?'

'And live where?'

'On your yacht. It's big enough, surely?'

'Well, I could, I suppose, but it would take me a while to sell; that's even if I can. The property market's hardly booming at the moment.'

There was a lull in the conversation, before they heard the father say, 'Look, I'm sorry. I'm sure we'd all have liked to have kept it, but I've got no choice. Jackson Developments has already made a generous offer. I'm also set to make about a quarter of a million on the development itself, once it's finished and the apartments are sold. You know, you can invest in it yourself, if you want. I've got a good relationship with Jim Jackson, and I know he's still looking for investors.'

Another pause followed, before they were just about able to hear Edward say, 'I'm sorry father, but we cannot let you do this.'

'Well, again, I'm sorry, son, but I can't see how you can stop me.'

'Then you've left us no choice. We'll be contesting the will. Expect a call from our solicitors.'

There followed the sound of heavy footsteps, followed by the cabin door being slammed open. A moment later the canvas awning's entrance was wrenched away to reveal Edward's head and shoulders emerging from the boat.

The second he saw Tanner and Jenny standing there, he stopped and stared out at them. Jumping off the boat, he asked, 'What the hell are you two doing here?'

'We've come to have a word with your father, but it sounded like you beat us to it.'

As Tessa stepped off behind her brother, she said, 'I sincerely hope you weren't standing there with deliberate intent to listen in on our private conversation?'

'We've only just arrived,' Tanner lied, with a thin smile. 'I don't suppose your father is in?'

'You can find that out for yourselves,' snapped Edward. 'Come on, Tess. I suggest we leave them to it.'

· CHAPTER THIRTY TWO ·

H AVING WATCHED JAMES Falcon's two children stomp back towards their rather flamboyant car, Tanner returned his attention to the boat to call out, 'Mr Falcon, it's Detective Inspector Tanner and Detective Constable Evans again, Norfolk Police.'

More footsteps followed, and the canvas entrance was once again torn open to reveal the over-heated face of James Falcon glaring out at them.

'I sincerely hope you weren't listening to all that?'

'Only in part. Your children don't appear to be very happy with you.'

'Ungrateful little shits. You spend half your life and more than half your money bringing them up, giving them the best education money can buy and a virtual open door into two of the largest financial organisations in the world, and what do they do in return? Attempt to stop you from cashing in on your rightful inheritance.'

'But it's their inheritance as well, isn't it?'

'Over my dead body!'

'I think that's what we're afraid of, Mr Falcon.'

'What? You think that those two are going to

177

come back and murder me over something that up until now they've shown not the slightest bit of interest in? Come on! The only reason they're kicking up a fuss is because it's not what they want. At the end of the day they're just a couple of spoilt little brats who are used to getting their own way, that's all. And before you say that I'm the one who spoilt them, I can assure you that I wasn't. It was their moronic mother, and was one of the many reasons why I decided to leave her.'

'That's as maybe, but unfortunately, someone killed your father. The reason for our visit is to let you know that it's also been confirmed that your brother's death was no accident.'

Raising his voice over the sound of his son's Ferrari roaring into life in the courtyard, James said, 'Well, it wasn't those two, if that's what you're implying. They literally worshipped the ground their uncle walked on. Their grandfather too.'

'Forgive me for saying so, but again, you don't seem to be very upset by the news that your brother was murdered.'

'I thought you'd said as much when you were here last. Besides, exactly how it happened is hardly going to change the fact. We're all going to die at some point. Personally, I think I'd rather be bashed over the head than have to spend years in painful suffering.'

'I wasn't aware we mentioned anything about how your brother was killed, Mr Falcon.'

'You told me someone dropped a boat on his head. Anyway; stabbed, shot, poisoned. I don't see what difference it makes.'

'It makes a difference because we didn't say, and yet, of all the ways he could have died, you were able to guess correctly.'

'Wow. So I must have done it then.'

'Well, if it wasn't you, and you don't think it was your children, who do you think it was?'

With a shrug, James replied, 'I've no idea.'

'How about the person who you said you didn't know, but who we've since found out is someone you've been having regular talks with: Mr Jim Jackson?'

'I suppose you overheard that as well.'

'We found that out by checking your phone records, Mr Falcon.'

'OK, so I lied to you about that. So what? Believe it or not, people lie about stuff all the time. It's hardly against the law. If it was, just about everyone would be lounging about in prison for having done so, no doubt yourselves included.'

'Perhaps. But it's not the fact that you lied, it's why you thought you needed to.'

'I didn't need to, I just did.'

'Yes, but why?'

'Because I don't like people knowing my business, as you two seem intent on.'

'That's because we're trying to find out who murdered your father and brother, Mr Falcon.'

'Er, no. It's because you seem desperate to pin their deaths on either myself or my children.'

'Believe it or not, we're trying to find out who actually killed them, and having you lie to us all the time is only giving us cause to think that you may have been involved, especially as you're the one who seems to have most to gain.'

'Oh, I doubt I'm the only one. There's Jackson, for a start.'

'So you think it may have been him?'

'I didn't say that. I'm just providing you with another more likely alternative, and I know for a fact that he's got some decidedly dodgy connections down in London.'

'What makes you think that?'

'Because he's told me as much. According to him, his main backers are the Camden Crime Syndicate. They have been for some time.'

Instinctively Tanner glanced over at Jenny. He'd heard the name before, many times. The North London firm had been behind the vast majority of criminal cases he'd been involved in when he'd been based down there. Although the activities of criminal organisations were rarely featured in the news any more, they still lay at the heart of drugs and prostitution, using their laundered money to invest in large-scale property developments throughout the country and beyond. If they did have money invested in the Moorings proposals, then he knew they'd stop at nothing to make sure it went through according to plan.

'What about you?' asked Tanner, studying James's face. 'Are you involved with them as well?'

'Me? I might be dumb, but I'm not stupid.'

'But you think Jackson is?'

'I'm not saying anything. I'm only pointing out to you that there are some far more likely candidates for murdering my father and brother than either myself or my children.'

Tanner paused for a moment. 'Going back to

Edward and Tessa. Do you have any idea why they're so intent on not letting you sell the estate?'

'Sentimental value, I suppose. We did spend every Easter and summer here as a family, when they were growing up, mucking about in boats and the like. That was before their mother and I separated, of course. They were good times, sure, but personally, I've never been much for sentiment, and needs must. You know how it is.'

'What about the will? Aren't you concerned they'll contest it?'

'You overheard that as well, did you? Well, they may think they can, but I'm afraid they're too late. I was able to call in a couple of favours last week to have the process of probate fast-tracked. It's a done deal. The estate legally belongs to my brother and myself. And as his will leaves everything to me, I can do with it as I please, at least that's what my solicitor has told me.'

'So you're going to sell?'

'Of course. And the sooner I can, the sooner I can get off this damned forsaken yacht, and head back to my home in Devon.'

· CHAPTER THIRTY THREE ·

ON THEIR WAY back to their car, Tanner said to Jenny, 'I'd better give Forrester a call. Hopefully, if nothing else is going on, we'll be able to call it a day.'

A few moments later, he was put through to Forrester who asked, 'How'd it go with Falcon junior?'

'Interestingly enough, we weren't the only ones there to see him. His children had driven up from London. They were in the boat having a rather heated conversation with him when we arrived.'

'I don't suppose you happened to overhear what they were saying.'

'As we approached, we did, yes,' replied Tanner, deciding to omit the fact that they'd deliberately crept up to the boat for that purpose.

'What were they discussing?'

'His children seemed to be a little miffed that their father was intending to sell Falcon's Yard.'

'Anything else?'

'Only that they genuinely didn't seem to know that he was, but they were certainly keen to try and change his mind.'

'Well, if they came all the way from London just to have a go, they must have been. I don't suppose you found out why?'

'The only reason we heard them give was that they didn't think it was what their grandfather would have wanted, and that they'd been expecting to inherit it themselves, as the will stated.'

'You still don't think they need the money?'

'It doesn't seem that way, no. It's their father who's struggling. They even offered to lend him some, but only until he told them how much he'd need.'

'And how much was that?'

'Five million.'

Forrester whistled down the phone. 'Sounds like he's in serious trouble.'

'His children left saying that they were going to contest the will, but when they'd gone their father told us that they were too late. Somehow he'd been able to fast-track probate, and with his brother dead, the estate was now his, to do with as he pleased.'

'Is it possible to get through probate so quickly? Doesn't that sort of thing normally take months?'

'He said he called in a couple of favours; which reminds me. We found out who the bulk of Jackson's investors are.'

'Dare I ask?'

'The Camden Crime Syndicate.'

The name was met by a cold silence from the other end of the line, prompting Tanner to eventually ask, 'Are you still there, sir?'

'I'm still here, Tanner. I assume you know who they are.'

'I'm afraid so. Rather better than I'd like.'

'If they're the ones behind all this, you know what we'll be up against?'

'I do, but it does explain a lot; for example, how Falcon junior was able to push probate through so quickly.'

'Did you ask him about that?'

'We did, yes. He said he wouldn't be stupid enough to get involved with them.'

'Did you believe him?'

'Not really. The man lies far too easily, and he doesn't seem to care who knows it.'

Forrester was silent for a while, before asking, 'What about the children?'

'To be honest, sir, it's becoming increasingly difficult for me to believe that they have anything to do with it. They seem intent on Falcon's Yard remaining within the family. If that is the case, why would they murder their own grandfather? And why then go on to kill the only other member of the family who wanted to keep the yard, and who was happy enough to stay on and manage the place? At this stage I think it's more likely to have been their father, or Jackson, or both of them working together.'

'Or maybe the Camden lot?' proposed Forrester.

'Very possibly, sir, yes.'

'Well anyway, the final report's come in from forensics. Unfortunately for us, other than the yard's employees, and Phillip Falcon himself, nobody else was inside the boatshed, or at least they've been unable to find any evidence that they were.'

'But Dr Johnstone still remains of the opinion

that he was murdered?'

'That's what his report concludes, yes, and forensics are backing that up in that they found blood splatter against the side of the boat and on the ground directly beneath him, in a way which suggests Phillip was hit on the head when he was standing up, not lying under the boat.'

'Then whoever did it knew enough about what they were doing to ensure that they didn't leave any physical evidence behind.'

'Which would tend to suggest the Camden connection,' proposed Forrester.

Tanner let out an audible sigh. Forrester was right. That was the only logical conclusion. He knew, just as well as Forrester did, that the only way an average person would be able to murder a fellow human being would be through intense hatred, fury and rage, normally as the result of an argument that simply got out of hand. Even if the assailant happened to be wearing gloves at the time, such acts of violence would always leave behind a trail that forensics would be able to follow in the form of hair follicles, broken nails, skin samples or even sweat. Only with training and practice was someone able to kill with such detached premeditated dispassion that they did so without leaving a single trace that they'd ever been there. And unless either James Falcon or Jim Jackson had somehow been able to acquire such experience, which seemed highly unlikely, the only conclusion to be reached was that it was a professional job.

'So what do we do now, sir?' asked Tanner.

'I don't think we have much of a choice. I'm

going to have to let Head Office know what we've found. They'll no doubt decide to pass it on to our colleagues down in London.'

· CHAPTER THIRTY FOUR ·

WITH THE SENSE that all their work so far was effectively going to have to be thrown out the window, Forrester told Tanner that they may as well go home. If nothing of any significance arose between then and the following day, he'd be giving Head Office a call in the morning with a view to handing over their casefiles to The Met.

After Tanner had filled Jenny in with the gaps of the phone conversation, climbing into the car she asked, 'So, I suppose that means we're going to be back on fifty-year-old missing persons cases again?'

'Probably, yes; however, on this occasion I think Forrester's right,' he replied, starting the engine. 'We don't really have much of a choice. We've no evidence to suggest that any of our current suspects were involved, and the only motive we have for both murders is to ensure the successful and timely completion of the Moorings development.'

'Which both James Falcon and Jim Jackson will directly benefit from.'

'I'm not arguing with you there. It just doesn't seem likely that either of them are capable of killing in such a professional manner. And if the two of them have been working in collaboration with the Camden Crime Syndicate, it's going to be one hell of a job to prove. I spent twenty-odd years trying to establish a connection to what we knew they were involved in, without much luck. In all that time I think I only managed to arrest about five people, none of whom we were able to charge. The evidence was never there, and even when it was, it would always manage to perform some sort of magical disappearing act.'

'Are you suggesting London CID is on their payroll?'

'Well, I had my suspicions. But it wasn't just that. Organised crime has come a long way since the days of the Kray twins. These days they're run like multi-national corporations, but instead of using credit cards and bank transfers, business is conducted with cash laundered through a vast network of pubs, corner shops and restaurants, all of which makes it incredibly difficult to trace. So if they are involved, then I think we're best out of it. They may not go around shooting people in the middle of a pub anymore, but murder still remains a big part of the game they play, and they've never been particularly fussy about who they have to kill to get what they want.'

Within less than five minutes of leaving Falcon's Yard, they'd parked their car and were strolling along the towpath, gazing over at the unwelcome view of the building site directly opposite their floating home.

With the bleak reminder that they still needed to find themselves a new mooring, they spent the rest of the evening poring over an ordnance survey map of the Broads, lit by a lamp hanging from the boom. It wasn't until gone ten that they came to the mutual agreement that they should have a go at searching the rivers and broads upriver of the medieval bridge that crossed the Thurn at Potter Heigham. Their thinking was that although it would be a pain to have to take the mast down every time they wanted to cross under the bridge to sail anywhere other than Horsey Mere, Hickling and Martham Broads, the medieval bridge acted as the perfect barrier against tourists, meaning that the waterways beyond offered more peaceful moorings than other parts, especially during the summer months.

Jenny ducked down into the cabin to begin getting ready for bed, leaving Tanner to fold up the map before turning off the lamp, plunging the canvas-enclosed cabin into darkness. As was his custom, he then stepped out through the awning, onto the narrow walkway that led around the outside. There he gave the boat a quick once over, glancing first down at the water level, to make sure he didn't have to either loosen or tighten the mooring lines, then over the boat's traditional white awning which hung over the full length of the boom, making sure it was secured around the base of the raised deck house. Lastly, he gazed up at the small flag on top of the mast, checking for wind, before casting his eyes over the cloudless midnight blue sky above, pierced by stars too numerous to count. Staring out over the peaceful river, watching as the surface danced in the light from a steadily rising moon, he saw a dense white mist rolling over towards them from the flat marshland beyond. As it swirled around the base of Hunsett Mill to begin seeping down through the reeds at the water's edge, his body shivered, as if someone had stepped over his grave. Something caught his eye. An old sailing yacht, very much like their own, drifted through the ethereal white mist towards them. Such a sight was normal enough, even at such a late hour, but the yacht had its canvas awning up, making it almost impossible for the boat to be steered.

'Jen!' he called out, his voice echoing out over the river. 'It looks like someone hasn't tied their boat up properly.'

'What's that?' came her muffled response from somewhere deep within the cabin.

'A boat's drifting downriver towards us, but its cover's still on.'

Even before he'd finished, he could hear her stumbling out to join him out on the walkway.

Peering towards it, after a moment she said, 'It must have slipped its moorings.'

'Or someone untied it on purpose.'

'Either way, it's headed straight for us.' Nudging past him to head around to the other side of the boat, she added, 'We'd better get ready to fend off.'

'Ah, my specialty!' proclaimed Tanner, following on after her. 'But do you mind if I use an actual fender this time? My leg's still sore from when we nearly ploughed into that pontoon the other day.'

'You're such a wimp,' said Jenny, already busy untying a white plastic fender. Passing it back to him, she untied another for herself before standing back up to join Tanner in staring out at the boat as it slipped inexorably closer towards them.

'Isn't it Harry Falcon's yacht?' asked Tanner, a few moments later.

'That's exactly what I was thinking. And I don't like the way it's lying either. Can you see how low its aft end is? If I was to hazard a guess, I'd say that it's been holed.'

'You mean it's sinking?'

'And quickly as well.'

'What if James Falcon is on board?'

'If he is, then he's about to go for a swim.'

'Unless, of course, he can't.'

Both of them remembered all too clearly what had happened to Tanner only a few months before, and thinking that the boat's current resident may be locked inside the cabin, incapacitated by either drugs or rope, or even both, Jenny said, 'We're going to have to board her.'

'Er, I think you're forgetting something.'

'What's that?'

'What you said at the beginning.'

'That the boat's sinking?'

'Yes, that. Surely you're supposed to jump off a sinking boat, not the other way round.'

'It's a fair point,' said Jenny. 'Tell you what. Stay here. I'm going to grab us a couple of life jackets.' She pushed past him to hurry back along the walkway, heading back inside.

'Er, and what happens when the boat goes past?'

'Don't worry. I should be back by then.'

· CHAPTER THIRTY FIVE ·

STANDING ON HIS own up near the mast, Tanner watched as Harry Falcon's old cabin cruiser came drifting ever nearer.

'How're you getting on?' he called down, in a bid to hurry her along.

'I don't suppose you know where they are?' came her muffled response.

'I've no idea,' he replied. 'If you can't find them, you'd better come back.'

'It's all right, I've got them.'

With the boat approaching fast, its sinking aft end arcing slowly around towards them, Tanner said, 'OK, but hurry. It's only a few feet away.'

A moment later, Jenny's head appeared back through the canvas awning. 'Here!' she called, throwing Tanner one of the fluorescent orange buoyancy aids.

Catching it with his free hand, Tanner dropped his fender to feed his arms through the holes and zip up the front.

Stepping lightly around the walkway to re-join him, Jenny did the same, just in time for the back end of the approaching boat to begin drifting past theirs, but it was nowhere near as close as they'd first thought it was going to be.

'I can't jump that!' exclaimed Tanner, judging the distance with his eyes.

'Of course you can,' said Jenny, before leaping over with graceful ease.

'Unbelievable,' muttered Tanner. She made it look so easy, as she had a tendency to do whenever she was on the water. She also left him with little choice. There was no way he was going to leave her stranded on a sinking boat, especially one which had been deliberately set adrift in the middle of the night.

Taking a deep breath, he launched himself over the gap, one foot landing where Jenny's had been. But the other was left hanging out over the side. Just as he was about to topple over backwards, into the murky waters beneath, Jenny grabbed one of his flailing arms to pull him safely on board.

'That was close!' he exclaimed, sending her a look of panicked relief.

But Jenny's focus was already on the boat. 'It's going down fast,' she said, stepping down into the well of a cockpit already half-full of water.

'Shit,' she said, grabbing hold of a padlock holding the cabin doors closed.

'Maybe there's no one on board?' proposed Tanner optimistically. 'Can you see anyone?'

Fishing her phone out, Jenny turned on its torch to direct the beam of light through the row of slats built into the tops of the doors.

'I can't, no,' she replied, pivoting the light around.

Just as Tanner was beginning to wonder how they were going to get off again, he heard Jenny say, 'Hold on, I think there's someone lying on one of the bench seats.'

'Is it James Falcon?'

'I'm not sure who else it would be,' she replied, her voice tense with anxiety. Tucking her phone away, she asked, 'Do you think you'd be able to break down the door?'

'I can try,' he replied, slipping down into the water as it sloshed about in the cockpit's well; but the task of breaking down a door which was already more than half-submerged soon proved impossible. The resistance of the water against his body simply wouldn't allow it.

After failing to force it open with his shoulder, he had a go at kicking against it with his foot, before giving up. 'It's no use. I can't put enough force against it. The water's too high.'

At that moment they heard someone muttering something inside the cabin.

Peering through the slats, Tanner could just about make out the silhouette of a head, then a pair of shoulders rising up from the end of the starboard side bench seat.

'Mr Falcon?' he called out. 'Can you hear me?'

'Who's that?'

'It's Detective Inspector Tanner, Norfolk Police. Someone's set your boat adrift.'

Tanner watched as the man he could now recognise pushed himself upright before swinging his legs off the bench, plunging them down into the treacle-like water surrounding him.

'What the...?' he exclaimed, staring down. 'What the hell have you done to my boat?'

'As I said, Mr Falcon, someone's set you adrift.

They must have put a hole in it as well; but don't worry. We're going to get you out.'

With James Falcon doing nothing more than stare at the water as it rose steadily over his knees, Tanner heard Jenny behind him say, 'I'm going to have a go at steering.'

Glancing around, he saw her start to peel back the awning from the cockpit, allowing her to see something of what was going on ahead.

'The boat will be heavy,' she continued, 'but hopefully I'll be able to guide her into one of the banks.'

As Tanner stepped out of the well to help her, he asked, 'What about Falcon? How are we going to get him out?'

'Try asking if he's got a key. If the padlock belongs to the boat, there should be a spare one knocking about somewhere.'

Nodding, Tanner leaned over to peer back through the door's slats. 'Mr Falcon. The cabin door has been secured from the outside using a padlock. Is it yours? Do you have a key?'

'A padlock?' the man asked, as if he hadn't understood the question.

Tanner watched as he stood up in the water to lift his hands up to the low wooden roof, directly above his head.

'I don't think so,' he continued.

Finally understanding the predicament he was in, he forged his way through the water towards the cabin's small wooden doors. With his fingers hooked around the slats Tanner had been talking to him through, he began pulling and pushing at them, shouting, 'Let me out! Let me out!'

'Do you have a key?' repeated Tanner.

'Just open the fucking door!' Falcon replied, as he attempted to prise them off their hinges.

'We can't, Mr Falcon. You've been locked in from the outside.'

'Then break it down, for fuck's sake!'

'I've already tried.'

'We'll see about that,' Tanner heard him mutter.

Taking the stance of a boxer, he pulled his arm back to punch hard at the slats, splintering the two in the middle, but doing no more than that.

'Mr Falcon, we need you to calm down.'

'Don't tell me to calm down,' the man snarled, throwing another punch at the door which landed with such force, it broke through all five slats.

Tanner watched as Falcon forced his hand through the jagged hole, the splintered wood tearing his skin as he reached down, frantically searching under the water on the other side for whatever was preventing the doors from opening.

Glancing around at Jenny, Tanner asked, 'Any luck with the steering?'

'She's too heavy,' she replied, her jaw set firm through gritted determination. 'I can't even move the tiller.'

Tanner turned back to watch as Falcon's hand tugged and pulled at the solid steel padlock with futile desperation. 'Is there no other way for him to get out?'

'Not that I can think of. If it had a lifting roof like ours, we'd be able to cut through the canvas sides.'

Fast reaching the conclusion that the only way

for them to save the man trapped inside would be to steer the boat into a fixed mooring, or to run it aground somewhere, Tanner climbed onto the bench seat opposite the one Jenny was kneeling on, saying, 'Here, let's have a go.'

With one of his hands taking the place of the two Jenny had been using, he took hold of the tiller's smooth rounded handle and began trying to heave it over towards him, hoping to force the boat into the dark mist-shrouded reeds sweeping steadily past. Unable to move it even an inch, with his feet braced against the edge of the bench seat where Jenny was perched, using both hands, he locked his teeth together and pulled.

It hardly moved.

'Shit!' he exclaimed, falling back against the tiller.

'Get me the fuck out of here!' screamed James Falcon, who'd given up with the padlock and was now battering at the doors with scratched and bloodied fists.

With the water lapping over the edge of the hole Falcon had made in the slats, Jenny asked, 'There must be something we can do?'

'Is there nothing we can use to break the door down?'

'The mud weight!' she exclaimed, kicking herself for not having thought of it sooner.

Springing to her feet, she leapt out of the cockpit to run down the side of the boat, heading forward for the bow locker where the 10kg lump of solid steel was kept as an anchor.

'Is that it?' he heard Falcon say. 'You're just going to sit there, watching me drown?'

Glancing through the splintered hole in the door, Tanner could see that the water had reached Falcon's chin, forcing him to hold his head back to keep his mouth clear of the rapidly encroaching surface.

'DC Evans has gone to fetch the mud weight from the forward locker,' responded Tanner, having another go at pulling at the tiller.

'What fucking use is that going to be?'

With Jenny returning with the conical-shaped lump of steel hanging from the end of a rope, Tanner stepped forward to take it from her, and then up on to the coach roof. Once there, with the weight hanging between his outstretched feet, he called out, 'You'd better stand back, Mr Falcon. I'm going to try and smash through the door.'

Assuming he'd heard, Tanner began swinging the weight between his legs like a pendulum, gaining height each time he did. When it passed through his legs for the third time, out over the cockpit, he let the rope slip through his hands allowing it to plummet down towards the cabin door beneath his feet.

An almighty splash of water erupted from where it landed, but the door itself remained untouched.

'It didn't work!' screamed Falcon, from inside. 'It didn't fucking work!' he repeated. But his shouts was soon replaced by pleading spluttering sobs. 'Please. Don't let me die. Not here. Not like this!'

Tanner threw Jenny a look of panicked desperation. The water was fast approaching the top of the cabin roof. There were only a matter of seconds before Falcon's head would be fully submerged.

Pulling in the mud weight hand over hand, until it rested on the roof between his feet, he muttered quietly, 'I'll have another go.' But his voice held little hope, and even less belief. By then he knew it was too late. If swinging the weight against the door hadn't worked the first time, there was no way it was going to now.

He heaved it up once again to swing it back and forth, but by that time the river's water had already begun creeping its way over towards Tanner's already sodden shoes, leaving nothing but the terrifying thuds of what he could only assume to be James Falcon's fists, pounding against the roof beneath his feet. Even before Tanner had swung the weight out for the third time, the sounds had softened before disappearing to leave nothing but the stillness of the night, and the River Ant slipping quietly through it.

· CHAPTER THIRTY SIX ·

TANNER AND JENNY remained with the boat until it had all but disappeared under the surface. No words passed their lips until they'd swum ashore. Dripping wet and freezing cold, they dragged themselves through a tangled bed of brittle inhospitable reeds, their shoes and socks sucked off by the swamp-like mud underneath. Eventually they stumbled out onto a wide desolate field, stripped of its produce months before, which now lay furrowed and empty, offering them nothing but a desolate muddy welcome.

Standing there, feet bare, clothes clinging to cold dirty skin, they tucked their hands inside the armholes of their life jackets for warmth and turned to look back at where they'd come from. The sight was clearly marked by the sunken yacht's tall wooden mast, piercing the midnight blue of the cold sky above.

Their limbs shaking as their bodies fought to keep warm, they began to take in their surroundings.

It was Tanner who broke the silence. 'I d-don't suppose you've any idea where we are,' his voice trembling from the cold.

'Somewhere near Barton Turf, I think.'

'Can we make it back to our boat from here?'

'Not without shoes, we can't.'

They both began searching their pockets for their phones, only to realise that they'd be as dead as the man they'd been unable to save.

A light caught their eye from an isolated house about half a mile away, at the far end of the field.

'I suggest we try there,' proposed Jenny, nodding towards it. 'They'll have a phone, and the walk will help warm us up.'

Burying their hands back inside their life jackets, they began trudging over the cold damp earth, scanning the overturned ground for stones or glass.

A little over fifteen minutes later they were picking their way over the gravel drive towards the front door of the cottage. By then, all but one of the lights had gone out, the remaining one coming from an upstairs window.

With guilty displeasure, Tanner tapped the heavy brass door knocker.

Hearing movement inside, they dug out their soaking wet police IDs in readiness to give whoever answered just cause for having disturbed them so late, along with a heart-felt apology.

The hall light was followed by the sound of a safety chain being put into place. After a click of the latch, the face of a bleary-eyed grey-haired old man peered out at them through a narrow gap.

With IDs in hand, Tanner said, 'Very sorry to disturb you at such a late hour. I'm Detective Inspector Tanner and this is my colleague Detective Constable Evans, Norfolk Police. We've been involved in an incident on the river and were hoping to be able to use your phone.'

Before the man had a chance to answer, a woman's voice came booming down from upstairs. 'Who is it?'

'It's the police.'

'The police!' the voice repeated, followed by the sound of hurried footsteps.

'My wife,' said the man, rolling his eyes at them. 'You'd better come in.'

He closed the door enough to take the safety chain off. By the time he'd opened it again they could see an elderly but robust woman come thundering down the stairs towards them, clutching a pink dressing gown around her middle. 'Well, Fred, aren't you going to let them in?'

With a heavy sigh, the man said, 'I was just about to.'

Reaching the door, she shoved the old man against the wall. 'You must forgive my husband. He's never been very good with people. But...good gracious, you're both soaking wet!'

'I know – I'm sorry,' replied Tanner, glancing down at himself.

'And neither of you have got any shoes on!'

'They came off along with our socks, when we were pulling ourselves out of the river.'

She turned to give her husband a menacing look. 'What on earth were you doing, leaving them outside like this?'

'As I said, I was just about to...'

'Never mind all that. Go to the kitchen, put the kettle on, get the hearth lit, and fetch some towels from upstairs, and a change of clothes. Something from the children's room.'

As the old man exchanged uncertain glances between the end of the hallway and the top of the stairs, the woman clarified her commands. 'Kettle first, then hearth, then towels, then clothes!'

'Of course,' muttered the man, and with a subservient nod, shuffled his way down the hall, heading towards the back of the house.

'We really don't want to be any trouble,' remarked Tanner, still standing on the porch. 'We only need to call for a taxi.'

'Nonsense! You need to come inside and get warmed up, that's what you need. Now, come in, and don't mind the floor. We're more than used to a little mud.'

Once in, Tanner borrowed their phone to make two calls. The first was to control, explaining briefly what had happened and to arrange for the necessary emergency services to attend the scene. The other was to DCI Forrester, during which Tanner offered to head straight back to the site of the sunken vessel, just as soon as they'd found themselves some shoes and a change of clothes. But Forrester told him not to be so stupid, and that they were to head for home, get some rest, and meet him there first thing in the morning. As long as the emergency services knew where to go, they'd no doubt be able to manage without them until then.

Within fifteen minutes of having been ushered inside the farmhouse, Tanner and Jenny found themselves huddled around the couple's Victorian kitchen hearth wearing ill-fitting shoes and unfamiliar clothes, sipping from steaming hot mugs of instant soup.

While the husband hovered by the door, the woman said, 'Make yourself useful, Fred. Call them a taxi.'

'Of course,' he replied, before catching Tanner's eye to ask, 'Where do you need to go?'

'Oh, it's not far. We live in a boat, about a mile or so upriver. If you tell them to take us to Falcon's Yard, we'll direct them from there.'

As the man left to make the call, his wife said, 'We'd offer to drive you ourselves, but our children took our car away from us last year.'

'How mean-spirited of them,' said Jenny, with a sympathetic frown.

'Oh, it was probably for the best. Neither my husband nor I can see much anymore, not enough to drive at least. Anyway...' Pulling up a chair for herself, she continued, 'So, you both live on a boat, do you?'

Jenny nodded. 'We do, yes. It's a forty-two foot gaff-rigged cruiser.'

'And you're policemen as well?'

Deciding not to point out the obvious, that only one of them was a policeman, Jenny replied, 'We are, yes. We work out of Wroxham Police Station.'

'And you live together, on board a boat?' she repeated, as if it was the most fascinating piece of news she'd ever heard in her entire life.

Jenny exchanged an aggrieved look with Tanner. It was looking increasingly likely that they weren't going to escape this socially awkward situation without being forced to endure a series of what they both considered to be highly personal questions.

Knowing how little Tanner liked to make small talk, Jenny took the lead. 'We do, yes,' she said, but given the way the old lady was looking at her, as if she had two heads, she decided to add, 'but it's only temporary,' even though it wasn't.

'Well, how very adventurous of you.'

Having heard that line numerous times since moving to the Broads and living on board a boat, Tanner chipped in with what had become his standard reply. 'If by that you mean uncomfortable, then I'd probably have to agree with you.'

The woman paused for a moment before letting out a bubbling laugh, slapping the tops of her thighs as she did.

Catching Jenny's eye, Tanner smiled and winked at her.

'I suppose someone was bound to find it funny, eventually,' Jenny responded, giving his knee a condescending pat.

From the doorway, the husband announced, 'There'll be a taxi here in about ten minutes.'

Relieved to hear that they wouldn't have to be there for too much longer, Tanner thanked the man, leading him to say, 'You mentioned earlier that your boat's moored up near Falcon's Yard.'

'Just upriver from there, yes.'

'I heard on the news what happened to old Harry Falcon.'

'It was most unfortunate.'

Standing just behind his wife, the old man asked, 'Is it true what they said; that he was murdered?'

'I'm afraid so. Did you know him?'

'Only by reputation. He was slightly older than me, but we both fought in the war. I wasn't in the SAS, like him, but I knew him. We all did. Everyone from around here, at least.'

With his interest piqued, Tanner leaned forward in his chair to ask, 'What was he like?'

'Well, as I said, I never met the man, but he was well known.'

'Through Falcon's Yard?'

'Through the stories that went around about him during the war.'

'And what were they.'

'Without going into graphic detail, they used to call him Hack'm Up Harry.'

Tanner raised an eyebrow.

'They say he used to take more pleasure than most in killing Germans, and that his favourite method of dispatching them was close up and personal, with a trench axe; hence the name. You know, it's funny, but it's always struck me as one of life's dark ironies that a soldier will be piled with medals for butchering people during a war, but locked up for life if they do the same thing at any other time.'

'Sorry, but are you saying he went around killing people after the war?'

'Well, not as such, no, but I know he found making the adjustment to home life difficult. We all did, to a degree, but from what I heard, he found it harder than most.'

'I assume that's why his wife left him, after they'd had children.'

'Oh, she didn't leave him.'

'I'm sorry, what do you mean?'

'She went missing.'

'She ran away?'

The old man shrugged. 'She could have done, I suppose, but the rumour mill said otherwise.'

'Like what, for example?'

'They were only stories.'

'Are you saying people thought that he killed her?'

The old man paused for a moment. 'Well, they were known for their blazing rows and violent behaviour, which grew far worse after the war. Then, one day, she just...disappeared. He told everyone that she'd gone to stay with her mother, which was fine, if it wasn't for the fact that we all thought her mother had been killed in the Blitz, at least that's what she'd told us.'

'What did the police say, or the newspapers?'

'I can't remember. Probably not much. It was hardly unusual for marriages to break down during that time. Nobody came back the same. Those of us who were lucky enough to make it back alive were suffering from what I think is now called Post Traumatic Stress Disorder. These days, soldiers are given psychiatric help. Back then we were told to simply get a hold of ourselves. Even the women had to make adjustments. Most of them had spent the time doing the work of men, making it difficult for them to revert back to being housewives again.'

Judging by the looks on their faces, it was clearly a subject which still struck a nerve, even after all the years they must have seen come and go since.

'I worked as a spot-welder for a munitions factory,' said the woman, her eyes glazed over, as if re-living distant memories.

Silence fell, interrupted moments later by an obtrusive knock at the door.

'That must be your taxi,' she said, pushing herself up from her chair. 'I've put all your wet clothes in these plastic bags. It's a shame you couldn't have stayed longer; I'd have washed them for you.'

'You've already done more than enough,' said Jenny, standing to swap her empty soup mug for a heavy bag filled with river-soaked clothes. 'Besides, there's a laundromat we use that's just down the road from us.'

After saying thank you and goodbye a number of times, they climbed into the back of a waiting white car, and directed the driver to head in the direction of Falcon's Yard, and to take the turning just before it.

· CHAPTER THIRTY SEVEN ·

Tuesday, 15th October

AT JUST BEFORE nine o'clock the following day, Tanner and Jenny were standing on board a police patrol boat positioned about ten metres downriver of Harry Falcon's stricken yacht. Beside them was DCI Forrester. Together they were watching a local marine salvage firm working to raise the sunken vessel using a series of inflatable bags, each of which had been sunk before being lashed to the yacht's sides to be slowly filled with air.

'We seem to be running out of suspects,' remarked Forrester, over the noise of the pumps driving air into the bags. 'I assume we're all in agreement that this is directly linked to the murder of his father and brother?'

'Unless it was some sort of a teenage prank that went horribly wrong,' said Tanner.

They watched in silence as the yacht slowly inched its way out of the water. When the coach roof began to appear, Forrester asked, 'So, any ideas?'

'Well sir, as you said, there don't seem to be all that many people left; even less who seem to have a reason for wanting James Falcon dead.'

'What about his children?'

Tanner thought for a moment. 'I suppose they could have. They certainly seemed determined enough to stop him from selling Falcon's Yard. But it still doesn't explain why they'd want rid of both their grandfather and uncle.'

'Maybe they're separate,' proposed Forrester, 'in that Harry and Phillip were murdered to ensure the sale of the estate, but James was killed to prevent it.'

'Again, it's possible, but for the children to have killed their own father, simply to stop him from selling what they believed to be their rightful inheritance?'

Entering the conversation, Jenny asked, 'Do you think what we found out last night could have anything to do with it?'

'What was that?' asked Forrester, curious to know what they'd neglected to mention.

'We were helped by an old couple,' began Tanner, turning to point behind them. 'They live in that farmhouse, where I called you from.'

'Yes, and? What did they tell you?'

'The old man said that he saw active service during the war, and that he knew Harry Falcon, at least by reputation. He said his nickname was Hack'm Up Harry, a name he'd earned for his preferred method of killing Germans. He also told us that Harry's wife didn't leave him, as we first thought.'

'What happened to her then?'

'Nothing was substantiated, but the rumours were that she went missing on a permanent basis, at the hand of her husband.'

'Are you seriously suggesting that Harry Falcon killed his wife?' questioned Forrester, sending Tanner a sharp look of condescending disapproval.

'That's what the man said, sir, yes.'

'But Harry Falcon was a decorated war hero!'

'Which I think was the reason he was alluding to.'

'What are you talking about?'

'He made the observation that although soldiers are rewarded for killing people during a war, society tends not to be quite so keen to do so when they do it during times of peace.'

'So you now think that Falcon was some sort of crazed psychotic serial killer?'

'The man we were speaking to was simply making the point that anyone who kills a fellow human being could be considered a murderer. Just because they've been ordered to do so during a time of war doesn't necessary alter the fact.'

'That's all well and good, Tanner, but the big difference is that during a war it's kill or be killed. There's no premeditation, and I can't imagine there's much of a stomach for it either.'

'Of course, sir, and I think he meant that for most soldiers that was the case; they killed because they had to. But for Harry Falcon it was different, in that he seemed to enjoy it.'

'And so he popped back home after the war and decided to carry on where he left off, by murdering his wife?'

'I'm only telling you what we were told last night, sir.'

'I appreciate that, Tanner, but what the hell has it got to do with him and his two sons being murdered some seventy-five years later?'

Tanner glanced around at Jenny. 'To be honest, we don't know. But we thought we should at least tell you what we heard, as it directly relates to one of the victims.'

'Yes, well, fair enough. But even if it's true, which I doubt, I can't see how it has a bearing on the here and now.'

'Unless the grandchildren found out that their grandfather had killed their grandmother?' proposed Jenny. 'Maybe that's what their uncle told them on the phone that day, and that her body is hidden on the estate somewhere?'

'And they're now trying to protect the family name by preventing the estate from being sold,' added Tanner.

'But surely, if that was the case, then James Falcon must have known?'

'Maybe not, sir. Younger children are often deliberately not told about such things.'

'OK, but why would his brother have told his children, and not him? And when they found out that their father was intending to sell the estate, why wouldn't they have simply explained to him the reason? I assume you didn't overhear them mentioning anything about it, did you?'

'We didn't, sir, no, but we didn't hear the whole conversation, only the tail end of it. And even if they had told him, I doubt it would have stopped him from trying to sell it. He never struck me as the type who cared much for his family's reputation.'

Massaging his bulbous double chin, deep in thought, Forrester stared at the stricken yacht. By then it was already halfway out, and had gallons of water gushing out through smashed porthole windows, making it look like some sort of macabre fountain.

'I assume this theory of yours would still have either Jackson or the Camden Crime Syndicate murdering Harry and Phillip Falcon.'

'I think so, sir, yes. But before you hand that part of the investigation over to our friends down in London, I'd like to ask your permission to get a search warrant for Falcon's Yard.'

'Is that really necessary? Surely after two murders having taken place on the estate, forensics would have found anything of interest.'

'Only if they knew what they were looking for.'

'What, like the skeletal remains of Harry's estranged wife?'

'Or anything else the grandchildren may not want us to find there. Other than sentiment, it's the only sensible explanation for them being so desperate to stop their father from selling it. For all we know, they could be drug dealers and have been using the place to stash their supplies. If we can find something, be it a body, drugs or whatever, then we'd be able to establish a motive for them having locked their father inside a boat before setting it adrift with a hole in it.'

Forrester thought for a moment. Eventually he said, 'OK, very well. In the meantime, I'll hold off on passing anything over to CID in London, at least until I hear back from you.'

- CHAPTER THIRTY EIGHT -

WITH FORRESTER HAVING to get back to the office, the boat's driver took all three downriver to where the DCI had left his car. Having watched him safely disembark, they motored back to continue overseeing the final stages of the salvage operation.

Once the vessel had been successfully raised, with the hole patched, they followed it as it was slowly towed downriver to where their medical examiner, Dr Johnstone, was patiently awaiting its arrival, along with a team of police forensic officers.

Disembarking the patrol boat, Tanner briefed Johnstone and the forensics team on what had happened. Leaving them to it, he drove Jenny back to the station where they wasted no time in applying for a warrant to search the entirety of the Falcon's Yard estate.

That done, they briefed Cooper and Gilbert on the overnight developments, including what they'd heard about Harry Falcon's wartime reputation, as well as what the rumours at the time had said about the disappearance of his wife.

As Tanner and Jenny were heading back to

their desks, Tanner's mobile phone rang.

Seeing it was his old family friend, Commander Matthew Bardsley, hopefully calling with news of the case revolving around his daughter, he excused himself and headed outside before answering.

'Hi, John. Sorry for calling you at work. I just thought you'd be interested to hear what I've managed to dig up about what you asked me.'

'Go on,' Tanner prompted, his heart already racing as he made his way around the side of the building.

'The witness they found hadn't come forward because he was a known drug dealer, who's thought to be working for the Camden Crime Syndicate.'

There's that name again, thought Tanner.

'He'd offered the information after being caught selling cocaine at a sex party.'

'Did he have anything to do with her death?'

'Only in that he was the first to find her.'

Holding his breath, Tanner asked, 'How about the Camden lot?'

'That was their original line of enquiry, but now they're thinking her death is linked to similar cases they've been looking into over the last ten years or so.'

'Similar, as in –?'

'Teenage girls sharing the same colouring, height and weight.'

'Are you saying they think Abigail was the victim of a serial killer?'

'That's how it looks, yes.'

'And what about the photofit DCI Baxter

mentioned? Is that of who they think it is?'

'Well, the dealer saw someone hurrying out of the passageway as he turned in, just before he found her. Apparently, he nearly walked straight into the guy, directly under a streetlight; so he had a good look. He's said to have had blood on his face and neck, and with the speed at which he was coming out, together with his expression, the witness felt certain that it was him who'd left her down there. Anyway, I'm afraid I haven't been able to get hold of the case files for you, but I have managed to get hold of a copy of the photofit. I'll email it over to you now.'

· CHAPTER THIRTY NINE ·

RACING BACK INSIDE the office, seeing Jenny at her desk, Tanner sat down in his chair to lean over and whisper, 'Have you got a minute?'

Glancing down at her watch, she replied, 'I've actually got two. What's up?'

After checking around the office to make sure nobody was within earshot, Tanner handed her his phone.

Displayed on the screen was the black and white photofit of a white male, probably in his late twenties, with a square jaw, high cheekbones, well balanced rounded eyes and dark, wavy hair.

'Who does that remind you of?'

'Er, my next date?'

'Seriously.'

'I must admit, I am being serious. I don't suppose you've got his phone number?'

Realising his request for her to answer without the humour was perhaps a bridge too far, he said, 'Don't you think it looks like Edward Falcon?'

'I suppose,' she replied, tilting her head to one side as she continued to stare at it. 'But then again, it could be one of a thousand good-looking young men, none of whom I've had the good fortune to wake up on top of, present company excepted, of course,' she added, with a cheeky smile.

'But it could be though, couldn't it?'

'It could be,' she replied, in a more serious tone. 'Why? What's it in connection with?'

'Matthew Bardsley just called me. This is the photofit my old boss refused to send me. He also told me that they don't think Abigail was murdered as part of a drug-related crime, but that she may have been the victim of a serial killer, one who they've been tracking for the last ten years or so.'

'John,' began Jenny, her eyes fixed gently on Tanner's, 'I know this means a huge amount to you, but you can't possibly think that Edward Falcon is a serial killer, and the very one who just happens to be responsible for taking the life of your daughter?'

Her words sent a wave of emotions crashing over his head, flooding his mind with a turbulent mixture of guilt, frustration, loss and love. He knew she was right. The photofit could be of any number of good-looking men. London was full of them. It could even be a younger version of himself. But he couldn't help how he felt.

Snatching the phone from her hands, he turned away. 'Of course,' he said, his words filled with indignation. 'I just thought they looked similar, that was all.'

Jenny's heart went out to him. She almost wished the man in the photofit was Edward Falcon, and that he'd step forward, out of the blue, to confess to being a deeply disturbed serial killer, unable to stop and desperate to be caught. At least that way John's life would finally be allowed to move on without the perpetual cloud of his daughter's murder constantly hanging over him.

Desperately she tried to think of something to say that might help, but everything that came to her mind sounded either contrived or insincere. So instead she thought she'd try to wrestle his mind back to what was going on with their own investigation, and not what was supposed to be someone else's.

'How long do you think it will take for that search warrant to come through?'

It was a fair question. It reminded Tanner that the warrant was to search Falcon's Yard for evidence that Edward Falcon had a motive for murdering his father, possibly his grandfather and uncle as well, which in turn would enable him to bring him in for questioning. If the man did also happen to have something to do with the death of his daughter, however unlikely that may be, he'd be able to find out about it then.

Checking his watch, he replied, 'Not for a while yet. We only put the application in a couple of hours ago.'

'Then we may as well head out for lunch,' proposed Jenny. 'Hopefully it will have been approved by the time we get back.'

· CHAPTER FORTY ·

DECIDING TO EAT out at the Bittern pub just down the road, Jenny did her best to keep Tanner's mind off the on-going investigation into his daughter's death by asking him to go over some questions, in preparation for her sergeant's exam. It was in a couple of weeks' time, but with so much going on, she'd hardly had the chance to study.

Despite having mixed feelings about her moving up a rank, Tanner was happy enough to help. Admittedly, he'd not done so before. His personal preference remained for her to move into another profession, one that wouldn't have her placed in harm's way on quite such a regular basis. The fact was that the longer they remained together, the more protective he felt towards her. He'd nearly lost her once before, and it had been hard enough then, when they'd only just met. Frankly, he'd no idea how he'd cope if the worst were to happen.

Putting his selfish interest in his own psychological well-being aside, if her focus remained, he knew Jenny would do well. She was both intelligent and hard-working, and was able to think on her feet, often in situations that would have many people running for the hills. She was also a fast learner and, most importantly, she had a sense of humour, which as far as Tanner was concerned was essential in such a job. Thinking about it, he wouldn't be surprised if she went on to become a DCI; maybe even higher.

When it was time for them to head back, Tanner quickly checked his email on his phone, to see if anything had come in from the local magistrate on their search warrant application. It hadn't. Neither had it when he checked again on their return to the office.

'What's taking them so long?' he muttered, half to himself.

'Has it still not come through?' enquired Jenny, in an empathetic tone.

'Not yet, no.'

'Maybe they don't feel the evidence we gave was compelling enough?'

'Then they would have said.'

Jenny thought for a moment. 'Is it worth chasing them up?'

'Probably not. Besides, there are other things we need to be getting on with.'

Silence followed, as Tanner logged into the Norfolk Police intranet. As he navigated to the relevant case files, he couldn't stop thinking about the photofit Bardsley had sent over, and how much he thought it looked like Edward Falcon.

Unable to concentrate, he took out his phone to open the photofit again. He then pulled up the picture they had on file of Edward to spend a few moments comparing the two.

'Sod it,' he eventually muttered.

Pushing his chair back he stood up, saying, 'I'm just going to make a call,' and headed outside.

'Matthew, it's John,' he said, hurrying around to the side of the building.

'Yes, John; what's up?' came Commander Bardsley's clipped but welcoming voice.

'I've had a chance to look at that photofit you sent over and – well, I think I might know who it is.'

'Really?' questioned Bardsley, with a clear note of surprise.

'I'm not one hundred percent sure, but I think it might be a suspect we're looking at in relation to a murder that took place here last night.'

'Do you have him in custody?'

'No, and that's half the problem. We haven't got enough evidence to bring him in yet. I'm waiting on a search warrant which I'm hoping will provide us with what we need, but it's taking forever and a day to be authorised, and I'm becoming increasingly concerned that he might do a runner whilst I'm stuck behind my desk, waiting.'

'Can't you just get someone to keep an eye on him?'

'That's the other half of the problem. He lives in London. Canary Wharf, to be exact.'

'Ah. I see what you mean.'

'He was up here yesterday. I witnessed him having a somewhat heated discussion with the man I believe he may have killed, but assuming he drove back to his apartment in London, I've got no way to keep tabs on him. And I can't ask Baxter. I doubt he'd believe me for a start, and even if he did, he'd only accuse me of poking my nose into what he thinks of as being his investigation again.'

'Would you like me to have a quiet word?'

'If you could just tell Baxter that he's also a suspect in another investigation – probably best not to say whose – and to keep an eye on him, I'd appreciate that.'

'OK, no problem. Who should I tell him it is?'

'Edward Falcon. He's a senior hedge fund manager at the Instathon Bank. I'll email you his address when I get back to my desk.'

· CHAPTER FORTY ONE ·

ACK INSIDE, NUDGING his way past Jenny's chair again, Tanner asked, 'Did I miss anything?'

'Yes. Cooper managed to make himself a coffee!'

'What, without help?'

'It's a first, I know,' she replied, wondering who he'd been speaking to who'd been able to lighten his mood so effectively.

Plonking himself down in his chair, Tanner rubbed his hands together with gleeful expectation. 'Right, hands up who thinks our local magistrates haven't bothered to come back to us on that search warrant yet?'

'I would,' replied Jenny, 'but I wouldn't want Forrester to see me and think that I was volunteering for something.'

'Fair enough.'

'Anything?' asked Jenny, having given Tanner time to log back into his computer.

'Nope! Unless, of course, it's been dumped in my junk file.'

A moment later he replied to his own question. 'It's not there either. Sod it. I'm going to give them a call.'

Picking up his desk phone, he jammed the number in and sat back in his chair listening for the various options being automatically read out to him. After making his selection, he eventually said to the girl on the other end, 'Hello, yes, I'd like to check on the progress of a search warrant application.'

'Your name, please?'

'DI Tanner.'

'And the number?'

'2564,' he replied, reading from his monitor.

'Did you say 2564?'

'That's correct,' he replied, placing his hand over the end of the phone to mutter over to Jenny, 'How many search warrant applications can they have?'

Using her fingers to count, Jenny replied, 'Well, there's yours, so that's one.'

'And when did you send it over?' the girl asked.

Resting his head in his hand with his elbow on the edge of his desk, Tanner replied, 'This morning, at 10:46am.'

'Oh, sorry. I was looking at yesterday.'

Hearing that, he deliberately slid his elbow off the desk, making his head fall sharply forward, as if he'd just been woken up.

Jenny snorted beside him.

'Ah! Here it is. Yes, we've received it.'

'And...?'

'And...?' repeated the lady.

Tanner sighed. 'And when are we likely to get a response?'

'I'm sorry, I've got no idea, but the note on the system says that one of our legal advisors has taken it in to be heard by the magistrate, so it shouldn't be long now.'

'OK. Thanks for your time.'

Seeing him replace the phone back into its cradle, Jenny asked, 'Did they say how long it would be?'

'No, but the magistrate's hearing the application as we speak. I suggest we start making our way over to Falcon's Yard. Hopefully it will have been approved by the time we arrive.'

· CHAPTER FORTY TWO ·

DRIVING FASTER THAN he should, Tanner dug out his phone to pass it over to Jenny. 'Can you check to see if the warrant's come through yet?'

Navigating to his email account, she scrolled down. 'I can't see it.'

Coming up to the entrance to Falcon's Yard, he indicated before turning in, only to be forced to slam on his breaks.

'What the…!' he exclaimed, the car juddering to a sudden halt.

Peering over the Jag's black leather steering wheel, Tanner stared up at a high makeshift wooden barrier that someone had erected between the two red-brick pillars that marked the entrance. Covering the barrier was an artist's impression of a large modern block of flats, with bold lettering splayed out across the middle which read, 'The Moorings. Luxury two and three bedroom riverside apartments for sale.'

Pointing over at a familiar logo, Jenny said, 'It's Jackson Developments.'

'I've no doubt. But what the hell does he think he's doing? He can't board up the entrance to a crime scene. He doesn't even own the bloody thing!'

'Maybe he does,' posed Jenny. 'Maybe James sold it to him before he was killed.'

'Even so, it doesn't alter the fact that it's still the scene of a double murder investigation.'

Taking his phone back from Jenny, he found Jackson's number to put a call through.

'Jim Jackson, please?' he demanded, as soon as it was answered.

'Sorry, but he's not available at the moment. Would you like to leave a message?'

'Is he in?'

'He is in, yes, but he's in a meeting.'

'Can you tell him that it's DI Tanner from Norfolk Police, and that I need to speak to him immediately.'

'OK, I'll put you on hold. One moment please.'

After being forced to listen to some nondescript jazz music, it wasn't long before Jackson's voice came over the line.

'Detective Inspector Tanner! What a pleasant surprise.'

'Good afternoon, Mr Jackson. Sorry to bother you again. I was just calling to let you know that I'm currently parked outside Falcon's Yard.'

'That's nice.'

'Yes, well, it would be if I was able to drive in. But unfortunately it would appear that someone's stuck up a seven foot wooden barrier, preventing me from doing so.'

'It's not a barrier, Inspector, it's a gate; one that leads into the site of the second phase of my Moorings development.'

'Yes, I got that from the fancy illustration that's been plastered over the front of it. But what

I fail to understand is why you think you have the authority to block off access to what is still the scene of an on-going murder investigation?'

'If you must know, I've bought the land, so I can do with it as I damn well please.'

'You've bought it?'

'That's right.'

'From who?'

'Who do you think? James Falcon.'

'And last night he was murdered, on board his father's boat.'

A moment of silence followed, before Jackson eventually came back with, 'I'm very sorry to hear that.'

'Coincidental, don't you think?'

With calm, almost clinical dispassion, Jackson replied, 'The money I paid for Falcon's Yard was being held in escrow by my solicitors. We exchanged contracts yesterday, at which point it would have been sent over to James's solicitors. Whatever happened to him last night would make no difference to the transaction taking place, or to me having paid for it.'

'Assuming you bought the property legally, that is.'

'I have the title deeds here, if you'd like to see them.'

'And what about the fact that Falcon's Yard is the scene of a double murder investigation?'

'My solicitor has already been in contact with your forensics department, who've advised us that they've finished with the site.'

Seething with anger, Tanner spat out, 'That's not for them to say! I'm the senior investigating officer! You have to ask me, not them!'

'Well, they seemed happy enough to give us the all clear. If you've got a problem with that, I suggest you take it up with them. But as I've already got men on site, and demolition is scheduled to start at eight o'clock tomorrow morning, I suspect you may be too late.'

'We'll see about that.'

Ending the call, Tanner muttered, 'Did you hear that? They're going to start demolishing the place tomorrow.'

'They can't be allowed to, surely?'

Dialling Forrester's number, Tanner replied, 'No, I'm sure they can't. Not legally, at least.'

When Forrester answered, Tanner blurted out, 'Sir, it's Tanner. We're at Falcon's Yard, but Jim Jackson has boarded up the entrance?'

'He's done what?'

'Boarded it up. I've just got off the phone to him. He says he exchanged contracts on the property yesterday, and forensics have given him the all clear to do with it as he likes.'

'But...that's not for them to say!'

'That's exactly what I told him, sir, but he seems to be of the opinion that it was for them to say. He's already got men on site with the plan to start demolishing the place first thing tomorrow.'

'Christ! Any news on that search warrant?'

'Still nothing. I was told before we left that it's being heard by the magistrate.'

'Then it should have come through by now.'

'Should I call them again?'

'I think you'd be better off going around there in person. If they have a query or even an objection, then you'd be in a better position to respond. Otherwise, we could end up waiting all week, by which time it sounds like we'll be sifting our way through a pile of rubble. Whilst you do that, I'll give head office a call. Hopefully they'll be able to push through some sort of court order to stop our Mr Jackson from demolishing what is still the scene of an on-going murder investigation.'

· CHAPTER FORTY THREE ·

WITH JENNY NAVIGATING, Tanner put his V12 fuel injected Jag's engine to good use, reversing out of the blocked off entrance to Falcon's Yard before spinning the tyres on the tarmac to begin tearing down country lanes, heading for the magistrate's court in Norwich.

Within less than half an hour he was turning into the court's car park, where he left his car over two parking spaces.

Engine off, handbrake on, Tanner and Jenny leapt out to leave the Jag's thirty-something year-old cylinder head ticking and pinging as it began to cool.

Launching themselves up the disabled access ramp, through an arched entrance with an elaborate royal crest displayed over the top, they were forced to rein in as they reached the security barrier, and two over-sized guards standing beside it.

Having emptied their pockets into some plastic trays before passing through a full body metal detector, and then retrieving their personal effects, they marched up to the reception desk where Tanner once again had to stop and wait.

The girl behind the desk was on the phone.

Tapping his formal ID on the desk directly in front of her, whilst clearing his throat and making a point of checking the time on his watch, the girl eventually engaged eye contact. 'May I help you?'

'DI Tanner, Norfolk Police. We're following up on a search warrant application that was sent through to you this morning.'

Her eyebrows knitted together. 'Didn't I speak to you on the phone earlier?'

'Probably, yes, but we still haven't heard back, and the situation has since become desperate.'

'Well, I'm sorry for you coming all the way over here in person, Mr Tanner, but there's nothing I can do to speed up the process. Unfortunately, these things take time.'

'I'm sure they do, but in this particular instance, we don't have any. So I'd like to speak with the magistrate in question, to find out what the delay is, and to help answer any questions he or she may have.'

Checking her computer screen, she said, 'It's Mrs Murphy. Shall I make you an appointment?'

Ignoring the question, Tanner asked, 'Where can I find her?'

'Well, she'll probably be in her chambers. But as I said, I'm afraid you won't be able to see her without making an appointment.'

'There's no time for that. Now can you please tell me where I can find her?'

The receptionist glanced over at the two security guards, who were already looking round to see what was going on.

As they began to waddle over, Tanner held up

his police ID for them to see as well, before turning back to the woman behind the desk. 'I'm here on official police business. If you don't tell me where I can find the magistrate who's ruling over my search warrant application, I'll be forced to charge you with obstruction of justice.' Looking specifically at the guards, he added, 'And by that I mean all of you!'

With the three courthouse employees left staring at each other, the receptionist eventually looked to her right and said, 'If you follow the corridor down, you'll find her chambers at the far end. Her name's on the door. But before you go, let me give her a call.'

Without waiting, Tanner said to Jenny, 'Come on,' and led the way down the corridor as directed, with the receptionist's cries of protest trailing hopelessly after them.

Having found the correct door, Tanner knocked loudly, waited for the briefest of moments, and pushed it open.

Inside they found a lady of some considerable years sitting behind a desk piled high with journals, reference books and box files. With a phone pressed to her ear, over the rim of her half-moon reading glasses she gave her two visitors a look of stern reproach.

'Excuse me, but did I say you could come in?'

'I apologise, Mrs Murphy...'

'That's Your Worship, to you!'

Unimpressed by her outward display of authority, Tanner repeated, 'I apologise, Your Worshipfulness, but we really need to speak to you about a search warrant application.'

Into the phone, the lady said, 'It's OK, Janet, they're here now. I'll deal with them.'

Replacing the phone back into its cradle, the formidable-looking woman glared back at them. 'You do understand that you have no right to come barging your way in here like this.'

She was right, of course; he hadn't, and had it not been for the urgency of the situation, he never would.

Realising that if he was going to get anywhere, he was going to have to change tack and go on the charm offensive, with more humble reverence, he bowed his head slightly. 'Again, I apologise, Your Worship, but the application is in connection with a triple murder investigation, and we've just heard that the building we so desperately need to search is due to be demolished at eight o'clock tomorrow morning.'

'I see,' she said, the words demanding her attention. Taking her eyes off the two police detectives, she looked down at a file open on her desk in front of her. 'There's nothing in here about the property you wish to search being knocked down tomorrow.'

'And that's why we needed to speak to you with such urgency. We only found out that the estate changed ownership this morning, and the building contractor who is allegedly the new legal owner has already had the entrance boarded up, with the idea that his demolition team will be moving in first thing tomorrow.'

'You say allegedly the new owner?' she asked, glancing up at him.

'Well, yes, Your Worship, but he has a reputation for adopting some highly dubious methods to acquire property, so I wouldn't put it past him if he's used such to acquire this one. Furthermore, he's one of the suspects in the investigation, so he could easily have an ulterior motive for wanting to buy the property and for it to be demolished the very next day, like destroying some key piece of evidence that we've yet to have a chance to find.'

Picking up a pen, the lady asked, 'What's the name of this person?'

'Mr Jim Jackson, the owner of Jackson Developments, based in Great Yarmouth.'

After making a note of that on the file in front of her, the magistrate looked back up at Tanner. 'Well, unfortunately, Inspector, I'm afraid this new information is going to be of little help with your search warrant application.'

Feeling his hackles rise, Tanner glared back at her. 'And why's that, may I ask?'

'Well, for a start, your application seems to be lacking credible evidence. Neither does it say what you'd actually be looking for. It's for those reasons that I've yet to approve it. Putting that aside for now, if you're correct in saying that it doesn't even belong to him anymore, then unfortunately you're going to have to submit a new application with the name of the property's correct owner, and maybe add in a slightly more convincing argument for me to grant you full and unrestricted access to what is, don't forget, private property.'

Tanner was dumb-struck. But his inability to

talk didn't last long.

'With all due respect, Your Worshipfulness, are you fucking joking?'

'I beg your pardon?' the magistrate demanded, staring at Tanner in open-mouthed amazement.

Feeling Jenny's hand rest firmly against his arm, Tanner tugged it away. 'Sorry, I didn't realise you were deaf. I said, are you fucking joking? I'm assuming you must be; after all, I'm attempting to investigate a triple murder, and the one thing that obviously connects them all, that being Falcon's Yard, is the one thing that you won't grant me a search warrant for, simply because I've incorrectly filled in one of the boxes, although I hardly think that's my fault, seeing that we only found out that the previous owner sold the property this morning, after we'd spent last night attempting to prevent him from being drowned inside his fucking boat!'

Even before he'd come to the end of his irreverent rant, the magistrate had picked up her phone to say, 'Could you possibly send security down to my chambers? It would appear that I need to have a couple of police detectives removed from the courthouse, forcibly if necessary.'

Replacing the receiver, she cast a forbidding eye over Tanner. 'I'm going to forgive your little outburst, Detective Inspector, seeing that you're clearly under some considerable pressure, but the law's the law, no matter how ridiculous you may think it is. If I was to grant you this search warrant as it currently stands, it would be thrown out of court, meaning that anything you did happen to find there would be inadmissible. So, if

I were you, I'd reverse yourselves out of here and find a more compelling argument for me to grant you what would effectively be unrestricted access to someone's personal residence, whilst making sure to accurately state who the property in question actually belongs to.'

'By which time the whole place would have been razed to the ground.'

Hearing the sound of at least two pairs of heavy footsteps come running down the corridor outside, the magistrate added, 'Then I suggest you apply for a court order to have them stopped. You can ask reception for the relevant form on your way out.'

· CHAPTER FORTY FOUR ·

T HE MOMENT THEY were back outside the courthouse, stomping over to his badly parked XJS Tanner put a call through to their DCI.

'How'd you get on?' asked Forrester. 'Were you able to speak to the magistrate?'

'We've just come out,' replied Tanner, which he thought was better than telling him that they'd been forcibly ejected.

'And?'

'We were told that we need to re-submit the search warrant application.'

'Why's that, dare I ask?'

'Basically, we got the legal owner's name wrong, given that Jim Jackson took ownership of it yesterday.'

'But that's ridiculous!'

'I couldn't agree more, sir. I don't suppose you've had any luck with getting a court order to stop Jackson's bulldozers from moving in?'

'The application's been sent over, but as it's gone five already, I doubt we'll hear back from them before tomorrow afternoon.'

'By which time it will be too late.'

'OK, well, don't worry. I'll chase them myself

first thing. With any luck, it won't take long; hopefully before Jackson's men have had a chance to do too much damage.'

But Tanner wasn't convinced by either possibility. Having witnessed local government bureaucracy in action, close up and personal, and with the speed at which Jackson seemed to work, Tanner was left with the opinion that by the time they were legally able to regain access to Falcon's Yard, it would have been transformed into a block of flats, half of which would already be rented out.

'Look,' continued Forrester, 'I don't see what we can do about it now. I suggest we call it a day and see how things stand tomorrow.'

As the call ended, Tanner looked over at Jenny. 'Do you want the good news or the bad?'

'Which would you recommend?'

'Well, the good news is that we can go home.'

'And I suppose the bad news is that Jackson is going to have flattened the place before we get a chance to go anywhere near it?'

'Correct.'

'OK, then I suggest we head back to our boat, open a bottle of wine, cook some food, and try not to think about it too much. For all we know, there's nothing there anyway.'

But by that time Tanner was convinced that there must be something at Falcon's Yard that someone didn't want them to find, whether it was Edward Falcon or Jim Jackson. Why else would Edward have been so desperate for the estate not to be sold, and Jackson so intent on having the place flattened just as quickly as it was humanly possible, even before he'd had a chance to clear out the fixtures and fittings?

As they began to make their way back to their boat, with Jenny quietly contemplating what they were going to eat, Tanner's mind was left to entertain some far more devious thoughts.

· CHAPTER FORTY FIVE ·

THE PLAN TANNER eventually came up with might be devious, but it was far from being the work of a criminal mastermind. In a nutshell, it was to get Jenny drunk to the point where he'd be able to convince her to sneak over to Falcon's Yard with him to have a look around, but not so much that she'd be unable to walk straight.

'More wine?' he offered, as they watched the sun drift slowly down behind Hunsett Mill.

Through the diminishing light, Jenny narrowed her eyes over at him. 'You know, if you want to have sex with me, you only have to ask. It's not like when we first started going out and you had to get me drunk first.'

'Who said I was trying to get you drunk?'

'Well, that's the third time you've asked if I'd like some more wine, so if it's not sex, then what is it?'

'Well, I was thinking...?

'Let me guess. You're thinking that we should sneak over to Falcon's Yard to have a look around, before the place gets demolished.'

'I wasn't, no, but now that you've suggested it, I think it's an excellent idea!'

'Oh, come on. You've been mulling it over ever since we got kicked out of the courthouse.'

'I thought I was the one who got kicked out of the courthouse?'

'You were, of course, but if you remember, I happened to be with you at the time.'

'Oh yes, that's right, you were. So anyway, what do you think?'

'What do I think of the idea of us breaking into Falcon's Yard half-drunk in the middle of the night to have a look around?'

'Uh-huh.'

Jenny scowled at him. 'If we did, and I'm not suggesting for a single moment that we do, you do know that anything we found over there would be totally inadmissible as evidence.'

'Well, yes, but with the place due to be demolished tomorrow, I don't see that there's all that much to lose.'

'And nothing to gain, either.'

'But if we did find something, then at least we'd be able to tell the magistrate what it was that we were looking for.'

'Without being able to tell her that we'd already found it, of course.'

'Well, yes.'

'OK, but even if we were to find something, and then used that knowledge to convince the magistrate to grant us a search warrant, it wouldn't stop the bulldozers from moving in at eight o'clock tomorrow morning.'

'It would if you stood in front of them.'

'I see. And what would you be doing whilst I was risking life and limb?'

'Er, taking photos? Anyway, I doubt they'd be prepared to stop for me. But you, on the other hand – now, that's something completely different!'

'Flattery will get you nowhere, John Tanner. It certainly won't get me standing in the way of a ten-tonne bulldozer.'

'I doubt they weigh that much.'

'And then there's the small matter of us getting caught breaking and entering, leading us to spend the next ten years in prison, followed by action-packed careers as traffic wardens.'

'I'm fairly sure they'd don't let hardened criminals become traffic wardens. We're more likely to become Lollipop Ladies, or at least you are.'

'Joking aside,' said Jenny, without even the hint of a smile, 'I'm not sure it's one of your best ideas.'

'It's not my worst, either.'

'Obviously not, no. I think that award goes to your decision to buy that car of yours.'

'Ha. Ha.'

'Who said I was joking?'

'Look, we won't get caught, I promise!'

'And what if we are? For all we know, Jackson's already installed an advanced security system with motion sensitive cameras and a couple of guard dogs.'

'OK, then we could just say that we were out looking for our cat.'

'We don't have a cat.'

'Exactly! Which is why we were out looking for one.'

Jenny offered Tanner a glimmer of a smile, before letting out a heavy sigh of capitulation. 'Very well, but if I hear so much as a dog bark, or even a cat meow, I'll be leaving you to it.'

'Not a problem.'

'Oh, and one more thing. We wait until morning, when I'm a little more sober, and there's a little more light. This idea is stupid enough without us wandering around Falcon's yard half-drunk unable to see anything.'

· CHAPTER FORTY SIX ·

Wednesday 16th October

HAVING BEEN SET for six the following morning, their alarm proved to be a rude awakener. If Tanner's plan to persuade Jenny to break into Falcon's Yard by getting her drunk had lacked a degree of sophistication, Jenny's plan to dissuade him had been far more cunning. She'd simply hoped that by delaying their clandestine extracurricular mission until dawn the next day, he'd change his mind the moment the alarm went off. It was only when she watched him roll out of their cramped but cosy bed through half-closed eyes that she realised her plan had failed.

Twenty minutes later, dressed but not showered, Tanner peeled back their boat's canvas entrance and stood on the walkway to watch briefly as the River Ant slipped silently through a chilly pre-dawn mist. The sun wasn't due to rise for another hour, but the sky above the eastern horizon was already brightening in anticipation.

'Are you ready?' he whispered back to Jenny, still in the cockpit.

'Just putting my shoes on,' she replied, in the same low voice the early hour seemed to demand.

Once out, they began following the towpath upriver. It wasn't long before they spied a series of wooden yachts hugging the riverbank ahead, their pretty white canvas covers stretched neatly out over elegant long booms.

'They've moved the boats out already!' exclaimed Jenny, still keeping her voice low.

Passing all twelve of Falcon Yard's hire boats, they soon came to the fence marking the property boundary. Jackson may have blocked off the main entrance with a sturdy seven-foot high plywood gate, but access near the river was easy enough. The low fence there was designed to keep livestock out, not people.

Scrambling over it, they stepped around a hedge, behind which they found the long narrow channel that Harry Falcon had dug out all those years before. There they discovered that Jackson's men had been far busier than they'd previously thought. Spanning the entire width of the dyke, about ten meters up from its mouth, was a long line of square wooden posts, each driven deep into the mud beneath to form a near watertight barrier. With the water on the other side considerably lower than that of the river, Jenny stated the obvious. 'They're draining the dyke! They must have banged those posts in yesterday.'

'Our Jim Jackson certainly doesn't hang about,' commented Tanner. Noticing just how much the sky had brightened since they'd left, he added, 'We'd better get a move on ourselves. I doubt we've got all that long before people start showing up.'

Breaking into a jog, they sped along the dyke, down to the boatshed at the end.

Crossing the planks at the front, Tanner came to a halt.

'I'd better have a quick look in here,' he suggested. 'You keep going to the main house.'

'But I still don't know what I'm looking for?'

'Just anything that you think looks out of the ordinary.'

With a shrug of her delicate square shoulders, she skipped into a run, leaving Tanner gazing up at the boatshed towering above his head. It was only then that he fully comprehended the overwhelming task he'd set the two of them. Jenny had been right. The idea that they would be able to conduct a meaningful search of the entire estate before anyone showed up for work was frankly ridiculous. It was made worse by the fact that they didn't even know what they were looking for. He turned to call after her, to tell her to come back, and to apologise for having dragged her out of bed at such an ungodly hour for no good reason, but she'd already disappeared around the corner.

Returning his attention to the boatshed, he muttered, 'In for a penny.' Wrapping his hand around the cold metal handle of the door, he turned it and pushed it open.

Pleased that it wasn't locked, he dug out his phone, and navigated to its torch app before stepping into the cold darkness beyond to begin following the beam around. The last time he'd been there was when they'd discovered the body of

Phillip Falcon, his head crushed under the weight of a toppled boat. Looking at the place now, it was if it had never happened. The boat which had been lying on its side was back on its stilts, and the only trace that a body had been discovered underneath was a dark patch on the concrete floor.

He checked the time on his watch before staring up at the boat, and the eaves of the roof above.

'Where on earth am I even supposed to start?' he asked himself, further regretting their excursion.

Spying a narrow balcony that led around the top of the building, underneath the roof's exposed bare wooden beams, he shone his torch along it until he saw something up near the front. It looked like a rolled-up carpet.

Remembering that the last time he'd seen something similar it had turned out to be the body of a bookshop owner, stripped of his clothes and doused in petrol, with his curiosity aroused he glanced around to see how he could get up there to have a closer look. Noticing a humble wooden staircase towards the back of the shed, he crept over to its base. There he began to climb, each sawdust-covered step creaking in protest under his weight.

Reaching the top, he pointed his torch along the length of the balcony, towards what could well be a body, or could equally be something far less ominous. The only way he was going to find out was to get closer.

He stared at the long narrow walkway. It was

hardly a sturdy structure, so before making his way down, he placed a foot on the first section and leant his weight forward. Confident it would support him, with one eye on the object at the end, the other on the balcony beneath his feet, he began creeping his way towards the front of the boatshed.

Reaching the object, he was still none the wiser as to what it was, but a gentle prod with his foot found it to be nothing more innocuous than a rolled-up sail, covered in a thick layer of dust. There was nothing inside it either, certainly not a dead body.

'What am I doing?' he asked himself again.

Glancing back up, he saw a circular porthole-like window that had been cut into the top of the shed's wooden outer wall, just beneath the apex of the sloping angled roof. Thinking he may as well have a look through it whilst he was there, he stepped over to peer outside.

Stretched out beneath him was the dyke, empty of boats and half-empty of water. He stared out at the flat horizon beyond, where a wide band of orange light marked the place where the sun was preparing to rise. He checked his watch again. It was already nearly seven o'clock, and all he'd achieved so far was to find a discarded old sail.

Deciding to give up with the boatshed, he was about to turn and head out when something caught the light of his torch, down in the dyke. Staring back out through the window, he shone his phone's light towards where he thought he'd seen it. But there was nothing there but the half-filled channel of water, its surface lying flat in the dawn's breathless morning air.

As he swung the torchlight over to the other side, he saw it again; a thin band of gold light, which looked as if it was lying just under the surface, opposite one of many metre-high electrical hook-up posts.

It's probably just a dead goldfish, he thought. But then it occurred to him that the dyke probably hadn't been drained in years, maybe not since the channel had first been dug out by Harry Falcon, all those years ago, and there was no telling what could be down there.

Retracing his steps along the rickety old balcony and down the sawdust-covered steps, he headed out of the boatshed, back along the dyke, scanning the water's surface as he did.

At the second electrical hook-up post, with the aid of his torch he peered down at the low-lying water.

There it was again, and it was no dead fish! From where he was standing, it looked more like a gold bangle, studded with brightly coloured jewels, caught around a long-submerged branch, just inches below the surface.

Crouching down to take a closer look, a cold shiver crept up his spine. He'd seen that bangle before. It looked almost exactly like the one in the picture in that missing girl's file: the wealthy socialite who'd disappeared without a trace back in 1964. He wasn't a hundred percent sure, but he could have sworn it was the same one.

He searched the ground for a stick, or something similar that he'd be able to use to fish it out with. A boat-hook would have been ideal. But there was neither stick nor boat-hook in sight.

Wrestling off his coat and jacket, the one with his spare phone inside, he undid the cuffs of his shirt to roll up his sleeves. The water was quite far down, but he thought he might just be able to reach.

Lying flat on the wooden walkway, he stretched down with his hand, but the surface was far lower than he'd expected. Bringing his arm back, he wriggled further out over the edge and tried again. He still couldn't touch the surface, and the item of jewellery was a good two inches underneath.

He had an idea.

Pulling himself back, he hooked the end of one of his feet around the electrical hook-up post. With what felt like a secure anchor point, he leaned out again, but much further that time, so that the entire top half of his body was hanging out over the edge of the dyke, with the only thing stopping him from falling into the murky water below being his foot, hooked around the post.

In that precarious position he reached down again. The tips of his fingers now touched the water. The bangle was tantalisingly close. Just another couple of inches and he'd be able to reach it.

He let out the breath he hadn't realised he'd been holding to stretch himself out even more.

Just as the tips of his fingers touched it, the end of his black polished shoe slipped off the corner of the post, sending him plummeting down, headfirst into the cold black water below.

· CHAPTER FORTY SEVEN ·

AS TANNER'S HEAD went under, cold shock contracted his chest. Desperate to breathe, he forced his legs down to kick against what he hoped would be the dyke's floor. But there was nothing there to kick against except decades of piled up silt. As something brushed against his legs he tried again, only to feel whatever had touched him wrap itself around his ankles. In sheer panic, he began clawing and kicking at the water, frantically trying to find something to grab hold of to help heave himself out. Feeling an object touch his hand, he reached out for it, opening his eyes as he did. It was the same beguiling band of gold that had enticed him down there in the first place. Seeing the branch it was caught around, he grabbed for it and pulled, hoping to God that it was attached to something other than the stupid bangle. As he did, something else slipped through the blackness towards him; another lifeless white branch. To his horror, he realised they weren't branches, but the skeletal remains of human arms; and peering out through the murky depths was a bony white hollowed-out face.

He spun violently away to make another

frantic bid for the surface, only to be met by another tooth-filled skull, grinning back at him.

With his body now desperate for air, blistering pain surged through his chest to clamp over his throat like a vice. As his vision began to fade, he reached up towards the surface in a silent plea for someone to help.

With his pounding heart beginning to slow, through shards of light dancing in front of his eyes he saw the arm of a living human being reaching down towards him from the surface, but the hand on the end wasn't Jenny's. It was his daughter's. He recognised the bracelet clasped around her delicate wrist – the one he'd bought for her nineteenth birthday.

Feeling himself slip further into the realms of unconsciousness, he knew he didn't have long. Half of him didn't even seem to mind; not if it meant being reunited with the girl his heart so longed to be with again.

· CHAPTER FORTY EIGHT ·

L EAVING HER MAN outside the boatshed, Jenny crunched her way over the courtyard to the main house. Outside the front door, she delved into her handbag for a pair of latex gloves. Once they were on, she tried the handle, hoping it would be locked, so giving her the excuse to go back to tell John as much.

Unfortunately, for her at least, it was open.

Stepping inside she began shining her phone's torch around the large open hallway, with its dark wooden floor and low beamed ceiling, wondering where on earth she was going to start. If she'd been of the opinion that attempting to search the entire estate on their own was a bad idea the night before, when she'd been half-drunk, now that she was standing inside the main house, cold-stone sober and in near total darkness, she was convinced it was. Even if she had a photograph, along with a detailed description of what she was looking for, she doubted she'd be able to find it. The main house was big enough, but the estate on which it was built was vast.

She spent a moment doing nothing but just stand there, following the beam of light around, wondering where to begin. But she didn't have a clue.

'If I was living here,' she asked herself, 'and had something to hide, where would I keep it?'

The question didn't help her much, as she didn't know what, if anything, had been hidden. If it was a body, then it would probably be down in the cellar, if the place had one. But even if it did and she knew for a fact that a murdered body had been hidden there, she wouldn't go down; not in a million years, at least not on her own.

The other obvious place to hide things would be the attic, but she'd no intention of going up there either.

'How about a bedroom?' she asked herself, thinking that she could probably just about manage one of those.

Having made up her mind, she crept quietly up the stairs, the banister in one hand, her torch in the other.

Reaching the landing, with no less than five doors to choose from, she began peeking into each room. One proved to be a bathroom; another looked as if it had been used for storage. Of the remaining three, only one seemed to have been used recently.

Spying a dressing table by the window, thinking it would be as good a place as any to start she stepped over to take a look. With the window overlooking the courtyard, providing an oblique view of the boatshed and the dyke in front, she peered out to see if she could see Tanner. With no sign of him, forced to assume that he was still exploring the boatshed she returned her attention to the table.

Amidst the clutter, her eye was drawn to what looked to be a large jewellery box which had a carving of a Broads sailing yacht on its front.

Struggling to believe that Jim Jackson was going to let all this be buried underneath about a hundred tonnes of rubble, Jenny left her handbag and phone on the dressing table, the light shining up at the ceiling, and picked up the box. Impressed by its weight, she opened up its delicate wooden lid to see what was inside. To her surprise, there wasn't all that much in there. Just a couple of cufflinks and a tie pin. Certainly nothing to justify how heavy it felt.

With the bulk of its weight feeling like it was in the base, she emptied its contents onto the table. She was about to give the inside a closer examination, when something caught her eye outside. Peering through the window she saw John, ambling towards the far side of the dyke, shining his torch over its glassy smooth surface.

'I'm not sure what you're going to find down there, Mr Tanner,' she muttered to herself, returning her attention to the box.

Tracing her finger around inside, she tried picking with her fingernails to see if it had a false bottom, but with her latex gloves on, she was unable to catch an edge. A little frustrated, she gave it a shake. There was definitely something moving about inside. Turning it over, she examined its base, rapping it with her knuckles. Sounding as if it was hollow, she tried prising it out, but again she was unable to. Instead, she had a go at sliding it out, but it still wouldn't move. As she contemplated the idea of removing her gloves to have another go, she turned it over in her hands only for it to slip through her fingers and land with a loud thud on the hard wooden floor.

'Shit!' She stared down at it through the early morning light. At first she thought she'd managed to break it, as the lid looked as if it had fallen off. But crouching down she realised that it hadn't come off as much as come away, revealing that there was indeed a hidden compartment, accessible only from where the lid's hinges were attached.

Holding open her hand, she tipped the box over for a purple velvet pouch to slide out to weigh heavily in her palm.

'Coins?' she questioned, feeling the way the contents clinked together as it moved.

Eager to find out what was inside she replaced the box on the dresser, and dug out a clear plastic evidence bag. Tugging open the pouch's drawstring, she began shaking out its contents into the bag.

It took her a full second to realise what she was looking at. They weren't coins that had been hidden inside, but about a dozen or so wedding rings.

As she wondered why someone would want to hide a collection of rings inside an old jewellery box, she found herself staring out of the window. Tanner was now lying over the edge of the dyke, reaching down for something in the water.

The idiot's probably dropped his phone, she thought, with an amused smirk, before seeing him lift himself back up to hook the end of his foot around the nearest electrical post and lean out even more.

'What are you doing?' she asked out loud, rising up onto the balls of her feet to try to see what he was trying to reach. 'You're going to go in if you're not careful,' she said again, just as his foot slipped off the post.

'Jesus Christ!'

With the evidence bag full of rings still clenched in her hand, she grabbed her phone and handbag and raced out of the bedroom, back down the stairs and out through the still-open front door. Tearing over the courtyard, she reached the dyke and began shining her phone's torch down at the water. But Tanner was nowhere to be seen, just a series of ever-expanding ripples spreading over the surface.

'John!' she called, darting the light back and forth.

With the ripples dissipating to leave nothing but an earie flat calm, cold hard fear gripped at Jenny's throat. Her heart racing, she called his name again, her eyes staring wildly about. But nothing came back in reply.

Fighting rising panic, she focussed the light at the epicentre of what was left of the rippling water. There, just under the surface, she saw something drifting up towards her.

It was a hand.

Thinking fast, she threw both the bag of rings and her phone onto the grass verge, pulled off her gloves and undid her belt, whipping it out from around her narrow waist. Adopting the idea she'd seen Tanner use, she fastened the buckle to form a loop. Dropping it over the same hook-up post,

she wrapped a foot around it. With a secure
anchor point, she threw herself over the edge of
the dyke, the belt tightening around her ankle as
she did. Leaning all the way down, she plunged
her arm into the cold dark water beneath to find
Tanner's face, staring back up at her. Desperately
praying that she wasn't too late, she grabbed hold
of his outstretched hand and heaved at it with
adrenaline-fuelled strength. The moment it
cleared the surface she used her other hand to
take hold of his forearm to heave again. As his
body began to rise, she let go of his wrist to grab
hold of his shirt collar and pull once more, until
his head finally broke free of the surface.

· CHAPTER FORTY NINE ·

A S WATER STREAMED off Tanner's head, Jenny desperately searched his face for signs of life, but there were none there to be found. His skin was limp and loose, water pooled around inside his mouth, and his eyes stared straight through her, as if she wasn't there.

'JOHN!' she shouted at him, desperate to be heard. But his face remained still, his eyes fixed, unblinking.

She knew what she had to do, and that she only had a matter of seconds to do it: get him out of the dyke, onto his back, check his throat was clear and begin cardiopulmonary resuscitation, as she'd been taught during her police first aid training. All that was well and good, but how was she going to get him out when the only thing stopping them both from going in was her foot secured to an electrical hook-up post by her belt?

Knowing she had to try, with one hand holding on to his collar, she swung her other hand up to grab hold of the edge of the walkway above. She attempted to heave his body up and out, but it was no good. She'd barely be able to lift herself back up, let alone Tanner as well.

Without a single clue as to what else she could do, she let go of the walkway to stare back at his face. 'JOHN! WAKE UP!' she screamed, giving him a violent slap across his face.

As his head shuddered with the impact, his eyelids flickered, then blinked. A moment later, his body convulsed violently, ejecting the water trapped in his mouth before coughing out what was left.

As Jenny did everything she could to keep his head above the water, a flood of raw emotion surged through her.

With tears erupting down her face, through a sobbing grin she caught his eye, gasping, 'My god, I thought I'd lost you! Are you OK?'

Tanner nodded. Gazing into her eyes with a confused look, he stuttered out, 'I - I thought you were...' He was about to say that he thought she was his long-lost daughter when he caught a glimpse of the bracelet she was wearing, the one that he'd bought her in Canary Wharf.

'You thought I was who?'

'I thought...I thought you were an angel,' he eventually replied.

'Just little old me, I'm afraid. Now come on, let's get you out of there before you freeze to death.'

Remembering what it was that he'd found in the dyke's deepest darkest depths, he whipped his head around to stare back at the water, half expecting one of the skeletons he'd seen come rising out to take hold of his shirt and drag him back down. But he could see nothing but the fractured light from a fast rising sun, dancing over the water.

Had he imagined them, as he had his daughter?

But the bangle he'd seen, before falling in – he hadn't imagined that.

'I think...' he began, as his mind struggled to separate what he'd actually seen from what his mind had imagined. 'I think there's something else down there,' he eventually said, turning to stare up at Jenny.

'We'll both be if we don't get you out,' she said, feeling her foot begin to slip through the belt wrapped around the post.

Forcing back the ghostly images that crowded his mind, he re-focussed on the here and now. Swinging an arm up, he took a firm hold of the edge of the walkway above, and with Jenny helping him, heaved himself up until he was able to get the edge of a knee over the side. As water cascaded from his body, he dragged himself over onto his hands and knees, trembling from a combination of cold and shock. Reaching back over the edge, he grabbed hold of one of Jenny's outstretched hands to help haul her up, until they were both out, taking in great lungfuls of air.

Seeing how Tanner was shivering, as Jenny reclaimed her belt from around the post, she said, 'We need to get you back to the boat, out of those clothes and warmed up.'

But Tanner wasn't listening. He was staring back down at the water.

'I think we need to get forensics down here, and just about everyone else.'

'Why? What did you find?'

'There's a body down there,' Tanner replied, a haunted look passing over his face. 'In fact, I think there may be more than one.'

· CHAPTER FIFTY ·

WITH THE DISTINCT possibility that yet another body had been found at Falcon's Yard, this one deep at the bottom of its half-drained dyke, Jenny didn't think twice before alerting control, telling them what Tanner had found, and asking for someone to bring a pair of bolt-cutters to gain entry through the barrier at the front. The fact that the discovery had been made without a search warrant was irrelevant. They had reasonable grounds for entering. What Tanner thought he'd found would hopefully be proof of that.

Whilst making the call, she hurried Tanner inside the main house, stood him in the kitchen and turned the oven on, as well as all four of the gas burners. Leaving him there, she rushed upstairs to see if she could find a towel, a change of clothes and a blanket.

Returning, she dumped what she'd found onto the kitchen table, threw the towel at him, and ordered him to get changed.

Leaving him to it, she put the kettle on and busied herself making him something hot to drink.

By the time she'd done so, Tanner had changed

into the ill-fitting but warm clothes provided, and was soon huddled in front of the stove, with the blanket draped over his shoulders and a steaming mug of instant coffee warming his hands.

The peace was shattered by the wail of an approaching siren.

Leaving Tanner where he was, Jenny made her way back out into the courtyard and over to the barricaded entrance to wait. A squad car pulled in and turned off its siren, leaving its roof-lights spinning. Recognising the two uniformed officers as they climbed out, she poked her police ID through the narrow gap between the two makeshift barriers, calling, 'It's DC Evans. Did you bring the bolt-cutters?'

'They're in the boot,' said the driver, nodding to his colleague to fetch them out.

With the approaching sound of another siren, the padlock was soon cut and the gates were dragged open, just in time to allow an ambulance in through the yard's entrance, closely followed by DCI Forrester's black BMW.

'I heard the news,' he said to Jenny, winding his window down.

'It was Tanner who found the body, sir,' she replied, one hand resting on his spotless car roof. 'At least he thinks he did.'

'Thinks?' queried Forrester, his frown of concern transforming into one of irritation.

'Well, yes, sir. He thought he saw the remains of someone when he fell in.'

'Is he all right?'

'Well, I had to help him out, and at first he wasn't breathing, but he seems OK now.'

'Where is he?'

'In the house, warming up in the kitchen. He was pretty badly shaken by the whole thing.'

'I'm not surprised!'

'But he did seem fairly certain that he'd seen at least one body down there.'

'Do you think he could have been hallucinating?'

'It's possible, I suppose, but there's something else as well.'

'What's that?'

Reaching into her jeans' pocket, she dug out the clear plastic evidence bag full of rings.

'I found these, sir,' she said.

'Whereabouts?' he asked, staring at the bag's contents.

'They'd been hidden inside the bottom of a jewellery box, in one of the bedrooms.'

'I don't suppose it's worth asking what either of you were doing, sneaking about here at such an early hour?'

'We believed we had reasonable grounds, sir, as demonstrated by what we've found.'

'You mean, what you think you've found?'

'Well, yes, sir.'

'OK, but Tanner better be right about there being a dead body or two at the bottom of the dyke. I'm not sure that finding someone's jewellery collection is going to warrant your supposed "reasonable grounds".'

'I think it's who the items may have belonged to that's of interest, sir, given that they're wedding rings. And judging by their size, I'd say they all belonged to women.'

After thinking for a moment, Forrester asked, 'What does Tanner make of them?'

'I've not had a chance to show him yet. I'd only just found them when I saw him fall in.'

'And that's another thing. How on earth did he manage to end up in the dyke?'

'I don't know, sir. It looked as if he was trying to reach for something, but again, I've not had a chance to ask him.'

'OK. Let me park up. Then I suggest you show me where Tanner thought he saw a body, before maybe heading in to have a bit of a chat with him.'

· CHAPTER FIFTY ONE ·

'HOW ARE YOU doing, Tanner?' asked Forrester, as Jenny showed him into what was by then a baking hot kitchen.

Startled out of his exhausted torpor, Tanner stared over at DCI Forrester. 'Er...better, thank you, sir,' before shooting a questioning look at Jenny as to what Forrester was doing there.

Answering with a shrug, she closed the kitchen door to squeeze past Forrester's portly frame and hurry over to the oven, turning it off, along with all four of the burning gas rings.

Having taken a moment to glance around, Forrester turned to face Tanner. 'I hear you've been having what I suppose could be described as an unauthorised swim?'

'I fell into the dyke, sir, if that's what you mean.'

'That was what I meant, yes,' he said, looking Tanner up and down. 'Before I address the elephant in the room, that being what the two of you were doing sneaking around Falcon's yard in the early hours of the morning without a search warrant, at this stage I'm more curious to know how you managed to fall into the dyke?'

'I – I thought I saw something, sir, just under

the surface, and was attempting to reach it.'

'And what was it that you thought you saw?'

Tanner glanced over at Jenny again before replying. He'd not even had a chance to tell her yet. 'An item of jewellery, sir.'

'It wasn't a wedding ring, by any chance?' asked Forrester, darting a look over at Jenny.

'No, sir. It was a gold bangle, one which I thought I'd seen before.'

'And why was that? Had you lost one?'

Tanner ignored his glib sarcasm. 'I thought I recognised it from the Missing Persons' report you gave me, sir, just before we got the call about Harry Falcon. The blonde socialite from 1964.'

Raising an intrigued eyebrow, Forrester asked, 'I've been told that you thought you saw a body as well?'

'That was after I fell in, sir. And there was more than one.'

'Well, Jenny's just been showing me the place where you went in, and I couldn't see a damned thing! And given what she's told me, that you very nearly drowned, I have to ask if you actually saw any of this, or if you haven't just imagined the whole thing? I mean, there must be a whole heap of crap down there.'

'I...' began Tanner, before stopping. The longer he was forced to think about it, the more he found himself doubting what he thought he'd seen; after all, Forrester was right. There must have been decades of discarded rubbish lying at the bottom of the dyke, and considering he'd nearly drowned, it did seem more likely that his subconscious mind had been projecting images that simply weren't there.

After sending Jenny a look of apology, standing a little taller he faced Forrester. 'To be honest, sir, I can't be sure of what I saw.'

'Shit!' Forrester cursed, snapping his head away.

At that moment they heard a commotion out in the courtyard. Hearing the noise burst into the house, Forrester opened the kitchen door to see a heavy set man with shaved grey hair and a bronzed lined face come storming down the hallway towards them.

'Who the hell are you?' the stranger demanded. 'And what the hell are you doing inside my house?'

Pulling out his formal ID, Forrester replied, 'Detective Chief Inspector Forrester, Norfolk Police. And you are?'

'I'm the legal owner of Falcon's Yard, that's who I am!'

From behind Forrester, Tanner clarified the man's statement. 'It's Jim Jackson, sir, of Jackson Developments.'

'Ah, Mr Jackson! I've been hearing a lot about you recently.'

'Nothing good, I hope.'

'No, nothing good,' confirmed Forrester, through a thin smile. 'And in answer to your question, we're here to investigate the murder of Harry Falcon and his two sons, Phillip and James, for which I'm sure you'll be delighted to learn that you're our prime suspect.'

'And yet you haven't questioned me under caution for any of them, let alone arrest me.'

After staring first at Tanner, then Jenny, Jackson returned to Forrester to ask, 'I assume you have a search warrant?'

Silently cursing Tanner for having placed him in such an awkward position, Forrester was left with little choice but to back up his senior DI. 'We don't, no, but I can assure you that we have reasonable grounds for being here.'

'Oh, I see. And what are they?'

'That there's a body submerged under the dyke; possibly more than one.'

'You're not serious?' demanded Jackson, staring around at all three of them.

Desperately hoping that there were human remains lying hidden at the bottom of the dyke, and that Tanner hadn't simply found himself entangled in a couple of discarded deckchairs, Forrester remembered the rings Jenny had shown him. 'And further items have been found to suggest that those persons may have been murdered. So until we find evidence to the contrary, this entire estate is the scene of an ongoing murder investigation, no matter what you may have been told by our colleagues in forensics.'

'Well, for your sake, there'd better be something there! This place is scheduled to be demolished today, and I've got a dozen men outside waiting to do just that, all who I'm having to pay by the hour. I've also spent a small fortune hiring the plant machinery. The fact that you haven't even bothered to get a search warrant before breaking into my private property means that if there aren't multiple bodies piled up down there, I'll be taking legal action against the whole fucking lot of you!'

· CHAPTER FIFTY TWO ·

FTER WATCHING JACKSON storm back down the corridor, Forrester turned slowly round to glare at Tanner. 'Thanks for that,' he said. 'Most enjoyable.'

'I'm sorry, sir,' Tanner said, his head facing down towards the stone clad floor, 'but I really did think I saw the remains of someone down there.'

'Yes, well, fortunately the phrase reasonable grounds is ambiguous enough to cover a multitude of hallucinations. And with those rings DC Evan's found, we should be OK. But before we leave with our tails tucked between our legs, I suggest we take a look to see what exactly is down there.'

With that, Forrester turned to lead them out of the kitchen and along the hallway. Once outside, they crunched their way over the courtyard, heading for the dyke, doing their best to ignore the many glares being directed at them from Jackson and his awaiting men.

Passing the boatshed, they were just in time to see a police diver emerge from the water at the same place where Tanner had fallen in. Seeing him remove the breathing tube from his mouth and perch his goggles on the top of his black neoprene-covered head, Forrester called out, 'Did you find anything?'

Climbing out, with water cascading from his glistening wetsuit, he turned to look back down at the dyke from where he'd come.

'Was that a yes or a no?' demanded Forrester, marching down the walkway towards him.

Wiping dripping water from his nose, the diver looked up to face the approaching Chief Inspector. 'We're going to need to finish draining the dyke,' he eventually replied. 'Then we're going to need more men.' Staring back down at the water, he added, 'We're going to need a lot more men.'

· CHAPTER FIFTY THREE ·

It was only when Tanner and Jenny returned from a trip to their boat for something to eat, and for Tanner to change into something more suitable, that they realised the true scale of what they'd unearthed. The courtyard into which Tanner purred his XJS was now littered with emergency vehicles, including no less than four forensic services vans and the old Volvo estate which they knew belonged to their medical examiner, Dr Johnstone.

'Looks like it's all hands on deck,' observed Tanner, electing to use a nautical expression he thought Jenny would appreciate. 'I'm not sure where I'm going to park, though.'

Forced to squeeze in between Forrester's car and a forensics van, they climbed out to make their way around to the front of the boatshed.

Rounding the corner they found the dyke a hive of activity. Four large white forensic tents had been pegged out along the grass verge, and crawling around inside the now empty dyke were about half a dozen forensics officers, their white overalls splattered with silty black mud. From the far end came the monotonous buzzing sound of an industrial-sized water pump, up near where

Jackson's men had banged in the makeshift damn.

With no sign of Forrester, seeing Dr Johnstone appear from out of the nearest tent, Tanner caught his eye to ask, 'Afternoon, doc. What have you found?'

'I think what I haven't found would be an easier question to answer. But assuming you're not referring to the three shopping trolleys, two bicycles and various incarnations of cameras, watches and phones, so far we've discovered no less than fifteen bodies, at least what's left of them, each weighed down with either chains or mud weights.'

Exchanging a look with Jenny, Tanner asked, 'Any idea who they all are?'

'Women.'

'Is that it?'

'For now it is, yes.'

'Do you at least know how long they've been down there for?'

'Difficult to say,' Johnstone replied, turning to look back at the tent. 'At a guess, I'd say that most of them have been down there for some considerable time.'

'As in months, or years?'

'Oh, years! At least ten. There's nothing left of them but bone, teeth and hair. But we've found three who I think are more recent.'

'More recent as in…?'

'As in one to three years. There's still some tendons attached, as are some of their toe and fingernails.'

'What about clothes and jewellery?'

'Some of both.'

'Wedding rings?' enquired Jenny.

'None that we've found, but we did find something which I thought may be of particular interest.'

Pulling something out of his pocket, he held up a clear plastic evidence bag containing a gold jewel-encrusted bangle.

'That's what I saw!' exclaimed Tanner, taking it from Johnstone. 'It's what I was trying to reach, when I fell in.' Staring at it through the plastic, he added, 'I swear it's the same one that I saw in the file of that missing socialite.'

As Forrester emerged from the tent behind him, Johnstone said, 'Anyway, as I'm sure you can appreciate, I do have rather a lot to be getting on with.' Turning to make his way to the next tent along, he added, 'And please don't ask me when I'll have more information for you. At this rate I'll be here until I can start collecting my pension.'

'Did he fill you in?' asked Forrester, as he approached.

'Only that they're all women, and that they've been down there a while.'

'Any thoughts?'

Tanner turned the bangle over in his hands, a part of him reliving the moment he fell into the dyke. It was left for Jenny to reply.

'With the wedding rings I found in the house, if Johnstone is correct in saying that the bodies have been down there for what could be decades, could it be that Harry Falcon is responsible?'

'It may explain what happened to his wife,' remarked Forrester. 'And half of Norfolk's missing women going all the way back to 1946, when he dug the dyke out,' he added. 'What was his nickname during the war again?'

'Hack'm Up Harry,' muttered Tanner, the name taking on a whole new meaning.

'Jesus Christ!' exclaimed Forrester. 'I can't believe the man was a war hero.'

'One who must have had some serious psychological problems, which would explain why active military service suited him so well. He was clearly psychotic. And don't they say such conditions have a tendency to skip a generation?'

'You mean...the grandson, Edward?'

'Well, it would certainly explain a lot. In fact, it would probably explain just about everything. He must have known his grandfather's secret – that he'd spent decades butchering women and leaving their remains weighed down at the bottom of the dyke. It may have even given him the idea to do the same, hence the three more recent bodies Johnstone said he'd found.'

'And why he was so desperate for the yard not to be sold,' chipped in Jenny.

'Maybe so,' said Forrester, 'but what it doesn't explain is what started all this.'

'You mean Harry Falcon, being drowned in his bath,' extrapolated Tanner. 'I'd have to agree with you there, sir. There's no reason for the grandson to have killed him.'

'And that means we still don't know who killed Harry Falcon, or why.'

'But it could explain why Edward may have killed his uncle, especially if he let slip that he knew what both of them had been up to, when he phoned them up that day. It also gives motive for Edward setting his father adrift, with a hole in the boat: to stop him from selling the yard, and so prevent anyone from uncovering the family secret.'

'OK, so what's your next step?'

'I think we need to head back down to London, sir, and arrest Edward Falcon for the murder of his father, his uncle and maybe even some of the women we've just dragged out.'

'But do we have enough to charge him? We're still lacking the physical evidence needed to tie him to any of this, and I can't imagine Johnstone's going to find much in the way of prints and DNA on the skeletal remains.'

'Well, sir, it's possible that London might have something on Edward, something they don't even know about yet.'

'I'm sorry, I'm not with you.'

Pulling out his phone from within his suit jacket's inside pocket, he opened his email to show Forrester the photofit picture he'd been sent the day before. 'I received this from them yesterday.'

As Forrester studied the image, Tanner explained, 'That's who they're looking for in connection with a serial killer enquiry.'

'Why on earth did they send you this?'

'To be honest, sir, they didn't. I had to ask the help of a family friend.'

'And how would a family friend have been able to gain access to a London CID case file?'

'Well sir, he's a senior member of the Metropolitan Police. Commander Matthew Bardsley. He was friends with my father, and has been close ever since.'

'I see,' replied Forrester, studying Tanner's face. 'Then you'd better remind me about him the next time I'm about to give you a bollocking.'

'Which I think may be now, sir.'

'I don't like the sound of that.'

'The picture,' continued Tanner, nodding down at the image, 'it's of someone seen fleeing the scene of my daughter's murder, sir.'

Forrester said nothing in response, but just lowered his head to examine the image.

'Anyway, sir. I believe the photofit to be that of Edward Falcon.'

More silence followed, before Forrester eventually looked over at Jenny to ask, 'I assume you know about this?'

Standing by her man, Jenny nodded. 'DI Tanner has told me, yes, sir.'

'Putting your relationship with Tanner to one side for the moment, as best you can at any rate, you've met the suspect, face to face. Do you think this could be him?'

After briefly casting her eyes down at the picture, she fixed them back on Forrester to reply, 'I do, sir, yes.'

Studying her face for a moment, Forrester eventually said, 'That's good enough for me, but it's going to complicate things somewhat.'

'Why's that, sir?' she asked.

Answering on Forrester's behalf, with glum seriousness, Tanner said, 'Because it means that we're going to have to work in collaboration with London CID.'

'We'll need them to share with us what they

know about Tanner's daughter,' confirmed Forrester, 'as we will about what's been going on up here, and why we think Edward Falcon may be the person they're looking for. We'll also have to explain to them how it was that we came by that photofit.'

'I'm sure Commander Bardsley will help smooth the way with that one, sir.'

'OK, here's what I suggest we do. If you can give your family friend a call, to warn him that we may need his support, I'll update Superintendent Whitaker with what's been going on, and find out who we'll need to liaise with in London about all this.'

'I can help you with that one as well, sir,' commented Tanner. 'It will be my old boss, DCI Baxter.'

· CHAPTER FIFTY FOUR ·

Thursday 17th October

RISING EARLY THE following morning, Tanner and Jenny were soon back on the train, heading for Canary Wharf.

The previous day, after clearing their actions with head office, Forrester spoke with Tanner's old boss, DCI Baxter. During the conversation, he told him about the photofit picture, and that DI Tanner had been sent a copy by a senior ranking officer of the Metropolitan Police. Knowing Tanner's family connection with Commander Bardsley, Baxter guessed straight away who that had been.

With that out the way, Forrester went on to tell him that they believed that they'd been able to identify the man featured, and that he was the same man they needed to speak to in connection with their current triple murder investigation. Eventually, Baxter agreed to send over the relevant case file, albeit begrudgingly, but only after Forrester sent him all they had in connection with the Falcon's Yard investigation.

Once both sides had a chance to study the contents of each, it was agreed that Tanner and

Jenny would head down to London, where they'd join forces with Baxter's team to place Edward Falcon under arrest. Tanner would then be allowed to question the suspect, but only about the events that had taken place in and around Falcon's Yard. The subject of his daughter's death was strictly off-limits. It was also agreed that the suspect had to remain in London, until such a time that he was either charged by them or released. In return for that, Baxter agreed to wait for them to arrive before moving in to make the arrest.

It was only after they'd boarded the train that Tanner received a call from Commander Bardsley, telling him that things hadn't gone according to plan.

'Bad news I'm afraid, but it looks like Baxter's gone and jumped the gun.'

'In what way?'

'He didn't wait for you. They moved in to arrest Edward Falcon in his flat during a dawn raid this morning.'

'Now why doesn't that surprise me,' said Tanner, rolling his eyes at Jenny sitting opposite him.

'That's not all.'

'Don't tell me that they accidentally managed to shoot him in the process?'

'Not quite that bad, no. Somehow he managed to escape.'

'From the penthouse flat at the top of a tower block?'

'I'm afraid so.'

'How on Earth did he manage to do that?'

'According to Baxter, he and his sister used the service lift, the existence of which hadn't come up when they'd been planning the operation.'

'You're saying he actually planned the operation?'

'His superintendent has already given him a bollocking.'

'And what was his excuse? Presumably to simply beat me to it.'

'He said that he was concerned Mr Falcon might do a runner before you arrived, so they decided to move things forward.'

'And yet, despite that, he's managed to do just that.'

'It looks that way, yes. So anyway, I wanted to let you know before you made the effort to come all the way down here.'

'Too late. We're on the train now, and the next stop is Liverpool Street.'

'Ah. Well, I'm sorry again.'

'It's hardly your fault. It's that idiot Baxter!'

'An All-Ports Warning has been put out for Falcon, so hopefully he'll be picked up, assuming he's planning on leaving the country.'

'I think the question is not if, but how, and from where?'

'Listen, as you're halfway down already, why don't we meet up for lunch? You never know, they may have picked him up by then.'

'That's kind of you. Thanks.'

'No problem. It would be good to catch up. How about I meet you at Liverpool Street station, at the base of the stairs on the main concourse?'

With that agreed, the call ended, leaving

Tanner to ask Jenny, 'Did you catch any of that?'

'Only that Edward Falcon has managed to get away.'

'My moronic old boss decided against waiting for us, and attempted to pick him up during a dawn raid on his penthouse flat this morning. But he must have been expecting it, to some degree, as he slipped the net using the service lift, something Baxter didn't seem to know even existed.'

'How about Tessa?'

'Her as well.'

'So, what's the plan now?'

'There's an All-Ports Warning out for them, so hopefully they'll be picked up before they can leave the country.'

'Do you think that's what they'll do?'

'Assuming Edward is the serial-killing psychopath we think he is, and that he now knows we're on to him, then I don't see what choice he'll have. And I can't imagine Tessa leaving his side, not when they seem inseparable.'

'But if they were able to avoid arrest by using a service lift, they must have planned for this. So I can't see them catching the cross-Channel ferry to Calais. Neither would they go to Heathrow.'

'They might try Docklands airport?' suggested Tanner. 'With their income, no doubt they could afford to hire a private plane. Maybe even a helicopter.'

'Personally,' said Jenny, staring out of the train window, 'if I wanted to leave the country without anyone knowing about it, I know exactly how I'd do it.'

'By boat,' guessed Tanner.

'To be more precise, a privately owned sailing yacht.'

'Yes, but they don't have one, or not one we know about.'

'No, but we know a man who does, or at least who did.'

'James Falcon!' stated Tanner.

'And as it's moored up in Dartmouth, it would be remarkably easy for them to drive down there and sail it out into the Channel. There isn't exactly passport control for them to go through. They wouldn't even need to notify the harbour master.'

'And presumably, once they'd sailed out into the Atlantic Ocean, they'd be able to effectively disappear.'

'They'd only need to make it out ten miles before they'd be in international waters, making their detention and arrest ten times more complicated.'

As they both took to staring out of the window, Tanner eventually continued, 'We're almost at Liverpool Street. I suggest we ask Matthew what he thinks before we do anything. With any luck, they'll have been picked up before we arrive.'

· CHAPTER FIFTY FIVE ·

THEY'D ONLY BEEN waiting at Liverpool Street station for a few minutes when Tanner caught a glimpse of the tall wiry figure of an out-of-uniform Commander Matthew Bardsley, weaving his way through the normal eclectic mix of London's travellers, glancing about as he did.

Attracting his attention with a raised hand, it wasn't long before Tanner was introducing Jenny.

'This is my colleague, DC Evans,' he began, deliberately keeping the introduction formal, 'although hopefully she'll be DS Evans by the end of the month.'

'You've got your sergeant's coming up, have you?' queried Bardsley, offering her a warm hand and a confident smile.

'I have,' she replied, returning the gesture, 'although I do seem to keep forgetting.'

'It's often the way, when you're busy.'

'Any news of our suspects?' enquired Tanner.

'Unfortunately there's been neither sight nor sound. I don't suppose you have any ideas as to where they may have gone.'

'Well, DC Evans thought of something, which I agree is a strong possibility.'

'We were wondering if they may be driving down to Devon,' she said. 'Their father – one of the victims – owned a yacht there, which we've been told he kept moored on the River Dart. It would be a relatively straightforward process for them to sail out into the Channel and effectively disappear, or at least make it as far as international waters.'

'It's an idea, I suppose,' replied Bardsley, 'but I'm not sure how they'd get down there. We're monitoring all train stations.'

'But couldn't they drive?'

'Well, yes, but DCI Baxter said that they'd sealed off the car park underneath their tower block before the raid, and that nothing came in or out.'

'They must have taken Tessa's Porsche,' Jenny realised, looking over at Tanner. 'Do you remember how Edward said that he was so ashamed of it, he wouldn't let her park it in the main car park, but that she had to leave it out on the street?'

'I assume you've got a number plate for it?' asked Bardsley.

'I should do,' Jenny replied, pulling out her phone.

A minute later, Bardsley was sending it over to Devon and Cornwall police, asking them to feed the number into their ANPR system, and to call him personally, should the number come up.

'What's ANPR?' asked Jenny, as soon as he had.

'Automatic Number Plate Recognition,' Bardsley replied. 'It's a relatively new system that allows us to search for any number plate that happens to drive past one of the cameras. We have over eleven thousand of them dotted around the country, making it difficult for anyone to go anywhere without being picked up.'

'And if they're already down there?' asked Tanner.

'I'll give the Dart's Harbour Master a call, to ask him to keep an eye out. Do you know the name of the yacht?'

Having already looked it up on Norfolk Constabulary's intranet during the train journey down, Jenny replied, 'Falcon's Reach. And I've got the phone number for the Harbour Master as well.'

Calling the number, Bardsley eventually said, 'It's going through to answerphone.'

Leaving a message to say who he was, and giving the name of the yacht they needed the harbour authority to keep an eye on, Bardsley ended the call. 'I'm not sure there's much more we can do,' he said, and began to propose that they may as well head off for lunch somewhere, when his phone rang in his hand.

'Bardsley speaking?'

Tanner and Jenny tried to listen in, but the ambient noise from the bustling train station prevented them from being able to.

'OK, thanks for letting me know.'

Without putting his phone away, Bardsley looked at Jenny. 'Looks like you were right. ANPR has already picked up that car. It's heading southbound on the A30, towards Exeter.'

'So, what now?' she asked, exchanging glances

between the two men.

'I think that's up to John here.'

'Me?'

'Well, you're the senior investigating officer.'

'What about Baxter?'

'He may have jurisdiction over what you can and can't do in London, but he doesn't for anything that goes on outside of it.'

'OK, but I don't see how we can get down there in time. Not if they're already as far down as Devon.'

'I know a way we can. Come on! You can update your boss on the way.'

· CHAPTER FIFTY SIX ·

TANNER AND JENNY were huddled together on the outer edge of London City Airport's helicopter landing area, with Commander Bardsley standing close by. Hovering just thirty feet above them was a gleaming black and yellow National Police Air Service helicopter, its giant blades battering them with thick hot air from its twin turbo engine. Without daring to move, they watched in awe as it began to inch its way down to the ground, its engine screaming ever louder.

The moment it touched safely down, and the blades began to slow, seeing the pilot inside the cockpit gesture for them to approach, Bardsley led the way forward, the three of them instinctively keeping their heads as low as possible.

Sliding open a window, the pilot shouted, 'Are you Commander Bardsley?'

'I am,' he shouted back.

'I hear you need a lift down to Dartmouth.'

'Myself and my colleagues, yes.'

Taking in the other people standing behind him, the pilot frowned. 'I was told there'd only be two passengers.'

'Sorry, no, three. Is that a problem?'

Glancing at his instrument panel, the pilot asked, 'Do I have time to refuel?'

'Do you need to refuel?' questioned Bardsley, feeling that was a far more appropriate question.

'I'd not made the fuel calculation based on three passengers, that's all.'

'How about if there are only two?'

'That should be OK.'

Nodding, Bardsley turned to face Tanner and Jenny to shout, 'Looks like I'm going to have to sit this one out.'

'But I thought you were coming with us?' questioned Tanner.

'The pilot's only got enough fuel to take the two of you.'

Seeing them exchange looks of mutual concern, Bardsley added, 'Don't worry, you'll be fine. It's just like taking a taxi, only louder.'

'And higher,' added Tanner, glancing momentarily up at the blades, still slicing through the air above.

Seeing the pilot knock on the window, gesturing for them to climb into the back, Bardsley opened the rear door for them before turning to shake them by the hand. 'Good luck!' he added. 'Give me a call when you catch them.'

'Will do!' confirmed Tanner, as he helped Jenny to clamber on board. 'And thank you for arranging the ride,' he added, following after her.

'You can thank me when you get there,' Bardsley replied, before closing the door and stepping back to wave goodbye.

· CHAPTER FIFTY SEVEN ·

WITH NEITHER TANNER nor Jenny having been anywhere near a helicopter before, let alone in the back of one, they found themselves fumbling nervously at their safety harnesses, before being able to secure them into place. Only then did they look out of the window to see Bardsley standing at the outer edge of the landing area, clinging to his coat as its hem flapped violently around him.

'All set?' asked the pilot, glancing around.

Seeing both of them nodding, the pilot gestured up at two headphones dangling from either side of their seats. 'If you put those on, we'll be able to talk more easily.'

Raising their thumbs, they unclipped the devices and, after spending a few confused moments attempting to work out which way round they went, secured the headsets over their ears and began adjusting the microphone levers into place.

As soon as they had, they began listening to the sound of voices crackling at them over the airwaves.

With permission to take off having been granted, the whine of the engine began to build as the blades only a meter or so above their heads began thrashing at the air.

Within seconds they felt a sudden jolt, as the helicopter lifted off the ground to begin a dramatic ascent, leaning forward as it did to head out over the Thames.

As both speed and altitude increased, it wasn't long before London's famous river disappeared beneath them, to be replaced by a seemingly never-ending series of concrete buildings, intermixed with occasional splashes of green.

Checking his watch to see that it was already gone two o'clock, speaking into the mic for the first time Tanner asked the pilot, 'How long do you think it will take for us to get there?'

'It shouldn't be longer than an hour and a half, but we do have a slight headwind to contend with. And then there's the fuel issue, of course.'

'The fuel issue?' questioned Tanner, a clear note of alarm in his voice.

As Jenny turned to stare round at him, the pilot said, 'Don't worry. As long as the headwind remains as it is, we should be OK, but we can always jettison some cargo, if we get low.'

'But...I thought we're the cargo?'

Turning to offer Tanner a wry smile, the pilot replied, 'You are!'

'Oh, great. A pilot with a sense of humour,' mused Tanner. 'I'm not sure which is worse, that or the fact that I'm about to be pushed out of a helicopter for being slightly overweight.'

'It's your own fault,' commented Jenny. 'I've been warning you about your diet for months.'

'Yes, and had I known that the dangers of overeating involved the possibility of being shoved out of a police helicopter when it was over a mile above the ground, then I'd have probably taken your advice to eat low fat cottage cheese sandwiches three times a day a little more seriously.'

A few moments passed as Tanner and Jenny did nothing but stare down at what had become a more suburban landscape passing by beneath them, before the pilot's voice came back over the airwaves. 'What are we looking for when we get down there?'

'We're hoping to locate a man and a woman, last seen driving a Porsche 911 towards Exeter; one of them is wanted in connected with a series of murders.'

'And you think they're heading for Dartmouth?'

'Dartmouth Harbour, to be exact. Their late father owned a yacht, which we've been told is moored down there. We think that they may be planning on using it to leave the country.'

'OK, well, if they've made it onto a boat, I'm not going to be of much use I'm afraid. I'll only be able to set you down on terra firma. And I doubt we'll have long to search the area when we get down there, due to the fuel issue.'

'Understood. If you can just get us to the harbour, hopefully we'll be able to spot them. If not, then we'd be happy enough to be dropped nearby.'

'Roger that,' confirmed the pilot.

With the headphones falling silent, Tanner and Jenny settled themselves down for what at first they thought was going to be a loud and uncomfortable flight. But it wasn't long before the hum from the engine behind them and the blades thumping at the air above took on a rhythmic hypnotic feel, and they soon found their heads rolling forward onto their chests.

· CHAPTER FIFTY EIGHT ·

'**D**ARTMOUTH HARBOUR IS coming into view,' announced the pilot, just over an hour and a half later, his voice pulling Tanner and Jenny out of their dreamless sleep.

Blinking his mind awake, Tanner leaned forward in his seat to stare out of the main cockpit window. Stretched out before them was a wide expanse of sparkling blue water, perfectly framed on either side by trees of vibrant green.

Jenny joined him to watch as the expanse of blue grew ever larger, and the trees fell back behind sloping granite cliffs.

'You can see Dartmouth Castle to your left,' said the pilot, indicating down at the medieval monument, its smooth rounded tower and battlement-topped walls glowing yellow in the late afternoon sun.

'On the other side is Kingswear Castle,' he added, pointing to a rectangular fort, rising out of the jagged rock on which it had been built.

Tanner and Jenny watched in envy as a small wooden gaff-rigged sailing boat drifted underneath them, its deep red sails pulled in tight as it tacked its way out to sea.

'Could that be them?' queried the pilot, seeing

what they were staring at.

'I wouldn't have thought so,' Jenny replied. 'It's an old pilot cutter. Having known the owner, I doubt it would have been to his taste. I think we'll looking for something a little more ostentatious.'

'Could we have a look, just in case?' asked Tanner.

'I'm sorry, we can't,' replied the pilot. 'We don't have enough fuel. Besides, if you look ahead, you'll see another reason.'

As the helicopter rounded the headland into the mouth of the River Dart, the harbour began to creep into view, with what must be hundreds of boats, either on swinging moorings to the side of the channel, or jammed into a crowded marina over to their right.

'If we started examining that lot, we'd be here all day. I'm afraid the best I can do is to set you down somewhere. Then I need to head off to the nearest airbase. But I'll come in as low as I can. Hopefully you'll be able to catch a glimpse of them before we land.'

'Understood,' confirmed Tanner, as he and Jenny began scanning the many boats scattered over the water beneath them.

As the helicopter flew in low over the marina, numerous heads turned to look up at them, some standing outside houses and shops, others on board their boats, all shielding their eyes from the glare of the sun as the machine thundered over their heads.

Spying a grass clearing nestled in amongst some trees, with a railway line lying in front of it and a car park to the right, Tanner pointed ahead.

'Do you think you'd be able to set us down over there?'

After checking the proposed landing area for telephone lines and electrical cables, the pilot eventually nodded. 'Looks good. And there's a footpath that will take you down to the marina.'

As the pilot began arcing the helicopter around to line it up for descent, Jenny caught a glimpse of what she thought was a Porsche 911, tucked discreetly under a tree in the corner of the car park.

With the helicopter still circling, she extended her seatbelt to lean over Tanner to see it again through his window. When it came back into view, she pointed down. 'Could that be Tessa's Porsche?'

'Well, it's a 911,' Tanner replied, 'and it's the right colour.'

Extending their focal point out to cover the concrete hardstanding outside the marina, and the series of pontoons beyond, it was Jenny's sharp eyes that spotted them.

'There, look!' she exclaimed, directing Tanner's gaze down towards a well-dressed young couple heading towards the entrance to the marina's pontoons; the girl walking at a brisk pace pulling a Louis Vuitton suitcase behind her, whilst the athletic man was pushing against the steel bar of a trolley, stacked high with bags, water bottles and other supplies.

When they saw them glance over their shoulders before hurrying away, they knew it was them.

'Looks like you were right,' said Tanner.

Leaning forward, he caught the pilot's eye to say, 'We've seen them. Any chance you can bring this thing down any faster?'

'Not without killing us in the process,' he replied, 'but I'll do the best I can.'

With the helicopter continuing its descent towards the flat plain of grass beneath, it wasn't long before the fleeing suspects were lost behind the large marina building.

The moment they touched down, the pilot looked round. 'This is your stop.'

Unclipping his harness, Tanner leaned forward to ask, 'Can you put a call through to the local constabulary, requesting backup?'

'No problem. Do you need an armed response unit?'

'Nothing like that, no, but someone with a boat might be handy.'

Seeing him reply with a firm thumbs-up, Tanner and Jenny took it in turns to thank the pilot before pulling off their headphones and climbing out of their respective sides, making sure the doors were closed securely behind them before ducking away.

Circling around the tail, Tanner joined Jenny on the other side. As the helicopter's engine was throttled up again behind them, they jogged down a grass incline to follow a path through a series of shrubs and trees, heading towards the railway line.

Checking for trains, they picked their way carefully across it, to end up on a concrete footpath on the far side.

'I can't see them,' said Jenny, peering over

towards where they last had.

'Me neither.'

As the helicopter thundered overhead, they broke into a run, following the footpath to the marina at the end.

Breathing hard, they reached the open entrance to a maze of floating pontoons. There they stopped to stare out over the dozens of gleaming white sailing yachts, their halliard cables clanking impatiently in the breeze against a forest of aluminium masts.

'They could be anywhere,' said Jenny, shielding her eyes from the glare of the sun as she stared around.

'Well, we'll see them when they set off.'

'By which time it will be too late. I think we're going to have to split up.'

'Not a chance,' objected Tanner.

'I can't see how else we're going to find them.'

'I appreciate that, but I'm not having you wandering down a pontoon on your own when there's the possibility of a psychotic serial killer and his twin sister waiting for you at the end.'

'Then what do you suggest?'

Tanner paused for a moment, but couldn't think of an alternative. 'OK, but the second you catch sight of them, you're to either call, or wave, or something. Better still, come and find me. Agreed?'

'No problem,' said Jenny, as they rattled down the slopping corrugated iron platform, heading for the pontoons at the end.

· CHAPTER FIFTY NINE ·

L EAVING TANNER TO cover the left-hand side of the marina's pontoons, Jenny went right, heading for the farthest end. As she did, she craned her neck to see over the myriad of boats, desperate to catch a glimpse of either Edward or Tessa Falcon. Whenever she reached the opening to one of the pontoon aisles, she slowed to stare down each, but all she could see were dozens of boats, all moored aft-in. There wasn't a single person on board any of them.

Approaching the farthest end, she stopped to look behind her, hoping to see Tanner over on the other side, but there was no sign of him either.

Beginning to regret her suggestion that they split up, she peered down the end of the pontoon's aisle. Again, there was neither sight nor sound of anyone. The entire marina seemed to be completely devoid of people.

It was time for her to start checking along the lengths of each of the pontoons, and the back ends of the boats moored up to them, just as she assumed Tanner must be doing at the other side.

Realising her heart had yet to slow since reaching the marina's entrance, after another fruitless glance around for Tanner she took a calming breath before beginning to pick her way along the slatted wooden boards stretched out under her feet, looking left and right to examine each of the boats' bathing platforms and cockpits, searching for signs of life.

Nearing the farthest end, she stopped where she was to crouch down, resting one of her hands on the footboards. Moored up at the end might be what she was looking for. It was a large light-grey inflatable RIB with a gleaming black outboard engine mounted on the back. Inside she could see a pile of haphazardly stacked shopping bags, water bottles and jerry cans, as well as that Louise Vuitton suitcase she'd seen Tessa Falcon wheeling behind her earlier. There was also the trolley her brother had been pushing along, still with some supplies left inside. What she couldn't see was the two people who must have dumped it all there.

They couldn't have passed me, she thought, glancing back. Maybe I passed them?

Remaining motionless, she spent a few moments carefully searching the boats that crowded around her for someone moving, or the sound of a voice. But the only movement came from the gentle undulations of the floating pontoon she remained crouched on, and the only noise from the constant clanking of halyard cables against the masts.

She briefly considered going back for Tanner, but if Edward and Tessa weren't beside the RIB, and they hadn't passed her going the other way, they must be hiding close by, possibly waiting for her somewhere back the way she'd come.

Without looking, she slowly reached around for her handbag, and the phone she knew was inside it. If she couldn't go in search of Tanner, she could at least call him.

As her fingers fumbled at the clasp, she glanced down to see what she was doing, when a blinding white pain burst over the back of her head.

· CHAPTER SIXTY ·

O N THE OTHER side of the marina, Tanner
had been undertaking a far less tentative
search. Instead of creeping along, as Jenny
had been, he'd been marching up and down the
pontoons' aisles, staring only briefly into the back
of the boats as he swept his way passed.

Since seeing the photofit of the man wanted in
connection with his daughter's murder, and
having become entangled in the bodies left to rot
at the bottom of Falcon's Yard dyke, he was now
certain that Edward Falcon was the man he'd
been searching for all this time. He was also
becoming increasingly convinced that it had been
no mere coincidence that he'd left London to join
the Norfolk Constabulary, or that the chosen
mooring for their new boat had been just upriver
from where Edward Falcon and his late
grandfather had spent years hiding the results of
their psychological imbalance. Going against
everything he'd believed up to the point when he'd
met Jenny, having seen the cold hand of justice
hammer down on those responsible for the many
murders surrounding the St. Benet's investigation
a few months before, he was slowly coming
around to the idea that there was more going on

in the universe other than just the material theories and mathematical principles he'd been brought up to believe in. He may not have been prepared to accept what the Catholic Church taught, nor any of the hundreds, possibly even thousands of other religions, all of which declared their beliefs to be right, making all the others wrong, but he was becoming increasingly convinced that there was more to life than what was preached by the scientific community.

With his mind so focussed on finding the man he was looking for, it was only when he'd finished searching up and down his half of the marina that it dawned on him that if Edward and Tessa weren't there, then they must be somewhere on Jenny's side. His frantic search suddenly became one of panicked desperation. What if she'd not found them, but instead, they'd found her?

Thundering back to where he'd last seen her, glancing only briefly down each of the aisles, he reached the final one. There he stopped dead in his tracks. He could see them, at the end of the pontoon, loading what was left of the contents of the trolley into a RIB. And there, lying inside the boat, was Jenny.

As the muscles on his shoulders bristled with dangerous intent, with his eyes staring out from underneath a pair of dark rigid eyebrows, primordial rage rampaged through his veins. If they'd hurt Jenny in any way, he'd make them suffer. If she was dead, they would be too.

Like a lion approaching his prey, he began pawing down towards them. He wasn't even too fussed if they saw him. He almost wanted them to.

It was Tessa who spotted him first, leading her to give Edward's arm a prod to garner his attention, just as he heaved the last of the five litre water bottles on board their inflatable craft.

'Going somewhere, are you?' enquired Tanner, coming to halt just a few feet away.

'As a matter of fact, we are,' confirmed Edward, pushing the now empty trolley to one side. 'It's certainly touching that you've come all this way to see us off, but please don't think that your presence here is going to stop us.'

'Unfortunately, I'm not going to be able to let you go anywhere, not with my colleague in tow.'

'I see. Does that mean if we were to let her go, you'd allow us to leave, unhindered?'

'In exchange for DC Evans' safe return, on this one occasion, I'd be prepared to turn a blind eye,' he lied.

Edward took a moment to study Tanner's face. 'You know, for some peculiar reason, Mr Tanner, I don't believe you. Besides, we need her for insurance purposes; just in case some of your colleagues show up who aren't quite as amenable as you're pretending to be.'

Speaking with forced dispassion, Tanner asked, 'I presume she's still alive?' If they found out just how much she meant to him, they'd never let her go.

'I've no idea. What do you think, darling?' he asked, glancing over at his sister.

'Oh, I'm sure she's fine,' she replied. 'I didn't hit her that hard.'

'Then I suggest you'd better let her go,' stated

Tanner. 'There's an armed response unit on its way, and in a hostage situation they're trained to shoot first and ask questions later.'

'Tell me, Mr Tanner,' Edward said, with a quizzical expression, 'are all policemen as bad at lying as you would appear to be?'

'What makes you think I'm lying?'

'Because you've just flown down from London on what I suspect was the off-chance of finding us here. If an armed response team was on its way then I think they'd have been here about two hours ago. Even if they do show up, they're not going to risk shooting one of their fellow police officers, especially not one as attractive as Miss Evans here.'

Realising he was going to have to take her back by force, clenching both teeth and fists, Tanner took a step forward, his eyes trained on Edward's.

'I wouldn't do that if I were you,' came Tessa's voice, from the other side.

Glancing around, Tanner saw her pull what looked like some sort of old-fashioned pistol out of a carryall bag, which she proceeded to point at his head.

'I hope you've got a licence for that?' he asked, surprised by how calm he felt.

'She doesn't need a licence,' replied Edward, on her behalf. 'If you knew anything about boats, you'd know that it's only a flare gun. However, I can assure you that at this range, it's just as lethal as a handgun, perhaps more so. I'm told it's possible for the human skull to channel a bullet away from the brain, whereas a flare would bury itself into your face and burn its way through.'

'The end result being that your sister would be charged with the murder of a police officer, as you're about to be for killing countless innocent women, just like your grandfather.'

Hearing that, Tessa began to giggle quietly to herself, as if she'd just been told a dirty joke at the back of a classroom.

'You must forgive my sister,' said Edward, his eyes still fixed on Tanner's. 'She's always been easily amused.'

As she began to laugh more openly, she lowered her flare gun, her face going red as she placed a steadying hand on her knee. 'I'm sorry,' she was eventually able to say, 'but I can't help it. Everyone always seems to assume that it's my brother who's the psychotic serial killer.'

'Everyone except our grandfather, that is,' added Edward, as Tessa regained her composure.

'I suppose it takes a psychopath to know a psychopath,' mused Tanner, as the full significance of what they'd said began to dawn on him. 'But that still doesn't explain why you thought it necessary to drown him in his own bath?'

'Because the decrepit old fart was developing a guilty conscience,' Tessa replied, aiming the gun at his head once more. 'Probably worried about spending an eternity burning in hell. Unfortunately for him, it was a little late in the day for repentance, not after the number of people he'd killed; maybe not those he'd massacred during the war, but certainly for all the women he'd had his way with afterwards; including our grandmother, I may add. Had his intention only been to confess what he'd been up to on his own, I'd have probably let him get on with it. But he made the mistake of extending his conscience to include me. He'd already told my uncle what I'd been up to. The next stop would have been you lot, and I'm afraid I'm far too young to spend the rest of my life locked up in some God-forsaken prison, especially for doing nothing more than killing a handful of stupid girls whose only contribution to society was that they were vaguely attractive.'

'Well, unfortunately for you, Miss Falcon, I have reason to believe that one of them happened to be my daughter.'

A broad grin full of amused realisation spread out over Tessa's face. 'Abigail Tanner! I thought I recognised your name from somewhere. Oh dear, you must be dreadfully upset with me. If it's of any consolation, she was one of the more intelligent ones.'

Tanner could feel a red mist darken his mind, like an executioner's hood. If it wasn't for the flare gun pointed at his head, she'd be dead already.

Hearing the distant sound of a siren come drifting over the marina towards them, Edward climbed on board the RIB to announce, 'It's time to go.'

'Shame,' said Tessa. 'I was having such fun as well. Oh well. Never mind. I've still got your young colleague here to play with.'

Keeping the gun aimed at Tanner's head, as the outboard engine spluttered into life, she swung her smooth tanned legs over the RIB's curved rubber side. With the mooring lines undone, she pushed away at the pontoon, and blew him a kiss. 'Au revoir, mon amour. I'll make sure little Miss Evans sends you a postcard.'

· CHAPTER SIXTY ONE ·

BLIND RAGE MIXED with an all-consuming guilt as he watched Jenny being sped over the water away from him. The flare gun that had been aimed at his head just moments before was now pointing at hers, as she lay motionless at the bottom of the RIB, as if already dead.

Fighting the futile gesture of diving in after them, he spun around, frantically searching the marina for a small boat like theirs to use to give chase. For what purpose, he didn't know, but he had to try something. But he was surrounded by row upon row of huge yachts and grossly oversized motorboats.

Then he heard the rumble of a diesel engine being started, somewhere close by, but he'd no idea which one it was.

Shielding his eyes from the sun's glare, he focussed towards where he thought the sound was coming from, trying to pinpoint its exact location. He thought it was along the adjacent pontoon, but with the way the sound was echoing around the marina, it could be the next one down, or even the one after that.

As he watched the RIB pass by the last of the

marina's moored-up boats to speed out into the River Dart beyond, out of the corner of his eye Tanner caught a glimpse of a whisper of thin grey smoke, rolling its way over the boats. Realising it must have come from the newly-started engine, he traced it back to its source. There he saw the head of a man bob briefly up above the coach roof of the yacht directly in front of him. The boat whose engine he could still hear gurgling away was moored up on the next pontoon along.

Breaking into a run, he clattered down the floating wooden walkway, back the way he'd come, to fly around the corner and charge back up the next.

Towards the end he saw an over-weight middle aged man wearing tan chinos and a powder blue polo shirt crouching down to untie the aft end mooring lines of a huge, elegantly sleek luxury motor launch.

Running up to him, Tanner pulled out his formal ID to call out, 'DI Tanner, Norfolk Police. I need to borrow your boat.'

With the undone rope in his hand, the man stood to mutter, 'Good luck with that.'

Reining himself in, breathing hard, Tanner shoved his ID into the man's face. 'I've got a murder suspect who's just kidnapped one of my fellow officers. Yours is the only one available.'

'Er, this is a forty-eight foot Sunseeker Portofino. It's probably the most expensive yacht in the whole of Dartmouth Marina. I don't mean to be rude, Mr Policeman, sir, but there's no fucking way I'm letting you go anywhere near her.'

With quiet, icy calm, Tanner replaced his ID to look the man up and down. 'And I don't mean to be rude, but I'm afraid you've got no fucking choice.' As adrenaline surged through his veins, Tanner snatched the rope out of the man's hands before shoving him back so hard that he stumbled away, tripping over the opposite boat's mooring line to plunge backwards into the water between it and the pontoon he'd been standing quite happily on just a few moments before.

Tanner looked on with guilty pleasure as he saw the man's head break the surface, his face almost purple as he coughed and spluttered out a series of unintelligible swear words.

Assuming he'd be able to pull himself out, Tanner cast the rope onto the boat and clambered up the side, heading for the raised fly-bridge at the top where he knew the driving console would be.

He took up position behind the wheel to stare first at the controls, then at the boat and the surrounding marina. Only then did he consider the task he'd set himself. It had only been a couple of months since he'd taken his Powerboat Level 1 & 2 course, something Jenny had insisted on, and although he'd motored their Broads cruising yacht several times since, he'd never driven anything quite like this. It looked big when he'd been down on the pontoon, but from up on the fly-bridge it was enormous.

Remembering the reason for him being there, he stared out at the River Dart. From his elevated view, he could easily see the RIB speeding its way towards row upon row of yachts, each tied to a buoy out in the channel. He tried to think back to what his powerboat instructor had taught him, but his mind was blank. All he could remember was what had been drilled into him time and time again; to tie what was called a kill cord around his leg, a simple device used to cut the engine should the driver fall overboard.

Finding it, just under the ignition key, he wrapped it around the top of his thigh, securing it in place with a plastic clasp.

Hearing the sound of the boat's owner dragging himself out of the water, shouting a tirade of abuse up at him as he did, and with the RIB becoming increasingly small, Tanner had no time to lose. Taking a deep breath, with one hand gripping the sumptuous black leather of the steering wheel, he placed the other onto the highly polished double chrome throttle and began easing it forward, as gently as he could. With the engine rumbling deep within its bowels, all forty-eight feet of resplendent floating luxury began gliding its way out of its berth, edging slowly towards the River Dart, leaving its bloated owner on his hands and knees, dripping wet and gasping for breath, evidently too exhausted from having heaved himself out to even stand up, let alone give chase.

His mind focussed on the job at hand, Tanner continued to manoeuvre the Sunseeker out past the other boats. Once clear, with the open channel of the River Dart beyond and the RIB in his sights, he began inching the double throttle forward, guiding the boat's direction with the steering wheel as it began slicing its way through the water.

As the boat's speed continued to build, with Tanner's heart seeming to be trying to keep up with it, it wasn't long before he was almost flying over the smooth flat river, the wind whipping at his hair, both hands locked firmly around the wheel.

With his eyes focussed on the water ahead, hoping to God another boat wouldn't cross his path, he risked a glance up at the fleeing RIB.

He was catching up fast.

· CHAPTER SIXTY TWO ·

JENNY AWOKE WITH a jolt with what sounded like a chainsaw filling her ears as the hard damp rubbery floor shuddered and bounced underneath. It was the intense throbbing pain in the back of her head which made her realise what had happened, and consequently where she must be.

Without moving, she inched open her eyes, just enough to take in her surroundings.

As she suspected, she was lying at the bottom of a RIB, the same one she'd discovered half-loaded with supplies before she'd been hit from behind. The front of her head was shoved up against the cold hard steel of a khaki green jerry can, which stank of the petrol she could hear sloshing about inside. Swivelling her eyes down the length of her body, she saw Edward Falcon sitting near the back behind a small steering console, both hands resting on the wheel, the chiselled contours of his face staring out from under the high collar of a midnight blue offshore sailing jacket.

Tessa must be up near the front, but without risking giving the game away that she'd regained consciousness, she could only assume that she was.

Tanner wasn't with her. They must have stowed her on board and motored away before he'd had a chance to find them.

Cursing herself for having failed to check behind her when she first saw their escape craft, she began to weigh up her options as to how she was going to get out of her current predicament. It was fairly obvious what their destination was; their father's yacht, which must be moored up to a buoy somewhere in the river's channel. The question was, would they let her go when they got there, or was it more likely that they'd keep her tied up inside a locked cabin until they'd reached the safety of international waters. And what then? Would they really be likely to keep her on board as their special guest, sharing their food and water until they arrived at their final destination, to then let her go with enough cash for a taxi ride home? More likely they'd ditch her overboard the second they felt she'd served her purpose.

Once those thoughts had rattled their way through her mind, she reached the conclusion that she only really had two choices; escape now, or die later. To do the former she'd have to jump overboard, before either Edward or Tessa had a chance to stop her. As long as they thought she was still unconscious, it should work, but the plan did have one major drawback. Once she'd gone over the side, it would be remarkably easy for them to double back and fish her out. Her only hope would be that they'd be too intent on reaching the yacht as quickly as they could to bother, especially if she was able to hold her breath to stay hidden under the surface, hopefully long enough for them to give up the search.

Having made up her mind that she had no choice but to at least try, she was about to leap up when she heard Tessa's voice call out from the front, 'There's a boat coming up behind us.'

Looking back to Edward, she saw his head whip round.

'Is it the police?' she heard him ask, his voice tense with anxiety.

'I doubt it,' came Tessa's more relaxed reply. 'A little too upmarket for them.'

With a dismissive shrug, Edward faced forward again. 'Then it must be some idiot driving too fast. Hardly the first.'

'Well, whoever it is, they're heading straight for us.'

Seeing Edward turn to look behind him again, Jenny took her chance. Like a lioness leaping for its prey, she sprang to her feet to launch herself over the side. It was only as she was going over, too late to stop, that she saw what the Falcon twins had been discussing: an enormous powerboat with a midnight blue hull, blasting at full speed towards them, its course set for running straight over the top of her.

· CHAPTER SIXTY THREE ·

AS TANNER'S BORROWED luxury powerboat began to bear down on the far smaller RIB, he could just about see Jenny, still lying sprawled out at the bottom, surrounded on all sides by tins of food, toilet rolls, jerry cans and other live-aboard essentials. Edward was sitting near the back, both hands holding on to the steering wheel. His psychotic sister was standing in a narrow space at the front, one hand twisted around a rope that led out to the boat's curved rubber bow, the other still holding the flare gun, but thankfully down by her side, not pointing at Jenny's head.

As the Sunseeker began closing in, his mind returned to what he was going to do next. He could hardly run them down, not with Jenny on board, and pulling alongside to politely ask them to follow him back to the marina was only going to result in a flare being shot either at him, or possibly into the side of Jenny's face. Alternatively he could blast past them, overturning their boat in his wake, but if Jenny was still unconscious when the RIB went over, with no lifejacket on she'd be likely to drown. He was just thinking that maybe he could pull up in front of them to block their way, or at least slow them down until a police boat arrived, when he saw Edward turn his head to look around at him.

That was when he saw Jenny leap up and launch herself out over the side, falling into the water directly in his path.

Blind instinct made him pull the steering wheel hard to starboard, banking the boat around with such force that Tanner was sent flying the other way, yanking the kill chord out from the ignition as his body was slammed into the port-side flybridge housing.

With the engine cut, the Sunseeker rocked violently from one side to another in its own giant wake, leaving Tanner to painfully heave himself up to stare frantically down at the surrounding water, desperately searching the surface for Jenny.

The RIB banked hard around, no doubt going back to look for her as well. As it did, its curved rubber bow ploughed straight into the first of the huge bow waves thrown out by the now stalled Sunseeker, sending the lightweight craft flying high into the air, and Edward tumbling straight out the back. But he couldn't have had his kill-cord on, as the boat's engine continued to buzz. With nobody left to steer it, the engine turned naturally to one side, leaving the RIB to begin arcing back around to start hunting him down.

Tessa also stumbled as the boat hit the wave, but although she was saved from following her brother overboard by the rope she had wrapped around her hand, the sudden jolt made her accidently fire off the flare, which blasted into the bottom of the boat where it began hissing and dancing like a demonic snake, its intense white heat setting fire to everything in its path.

Tanner watched as Tessa clambered over the supplies, desperate to keep it from burning her feet. At some point she must have caught sight of her brother in the water. With the boat having nearly completed a full circle, all set to run him down, he saw her leap for the wheel, just managing to reach it in time to steer the boat away.

Then Tanner saw the flare had found the jerry cans, immediately igniting the petrol that must have been spilt down their sides.

Knowing they could explode at any moment, Tanner took cover behind the flybridge surround, from where he watched Tessa stare down at the burning cans. She must have known what could happen, as after hesitating for the briefest of moments, she too launched herself overboard.

But the RIB hadn't finished with her yet. With no one at the helm, and with the engine still buzzing madly as the supplies on board burned, it began to circle back around, hunting her down like a burning shark sent from the depths of hell.

· CHAPTER SIXTY FOUR ·

TANNER WATCHED AS Tessa began stabbing madly at the water, trying to swim frantically away from the rapidly approaching RIB. But he could see she needed to fight her instinct to do so. Instead she had to swim to the side, out of its path. Within a matter of seconds, he knew it was too late. Just as she turned her head to look back, the boat ploughed straight over the top of her, the sound of her skull cracking against its base, leaving the propeller to carve its way over her body.

As the RIB continued on its way, what was left of Tessa Falcon rose to the surface, her head facing down as a dark circle of blood began spreading out from her chewed-up remains.

Dragging his eyes away, her confession to having murdered his daughter still reverberating in his mind, he remembered Jenny, and rushed around the flybridge, searching the water, pleading with God that she'd been spared a similar fate. But there was no sign of her. All he could see was Edward Falcon, treading water as he watched with hopeless agony as the RIB circled back around to once again run over what was left of his sister.

Then came the sound of an all-too familiar voice from somewhere near the back of the Sunseeker.

'What the hell are you doing up there?'

As a surge of relief flowed through his body, he spun round to see a bedraggled Jenny Evans attempting to claw herself out the water, onto the Sunseeker's low-lying bathing platform.

'I thought I'd borrow a massive powerboat to see if I could run you over,' he called back, a wide grin spreading out over his face.

'And you damn well nearly succeeded,' she replied, looking none too happy as she attempted to hook a knee over the edge of the platform, only for it to slip off and fall back into the water.

'Yes, sorry about that,' said Tanner, content enough to stand there, staring down at her. 'To be honest, I was trying to catch up to you. Had I known you were about to leap out directly in front of me, I'd have slowed up a little.'

'Are you going to help me out, or what?' she demanded, dark lines of mascara running down the sides of her face.

Apologising, he leapt into action.

Taking the flybridge steps two at a time, he landed on the main deck to continue down onto the bathing platform, where Jenny was waiting with an outstretched hand.

Heaving her out so that they were both standing, they couldn't help but grin at each other.

'I must look a right state,' she apologised, using the backs of her hands to wipe self-consciously at the water under her eyes. But doing so only served to smear the mascara to leave her looking like an American Footballer.

'You look perfect,' replied Tanner, trying not to laugh.

The sound of a fast approaching police motor launch reminded Jenny why they were there. 'What happened to the Falcon twins?' she asked, turning to stare down at the water behind them.

'Didn't you see?'

'See what?'

'Tessa's dead.'

Jenny paused for a moment. 'And Edward?'

'I've no idea,' replied Tanner, with total dispassion. 'The last time I saw him he was treading water, watching his sister being repeatedly run over by their RIB.'

· EPILOGUE ·

Friday, 25th October

A LITTLE OVER a week later, Tanner was sitting in his XJS watching Jenny come tottering out of Wroxham Station, a particularly glum expression clouding her face.

'How'd it go?' he asked, opening the passenger door for her.

'Oh, fine.'

Tanner waited for her to climb inside before asking, 'Do you think you passed?'

'Dunno,' she replied, with a noncommittal shrug. But Tanner had spied the corners of her mouth lift just enough for him to know that she was deliberately trying not to smile.

'You found it easy, didn't you?' he stated.

'Well, a bit, yes,' she admitted, with an expanding grin.

'God damn it,' he cursed, pretending to be upset. He wasn't, of course. He was hardly surprised, either. Despite the Sergeant's Exam being incredibly difficult – at least it had been for him, the few times he'd helped her prepare – it had become blindingly obvious that she was going to sail through. Jenny appeared to have a brain like a sponge. His was more like a tub of ice cream that had been left in the freezer too long. You could get stuff into it, but it was an effort.

'To be honest, I'm not sure why you found it so hard,' said Jenny, staring nonchalantly out of the window.

'I think that's because I'm normal,' Tanner replied, driving out of the car park. 'So, I suppose celebrations are in order?'

'I haven't passed yet!'

'Oh, I suspect that's just a formality.'

Silence followed, before he eventually said, 'You know, I'm still not entirely happy with the idea of you moving up the ranks quite so quickly. At this rate, I'm the one who's going to be calling you sir.'

'You mean ma'am,' she grinned at him.

'You know what I mean,' said Tanner, in a more serious tone.

'Listen, John, I know you'd rather I didn't move up to the rank of sergeant, but this is what I want.'

'I know. I just can't help worrying about you, that's all.'

'Well, don't! I'm more than capable of taking care of myself.'

If she had what Tanner considered to be a normal job, like being an estate agent, or working in IT, then he had no doubt that she could. But there was nothing normal about working for CID. The fact that she'd been directly in harm's way no less than twice since he met her was proof of that.

Once again, the car fell silent. Jenny knew how Tanner felt. She was all too aware that there were risks associated with the job. However, it was what she loved doing. Besides, starting anything more normal after what she'd been through over the last six months would seem incredibly dull.

Thinking it was probably best to change the subject, she eventually asked, 'I don't suppose there's been any news of Edward Falcon, in my absence?'

'Nothing, no. But I did get a call from Matthew earlier.'

'Oh yes?'

'A yacht's been reported missing from its moorings in Dartmouth harbour. The last time the owner was on board was the weekend before we were there, so it's looking likely that Edward must have hidden there until we called off the search, and then taken it out to sea.'

'So, he could be anywhere?'

'Quite possibly, yes. Either that or he drowned, and his body's yet to wash up. There's been some news about our Jim Jackson, as well.'

'Oh, do tell!'

'He was picked up today by the SFO.'

'The Serious Fraud Office?'

'That's the one. Apparently, they'd been watching him for months. They also arrested someone working in the local council's planning office.'

'Does that mean we're not going to have to find a new mooring?' asked Jenny, with hopeful expectation.

'Well, they'll have frozen his assets, both personal and business, so we shouldn't have to, no.'

'What about the diggers?'

'Assuming Jackson was hiring them, hopefully they won't be there for too much longer. And it's not as if they'd laid any foundations, so it should grass over fairly soon.'

'So, celebrations really are in order then?' mused Jenny, with triumphant glee.

'Er, only if you passed your Sergeant's Exam.'

'Yes, well; as you said,' she continued, 'I suspect that's just a formality.'

DI John Tanner and DC Jenny Evans
will return in

THREE RIVERS

A LETER FROM DAVID

I just wanted to say a huge thank you for deciding to read *Moorings*. If you enjoyed it, I'd be really grateful if you could leave a review on Amazon, or mention it to your friends and family. Word-of-mouth recommendations are just so important to an author's success, and doing so will help new readers discover my work.

It would be great to hear from you as well, either on Facebook, Twitter, Goodreads or via my website. There are plenty more books to come, so I sincerely hope you'll be able to join me for what I promise will be an exciting adventure!

David-Blake.com
facebook.com/DavidBlakeAuthor
facebook.com/groups/DavidBlakeAuthor
twitter.com/DavidDBlake

ABOUT THE AUTHOR

David Blake is an international best-selling author who lives in North London. At time of going to print he has written sixteen books, along with a collection of short stories. He's currently working on his seventeenth, *Three Rivers*, which is the next in his series of crime fiction thrillers, after *Broadland*, *St. Benet's* and *Moorings*.

When not writing, David likes to spend his time mucking about in boats, often in the Norfolk Broads, where his crime fiction books are based.

www.David-Blake.com